RUSSIAN SLEEPER CELL

NATHAN MONK

Russian Sleeper Cell

Nathan Monk

NathanMonkTour@gmail.com

CharityInstitute.com

ISBN-13: 979-8-218-07945-1

Printed in the United States of America

First Edition

10 9 8 7 6 5 4 3 2 1

Dedication

For Father David

RUSSIAN SLEEPER CELL

A NOVEL

NATHAN MONK

"Man will never be free until the last king is strangled with the entrails of the last priest."

- Jean Meslier

Prologue

The Mission

The face of Sister Mary Margaret looked almost angelic as her frozen body lay outside the doorstep of The Mission. The blood encircling her made an almost perfect halo. The shadowed frame of Sergeant Stephens soon engulfed the scene as he leaned down to examine her further. The halo confused him so much that he nearly didn't mention the oddity of it out loud for fear of sounding strange to his partner, yet the peculiarity of it forced him to acknowledge it to someone. He took a step back and paced between his partner and the corpse for a few moments attempting to find the right words to say to draw attention to the unnatural design of the blood without making himself seem foolish.

"If I were a superstitious man, Larry," Stephens said to Sergeant Decker, finally breaking the silence, "I would just about say that was a halo around her head."

"You know," Larry remarked back, "I was thinking the same thing but couldn't come up with the right damn word for it."

Everything about the situation sat uneasy with them: in theory, it was a brutal murder, but the scene seemed almost beautiful. This looked more like a burial than a homicide. It was obvious to the trained eye that the nun had been killed somewhere else and that her body had been dragged back to this place where she would have been found. Whoever did this wanted others to know where she was; this was done with love. But why? Despite the nasty gash across her neck, her face had a look of peace unbefitting the grotesqueness of her demise. Though her complexion was now a blueish grey color, she seemed almost alive, stuck somewhere between Heaven and Earth.

Then there was the issue of that dammed bloody halo; Stephens couldn't shake the strangeness of it all. After a few more moments of silence, he looked back at Decker with a curious thought. "You think that was on purpose?"

"The murder?" Decker asked, barely looking up from his crossword puzzle he had stolen from the morning paperback at the office. "It seems like a pretty intentional cut to me. No one could do that to themselves; the odds of it being an accident have to be next to zero. Whoever did this knew exactly what they were doing, I figure."

"No, not the murder itself," Stephens said, shaking his head. "That is clearly on purpose. I mean that goddamn halo."

This was the first time either of them had cursed so far that morning, which was a remarkable feat. Usually they could barely reach the precinct's front door before offending God and His mother. Neither one of them had agreed not to swear in front of the nun's corpse but they did so rather instinctively until now. Now being the first of them to slip, Sergeant Stephens set off a chain reaction of vulgarities that would soon follow as if it were a necessary tool to solve the case.

"Fuck if I know," Decker replied without looking up from his puzzle. "It sure is strange; I will grant you that. It does seem like an awful lot of blood. I wonder if she hadn't yet died by the time the perp dragged her up here. That's all I can make of it. Unreal."

"Unreal, indeed," Stephens agreed.

"No." Decker was holding the crossword up. "Six letters, seeming fake."

Stephens shot a look that caused Decker to finally fold up the crossword, placing it in his back pocket before leaning his meaty head over the frozen frame of the sister. He began to rub away the goosebumps from his arms that had surfaced when he realized that Sister Mary Margaret was, in fact, smiling. Not a massive grin but just a soft Mona Lisa smile, so faint yet almost tender. Had either of them been Catholic, the word eluding them both was incorruptible. Her spirit seemed to somehow remain with her torn body, preserving it in a type of holiness.

"Yes, sir," Decker said to no one in particular, fidgeting with his pen and wishing he could finish the last few lines of his puzzle, "this is weird as shit. I'm not going to say it's a miracle or anything wackadoodle like that, but then again … it's just weird."

"Maybe we should tell someone about it," said Stephens.

"Like the newspaper?" Decker used this as a moment to retrieve the crossword from his pocket and use it as a prop for emphasis.

"No." Stephens was almost indignant at Decker's reply. "Not the fucking newspaper. Like someone within the diocese, I don't know. How do they make someone a saint?"

"They don't do that anymore, you idiot." Decker laughed. "They are all full up on saints. There hasn't been a new saint since the medieval ages or something like that. The saints were chosen because a person, like your family or whatever, paid to have that person become a saint. That's how they paid for the Crusades, you know."

"No shit," Stephens said, surprised.

"No shit," Decker echoed back to Stephens matter-of-factly.

Sergeant Decker had no clue what he was talking about. He had grown up in an obscure cult-like branch of the Baptist Church that believed only the 1611 King James Bible could be read because of its advanced revelations. This made Decker many things, but an authority on the Catholic Church, or how it operated, was not one of them. However, he spoke with such authority that Sergeant Stephens instantly believed him and logged this extremely incorrect information into the permanent file in his brain on Catholic trivia. He would repeat this incorrect information many times over the course of his life. It wouldn't be until he was in his seventies, still telling this false information to others, that someone would finally correct him and he went home to research it. Sadly, by this point, Decker would be long dead from a heart attack, so Stephens would be unable to tell him what a dolt he was.

"It's a pity; she would have been a good saint," Stephens said.

"What's a five-letter word for a public servant?" Decker had ceased using the paper as a prop and was now back attempting to close the only case he could today.

"Mayor?" Stephens offered.

"No."

"Got any letters yet?"

"Yeah, second letter is O."

Stephens thought for a moment. "Police?"

"I'll be goddamned." Decker chuckled. "Now that's funny."

"That's six letters," Stephens grunted.

"Yeah, I guess it is." Decker shrugged; counting was never his strong suit. Then again, neither were crossword puzzles, nor was fighting crime, but these inadequacies didn't stop him from attempting all three. Frequently at the same time.

Stephens and Decker would spend the next few months attempting to piece together what had happened that night. They would interview several folks who had stayed at The Mission. Some individuals would give helpful clues; others would make up stories just for the free coffee and donuts. They would even interview the killer a few times. Eventually, the story would pull itself together enough for them to make an arrest and close the case a few days before Christmas. Stephens would then spend Christmas Eve alone in his home eating ramen noodles while watching *It's a Wonderful Life* on network television. Meanwhile, Decker would unwrap a gift of a bathroom edition crossword puzzle book that his wife had given him. They would both feel satisfied with their crime-fighting detective work.

Downtown, hundreds of cold and hungry people would line up outside of The Mission for their traditional Christmas Eve meal and the "room at the inn night" that allowed anyone to stay at the shelter, regardless of how many days they had stayed that month. Instead of finding a warm meal and a place to stay in memory of the manger, they would find an unceremonious note attached to the door that read:

Permanently Closed.

***

Few of us will ever know that a day will be our last. Even for those of us who are given a terminal diagnosis, we are only given a timeframe. We walk around with the idea of death looming over our days but rarely the certainty. Even for those who choose to make an early exit, they only presume that this day will be their last, but a million little variables could change that absolutism into choosing instead to live yet another day or decade. Some of us dread the thought of death, looking at every possible scenario as potentially the weapon of our demise from a paper cut to the logs precariously taunting us from the back of an eighteen-wheeler giving us flashbacks of what could be our final destination.

Sister Mary Margaret did not know that today she would be murdered, so she moved about the day with the same feeling of life she always did. Yet, as she moved throughout the mundanity of her day, death was stalking behind her, lurking behind each corner and in every shadow. The line of those seeking shelter nearly wrapped around the building. They had no idea that the normalcy of waiting for food and a meal would eventually make each one of them a suspect.

It was an unseasonably cold evening, which meant that more people than usual were attempting to seek shelter from the harsh elements. The demand always outweighed their ability, yet it was more pronounced on nights like tonight. It was Sister Mary Margaret's personal custom not to enter through the staff door in the back of the building. Instead, she would enter through the same door as the clients. She would ceremoniously walk up the line of souls seeking refuge and welcome each one with a smile while looking at them directly, greeting each one by name if she knew it and introducing herself if she did not. To her, simple little greetings and moments of acknowledgment made all the difference. When the line was especially long, the questions would cease to be about what was on the menu for the evening but if they would have enough room for everyone. With each step she took, she assured them that the sisters would make certain everyone would have a space to stay for the night. After her long journey to the front door, she fumbled around in the pockets of her habit to find the keys. They were nowhere to be found, causing her to wonder if she may have left them in her car or, possibly worse, back at the abbey. Mary Margaret offered up a quick prayer to Saint Anthony and then shuffled around in her pockets once again.

"Thank you, Tony!" she exclaimed as she felt the small circular keychain.

Though nothing was impressive about the building itself, being nothing more than a cinderblock structure that housed three separate non-profits, to hear the clients tell it this place was a place of hope. Yet, it contained in its unimpressive walls the keys to the Kingdom. To the sisters, especially Mary Margaret, there was nothing more holy or sacred than the souls they secured within these walls. Though they worked in tandem with the other organizations attached to the building, the shelter's residents would be the first to say that The Mission was the bedrock of security for each of them. The Mission strived to see the sacredness of each person they served. Sister Bernadette often said, "Each day, we strive not to have a job tomorrow." She said this to mean their purpose was to end the cycle of homelessness and not to be part of the problem.

As true as this might have been for The Mission, located to their right was The Coalition and to their left was the Fishes and Loaves Food Pantry. One was tasked with providing food to the community and the other was designed to provide funding for the organizations that served the poor and marginalized. It seemed that neither one worked particularly hard toward ending hunger or getting to a point where they would no longer have to ask for funds. Instead, they worked hard to be the band-aid over the bullet wound of poverty. They were not striving to be unemployed as Sister Bernadette was. No, they had already seen what happens to the jobless in this country and wanted to be very secure in their futures. Instead of those living on the streets being their clients, they were the commodity: the poor were the product.

If Sister Mary Margaret could have changed anything at all about the building, it would have been the collage of instructional notes surrounding the entrance to the building, which had become a hodgepodge of handwritten rules and admonishments that were then placed inside plastic inserts for protection before being taped to the door, rarely ever being read. She hated all those rules. They seemed to her a rather cruel introduction to life at The Mission. It was not at all how she envisioned this place when she heard about it over the Catholic radio station her grandmother used to listen to when she would visit her for the summer.

Nothing about this place at all looked like she imagined. In her mind, as a child, she thought that The Mission would look like a grand cathedral with rooms and that each room would look more beautiful than the next, kind of like that mansion with many rooms that Jesus described he would build with his Father. This vision made her realize from a young age that she wanted to be a nun so that one day she would work at The Mission helping the helpless. Instead, upon arrival, she was met first with a "No Loitering" sign. Sure, some of the notices gave helpful information like the hours of operation or the days of the week one could do laundry. There was also one that was just a symbol of guns, knives, and needles with a red crossed-out circle surrounding it to indicate that these were banned paraphernalia. In the center of all these notes was one with a quote from Mother Teresa that was no longer legible but had once read, "Find your own Calcutta," yet next to it was another notice that said, "No food on Sundays."

The reality of the place was much darker than the idealistic mansion she had created in her mind as a child. Each day, as she made her way inside, she surveyed the cots nuzzled head to head in the room that would triple as the chapel, sleeping area, and dining room. This was not a grand cathedral in honor of the Lord, just a windowless building with fading murals on the walls that one of the clients had painted for free in exchange for an extra week's stay at the shelter. This place was not the temple; it was the manger.

Inside, Mary Margaret found Sister Meredith was already preparing the tables. Tonight, the meal would be provided by a local Methodist congregation, so the other sisters had the night off from cooking.

"Sister," Meredith said with a nod, "once I am done here, I need to discuss something with you. Why don't you go on into the office and I will meet you there in a moment?"

"Of course, but are you sure you don't need any help?" Mary Margaret asked sweetly.

"No," Meredith said, pointing toward the office with her nose as both hands were full of condiments and disposable placemats. "Meet me there. I'll be faster without your help."

Coming from anyone else, this may have sounded like an insult, but from Sister Meredith it did not. At least not to Mary Margaret it didn't. She was correct, but not because Mary Margaret was particularly slow, it was just that Meredith was faster when no one was distracting her. It was simply how she was wired; at this age, she wasn't interested in changing her personality to accommodate the feelings of others. Mary Margaret left the other sister to her solitude and made her way to the office, taking a seat as commanded.

Though they called it "the office," it was, in reality, nothing more than a glorified broom closet with a desk and two chairs. The walls were covered in an out-of-date calendar and a cork board with more rules plastered across it. A cheap crucifix hung on the wall behind the desk that was slightly off-tilt. It was made of thin wood and had a brass corpus that was missing a nail and needed a good polishing. Just a generic replication of Jesus at his worst moment, the same kind of crucifix one might see adorning the rooms of hospitals. Mary Margaret nervously fidgeted for a few moments waiting for Meredith to arrive.

"I'm going to cut right to the chase," Meredith said plainly as she entered the room before making her way to the desk, moving a few papers around to busy herself.

Cutting to the chase was maybe one of Sister Mary Margaret's favorite qualities about Sister Meredith. She also always told you she was going to cut to the chase. Mary Margaret was a very nervous person by nature and she appreciated people who got straight to the point without making too much of a fuss.

"Levi is missing." Meredith relayed this information with a tender tone that was a bit out of character. "He hasn't been seen for days and that is just how it is sometimes."

Levi had been with The Mission for as long as anyone could remember. He was the first person ever to greet Mary Margaret when she arrived as a young novice. His frame was tall and slender. When he gave her the tour of the facility, he'd had to duck as he walked through the doors due to his height. Even though he was much older than most who stayed at the shelter, his hair remained nearly jet-black, except for a single streak of stark white that ran directly down the center of his scalp. This earned him the nickname of skunk on the streets. He didn't care for the name much as he thought it might have a double meaning. Sister Mary Margaret never called him skunk and he liked that very much about her.

Levi was gentle and kind, except when he wasn't. Before his white streak appeared, they used to call him

The Jackal, a reference to his mood swings being like Dr. Jekyll and Mr. Hyde. He didn't much care for being called skunk, but he preferred it to The Jackal, though he would have much preferred that everyone just called him Levi, as Sister Mary Margaret did. He tried hard not to let the nicknames get to him. It wasn't as if he hated nicknames; he had even given one away himself once to Sister Mary Margaret.

"You are Sister M&M," he once told her, "because you are as sweet as candy."

He wished that others saw the sweetness in him instead of naming him after a madman or a smelly animal. It wasn't as if he enjoyed losing his temper, but sometimes the spells overtook him. He suffered from a traumatic brain injury, the result of a worksite injury many years ago. In his previous life, he had worked on an oil rig, and one day a pipe came loose, careening toward one of his shipmates. Levi believed that his brute strength alone could stop the metal as it crashed down toward the other man. Instead, he woke up weeks later at the local hospital. He should have died; some days, he wished he had. For years he walked around with the business card of a personal injury attorney in his pocket. He meant to call him, but he had to meet with his landlord to discuss why he had gotten behind on rent. Then he was busy making arrangements to move his items into a storage unit. He slept under the stars on the nights it didn't rain and inside the storage unit on the evenings it did. He opened a PO Box so his work could send him a check that never came. Walking the streets for miles each day searching for food was hard work. He sweated through that attorney's business card for nearly two years until, one day, someone asked him if he had something they could write a note on and he gave them the card. That was the last he ever saw of it and the last he ever thought of it.

That is the nature of a traumatic brain injury.

All that Sister Mary Margaret could think about was wanting to rescue poor Levi: from wandering around in his shattered mind and these shattered streets. Sister Meredith had an entirely different worry, which was to convince Mary Margaret not to go wandering at all. For nearly thirty minutes, Sister Meredith explained to the young nun all the reasons why she could not go looking for the lost sheep, and those words were not penetrating. With each plea she could see in Mary Margaret's eyes her intention to walk down the hallway, grab her coat, and make her way outside to search for her missing friend.

"You cannot go," Meredith finally said with a sternness that nearly made Mary Margaret cry on the spot. "I forbid it; that is the end of it."

"Yes, I understand," Mary Margaret meekly stuttered, fighting back the tears.

"No, lying!" Meredith shouted. This caused the waterworks to finally burst, which caused Meredith to realize her error in phrasing. "Not you, child. Them!"

Sister Meredith was pointing toward the clients who had begun to make their way into the main hall and had begun to lie down before dinner. They did this to secure the best beds before the meal was served. Two beds were most favored, the one near the bathroom and the one near the back exit door, where they could sometimes sneak out and have a smoke after lights out. The two sisters were never able to finish their conversation as they now had to check on the guests before chaos ensued, but before they made their way out to the lobby, dinner was announced and all the men got up to enjoy their meal.

Mary Margaret enjoyed meal time the best of all because it felt the most like how she imagined it should be. Instead of just slopping food onto trays, the guests sat at the tables and were served a proper meal like they were at a restaurant. They got to choose which items they preferred to eat and which drink they would like to drink, and they were allowed to get seconds if they so chose. On occasion, the dinner guests would even tip the servers. The volunteers had a jar in the kitchen that they would place these small offerings into and then they gave the funds back to the work of The Mission.

Though the meal was lovely, Mary Margaret could only think about how cold it was tonight and that Levi was out there, somewhere, probably very lost and confused. The only other thing that crossed her mind was when Sister Meredith said to her, "Promise you won't go looking for Levi." In that very moment that she had finished the sentence, maybe even before she had fully said Levi, one of the ladies from the Methodist church had knocked on the door to ask a question, which pulled Sister Meredith away from their conversation. As a result, Mary Margaret had not said the words, "I promise." Because of this, she felt she was not bound to any such promise since no promise had been given, only a request for a promise made. There was the issue of being forbidden, but then again, Meredith was not her superior. Meredith may have been a great deal older than Mary Margaret; still, seniority was not the same thing as superiority, and Meredith only had the former and not the latter. Since she had already survived thinking Meredith had called her a liar, she was sure she could endure it again.

At this moment, she resolved to escape and go search for Levi.

She waited for the folks from the Methodist church to leave and for the lights to be turned off. Then she waited some more for Meredith to make her own sneaky maneuver to the back patio for a brief smoke. This would be the moment of her grand escape.

Though The Mission was far inland, the winds coming in from the waters cut deep that night. The humidity only worsened matters and it was not yet the coldest part of the evening. The previous year, two people froze to death on the streets and Sister Mary Margaret was not about to let Levi become a statistic.

About a mile from The Mission, under the bridge by the water, there was a vent that could be opened and it led to a little room of sorts. It was supposed to be an overflow from the drainage pipes, but they had long ago clogged, making this a relatively dry place. It was here he went when he had to "hide Mr. Hyde." That was what he called it when he couldn't stabilize his moods anymore. He would hide for a bit until he felt safe to be around people again. Usually, it was only a day or two at the most for him to emerge. It was never long enough to be alarming or for anyone to take much notice. But this time was different.

Sister M&M walked in a rush, constantly looking over her shoulder, afraid that Meredith would go searching for her to stop her plan. When she finally reached the bridge, she could see the grate had been moved to the side and was hopeful that Levi was inside. Before she even reached the grate itself, she began to call out Levi's name into the void, but a low growl greeted her before a familiar gruff voice rose from within the darkness.

"I knew you would find me. I fucking knew it, you fucking bastards," Levi howled.

"Levi, it's me. Sister M&M. I heard you hadn't been by in a while.'

"Do you have any identification?" Levi asked sternly.

"I don't; I am sorry."

"Who sent you?" Levi demanded.

"No one sent me, my love," Mary Margaret said with the sweetness that earned her the moniker, "I just came looking for you to make sure you were all right."

"You are going to die, bitch!" Levi screamed as he began to charge at the sister. As he emerged from the darkness, their eyes met. At that moment, Mary Margaret knew she had made a grave mistake in going there. She could see in his countenance that something was indeed different about Levi this night than any other night. In the slow motion of adrenaline, she wondered what might have happened: could he have lapsed on a medication? Maybe he took something he wasn't supposed to. His traumatic brain injury was degenerative; was it possible he had fallen further down the rabbit hole than ever before? The real Levi was being held hostage in his mind, and this imposter, the one crashing toward her, had taken him captive. He began to thrust towards the specter in his mind, the one standing in the exact location where Mary Margaret now stood, and she began to run, not from the Levi she knew but the one that was now possessed by trauma.

As she ran, she held up the skirt of her habit, along with her rosary that dangled from her belt. She was making great speed, but with Levi being nearly seven feet tall, he gained on her substantially with each stride. His gait was so broad that he seemed to sail across the air as he pursued her. Thinking she heard a noise, Mary Margaret turned around. Though Levi was gaining ground, he was still further behind than she'd thought. Because she was looking backward, she did not see a small patch of ice that had formed on the road ahead of her and she fell for the first time.

"Fuck!" she screamed as she pulled herself up quickly.

She darted around a corner, but it was not as brilliant an idea as she initially thought. There was only one way out, down an alleyway between a discount bread market and a liquor store. At this point, anything was better than being caught, so she continued to run toward the escape route. Part of her hoped that when she turned into the alley, one of the clients from The Mission might have snuck out for a cigarette and would see her, but tonight was too bitterly cold. No one would be so foolish as to be outside—no one except for her and Levi.

A chill ran up her spine as she felt a hand graze across her back. She tripped a second time, but before fully hitting the ground, she kept running. She thought she must have looked like the Roadrunner as he spun his legs just before taking off. All of this fear and anxiety was building up inside her, yet her brain was playing it out like a cartoon. Her lungs were burning from the freezing air. It had been a while since she had run any substantial distance and she could feel she didn't have much more in her. Her body was giving up.

Escaping the alleyway, she reached a small park on the other side. She fell a third and final time just before she made it to the swing set. As she fell flat on her stomach, she thrust her head up first as she pressed against the ground to lift her body. In this moment of exacerbated weakness, Levi jumped on top of her, straddling the small of her back and pinning her down with his giant body. He kept her head held up by her veil and bandeau. With a singular motion, he cut her across the throat. The blood flowed slowly at first before it began to rush in earnest. She reached for her throat to hold back the bleeding in vain. She fell onto her back, looking up toward the stars, which were remarkably visible on this crisp night. *What a beautiful last moment on Earth,* she thought. Instead of the stars, her eyes were met with the face of Levi looking down at her. He had returned to himself as Sister Mary Margaret watched his eyes shift back and forth in terror. He had finally been allowed to leave whatever place of torture he had been held captive in, only to awaken to this hell.

"Sister!" Levi screamed as he placed his hand over hers, trying desperately to hold the blood in. "Did I do this? I'm so sorry."

She was gasping for air and having a difficult time getting the words out. So many words were traveling through her mind, things she wished to say to him. She couldn't make the words escape her. He kept apologizing and she kept trying to forgive him. Looking up at him, she released her hand from her neck and ran it through his beard.

You didn't know, she thought but could not say.

She smiled up at him, hoping he could feel all of the love and forgiveness that she was giving him. Could he hear her heart? Levi's eyes were filled with tears, but Sister Mary Margaret kept smiling until her eyes finally closed. Levi held her there, wailing and covered in blood and tears. Soon, the tears were replaced with determination as he realized the danger he was now in. He lifted Sister Mary Margaret; she nearly disappeared into his long arms. There was no one out on the streets; not even the police patrolled because they figured everyone was too cold to commit crimes. The entire time he walked with the sister in his arms Levi kept talking to her, hoping her soul was still close enough to hear his words.

"I am so sorry, Sister M&M. I didn't mean to; I didn't see you. I promise I didn't."

When Levi finally made it to The Mission, someone was standing outside smoking a cigarette. He stood in the shadows, with Sister Mary Margaret in his arms, waiting for the smoker to sneak back inside. Before even finishing the whole cigarette, the man snuck around the corner and went back inside. Without hesitation, Levi snuck across the road up to the front door of The Mission. He gently laid Sister Mary Margaret down on the ground. He pulled out one of those pieces of paper, the one with the disappeared quote from Mother Teresa, and wrote, "I'm sorry. I didn't mean to," on it, placing it under Sister M&M's shoulder. He realized that he had placed the sister with her feet facing the street and feared someone might trip over her or jump the curb and hit her. He gently took her by the shoulders and turned her. As he did this, the blood that had dripped on the sidewalk made a circular image that haloed her head. It was this motion that dislodged the note just enough that it would blow away. Just before he left, he noticed that her smile had not yet wholly faded. As he looked down at her face one last time, he felt forgiven. With this, he disappeared into the darkness.

***

Neither Sergeant Stephens nor Sergeant Decker were particularly intelligent men. Though they both fashioned themselves to be the American Sherlock Holmes, in actuality they had blundered more cases than they ever solved. They trampled on evidence, improperly executed a few warrants, and falsely accused the wrong person twice. Both times it resulted in a conviction, one of them being a death penalty case. Those innocent men were never exonerated.

It was only by pure dumb luck that a store clerk mentioned seeing a giant of a man outside The Mission the night that Sister Mary Margaret lost her life. When they asked around, they were directed to Levi, who promptly confessed when asked directly. They arrested him on December 17th, 1984. On December 24th of that same year, the bishop closed the doors of The Mission for good. He was unconcerned with the irony of such an action. He had long looked for an excuse to close down this project and the death of a nun at the hands of an undesirable was as good a reason as any.

The building remained in the care of the diocese until such a time as it would be financially beneficial to sell it. Unfortunately for the diocese, such an opportunity never presented itself. The city continued to blight the area, using it as its own personal wasteland for every project they didn't want to be on the more prominent sides of town. And then, one day, to the great surprise of many, the Pope announced Sister Mary Margaret as a candidate for sainthood. Now retired, Sergeant Stephens wished he could call his late partner Decker to let him know how wrong he was.

Because of the uniqueness of the situation and because a new bishop had recently been appointed to the diocese, this more ambitious bishop saw an opportunity. Should Sister Mary Margaret be canonized as a saint, then the former mission where she had worked and died would become a holy site: a place of pilgrimage. There would be no end in sight of the number of faithful who would travel and, of course, spend money to see this place. So, on the anniversary of her death, December 17th, 2021, the bishop announced that they would soon reopen The Mission and dedicate it to her memory.

And that is precisely where our story begins, as Father Caspian began as the new administrator of the Sister Mary Margaret Mission for Those Experiencing Homelessness.

CHAPTER ONE

F*uck* was the first word that entered Father Caspian's mind as his eyes flickered open that morning. By the time he had got around to writing his morning journal entry, he had expounded upon the thought from a simple expletive to, "I have royally fucked up." Those five words were all he could muster to pen before finding a less wrinkled clerical shirt to place on then making his way downstairs to have his breakfast. It was not his surroundings that had made him feel this way; the rectory was lovely. He was assigned to the Basilica of Saint Raphael, a French-styled miniature cathedral that nearly dwarfed the competitors in neighboring New Orleans. However, they might not compare to any actual French cathedrals. He could not be sure of that as he had not yet ever traveled to France, or anywhere else outside of the United States for that matter. He was, however, a bit of an expert on New Orleans as he had attended a local seminary in the city of Southern decadence. He could never have imagined then that his time at school was what would have ultimately led him to this respite he was now enjoying just outside the city of Mobile in Alabama.

The town was quaint and excessively Southern. Before moving to Alabama, Caspian had always assumed that the South was just one big pile of rednecks. Instead, he quickly learned that he didn't even have his pejoratives correct. There was a vast difference between rednecks, hillbillies, and trailer trash. Some of these lines could be blurred depending on how close your proximity was to the Appalachian Mountains and if you were along a ridge running east or west. He had also wrongly assumed that he knew much about the South from his time in New Orleans as a seminary student. This was also incorrect. New Orleans might be geographically located within the South, but it is no more a Southern town than Miami, albeit the southernmost tip of the country. No, New Orleans has a culture all to its own that is rooted in Haitian, Creole, French, Irish, Native American, and Cajun, to name a few. It is Southern in its rugged independence and yet entirely different from any other community along the panhandle. For one, New Orleans does not frequently have sweet iced tea, as one would often read about in Southern literature.

In contrast, the communities surrounding Mobile only serve sweet tea and Coke. Now, it should be noted that by Coke they mean any soda pop beverage one might have in mind. So if a person were ordering a soda pop, they would do so as follows:

"And what would you like to drink today, darling?" the waitress might inquire.

"I'll have a Coke," the patron would respond.

To which the waitress would smile without any sense of irony whatsoever and say, "What kind of Coke would you like?"

"Sprite," the patron could say back and the server would go to retrieve the non-Coke coke.

It appeared to Father Caspian that this was not about brand loyalty but simply that everything one could consume, from root beer to Dr. Pepper, was classified under the "Coke" category. In a similarly confusing fashion, all a person would have to do to obtain a sweet tea is order "tea" without any description whatsoever. They would not need to indicate that they wished to have a sweet tea or an iced tea. The presumption would be that you were defaulting to sweet tea and if you wished to order something other than sweet tea, you would need to clarify this beforehand by saying, "I would like an unsweet tea," or, "Do you serve hot tea?" and it was not always the case that an establishment would serve hot tea. Though most did serve tea unsweetened, it had also become clear to Father Caspian that those that consumed unsweet only did so for health reasons and not because they disliked the taste of sweetened tea, because if you ordered an unsweet tea, the waitress would bring you out a small canister full of pink, blue, and white sugar and sugar alternative packets so you could pick which way you'd like to convert your previously unsweet tea into a sweet tea.

Father Caspian did not feel he had "royally fucked up" due to his surroundings or because of ordering colloquialisms. He found all of this exceptionally charming and was rather enjoying the Southern life. What he despised about this current iteration of his existence was his station in life.

For the outside observer, there was nothing particularly unpleasant about his life. His needs were met, he had food every day, and his living arrangements were rather nice. The basilica was exquisite and a pleasing place to celebrate your faith. The ceilings were remarkably high, and as you walked down the center aisle, to your right, if you were facing the altar, some pews were cut at three-quarters length that abutted a spiral staircase that led down into underground catacombs where many priests, nuns, and benefactors of the basilica were buried. The place was rich in history and, during the sunrise, the light hit the stained glass in just such a way as to make the entire basilica feel as if you were living inside of a rainbow. Since Caspian was a child, he had always fantasized about catching a rainbow and being able to run through the bottom where it touched the ground and seeing the splashes of color consume everything around him. Being inside this basilica was probably the closest he would ever get to that feeling and he enjoyed it immensely.

Between the basilica and the rectory was a small courtyard surrounded by wrought iron fencing. It had two giant statues, one of the Sacred Heart of Jesus and another of the Virgin Mary as she appears on the Miraculous Medal. Each sculpture had been there a while as they had a lovely patina. There were rose bushes encircling both figures that let off a pleasant aroma. The garden's centerpiece was a rather large tree drenched with Spanish moss. He could easily walk from the back end of the church, exiting the sacristy and directly into the rectory kitchen without going through the front portion of the building where the receptionist's office was. Two large French doors with stained glass separated the office space from the kitchen for some added privacy. During the day, they did share the joint space with the church staff, but by evening time, he could easily go downstairs in his robe and enjoy a nightcap with the pastor of Saint Raphael's, Father Kilpatrick.

Usually, it would be customary to call a priest by their first name, as with Father Caspian, but Father Kilpatrick did not like this custom and preferred to be addressed by his title and last name in public. However, Caspian was able to address him as Michael in private.

The upstairs of the rectory had four separate rooms, each decorated with what appeared to be period furniture. The rooms did not have individual television sets, but a lounge room in the center of the apartments had a television, a Bluetooth jukebox, and a pool table. There was also a bar at the far end corner to entertain other clergy that might visit from time to time. The bishop considered the basilica one of the crowning jewels of the diocese and he would often place visiting clergy to stay there. After having been there for just a short while, Caspian could certainly see why. In many ways, this was quite a step up from where he had served all the way on the other side of the country in California. The rectory at that parish was more like a dormitory and considerably smaller. It was not as old but was in much more disrepair. It smelled of mildew and still had a faint scent of cigarette smoke that would occasionally ooze from the walls. The smell was still stuck there from back when it was a bustling place and all of the priests used to smoke. In every sense, he loved the basilica far more than his previous home back on the West Coast as it smelled of cedar and mothballs.

The reason his first thought that morning was, *Fuck,* which ultimately evolved into "I have royally fucked up" by the time he found his journal, was simply because he was not the pastor of this basilica. He was only attached to the facility as a part-time associate. In many ways, he was fortunate; it wasn't as if he had been relocated to this facility due to any scandal or public shame, other than the fact that he was just not a very good pastor. Previously, he had been stationed at a medium-sized parish with an aging congregation for a brief time. In that short time, he had accumulated a great deal of complaints about his homilies, his demeanor during confessions, and that, as one parishioner put it, "I am not sure that Father Caspian has a clear understanding of the Catholic faith, much less how to administrate a parish properly." Now, usually, this would not have been the worst chastisement a priest could receive during the course of their career, but, unfortunately for Caspian, this complaint came from one of the members of the parish council. They also happened to be the chief benefactor of the parish. After less than a year of serving his first full-time pastoral assignment he had been moved into acting as a supply priest for the diocese to fill in for other clergy when they were sick or on vacation.

Shortly after the removal from this post, he'd had to attend a diocesan retreat. He had dreaded that because this meant he was in trouble and he hated being in trouble. However, he was pleased to learn that his former classmate would be one of the speakers. They had dinner the first evening of the conference. This former seminarian friend of his had now been elevated to the bishop of the diocese that oversaw much of the panhandle, which included

Mobile, and, upon hearing of all of the discontentment that Father Caspian was feeling, the bishop offered him the opportunity to switch diocese, move to the South, and assist him with a new project that he was working on. At the time, Caspian welcomed any change that might come his way. So, after some extensive paperwork, he moved across the country to take on yet another job he knew absolutely nothing about: reopening The Mission, which had now been renamed the Sister Mary Margaret Mission for Those Experiencing Homelessness. And it was this assignment that he had gleefully accepted that made Father Caspian feel royally fucked this morning.

The feeling was for two very distinct reasons:

1. His classmate was already a bishop and he couldn't even maintain a job as a pastor
2. He had absolutely no fucking clue what he was doing at the shelter any more than he knew how to administrate a parish.

However, Father Caspian was in too deep at this point and he couldn't imagine having to go back to school to learn a new trade or starting life over in his forties. Instead, he decided that any opportunity was better than none, even if he did feel royally fucked about the whole ordeal at this particular juncture.

After his moment of existential crisis, he enjoyed a bowl of cereal with Father Kilpatrick before he began his half-mile walk to the wrong side of town where The

Mission was located. One thing Caspian noticed about living in the South was that people were not too keen on change and, even though The Mission had been renamed, that did not stop nearly everyone in the town from continuing to refer to it as The Mission. In order to blend in, he too continued to refer to it as The Mission.

As he made the final block to The Mission, he could see a man sitting on the stoop outside the front door in the distance. He always called it a stoop, but in reality, it was an old planter bed that had long ago stopped being used for plants and became a community ashtray/trash can. Above the planter was small sign printed on plain paper, placed inside a plastic insert, and taped to the window that overlooked the planter, which read, "Do not dispose of cigarettes or other rubbish in the planter." This pleading, however, seemed only to increase the amount of rubbish placed inside the former planter.

The man sitting upon the planter's edge was smoking a cigarette and Caspian made a mental note of this as he approached. Caspian had never seen this gentleman before, so he slowed his stride to see how he would handle it as the man had nearly completed his cigarette. After taking another drag, the man pulled the cigarette close to his face, examining how close the embers were to the butt. He then determined he had enough tobacco to inhale one last drag before reaching into his bag. He then pulled out a small green and brass container, setting it atop the planter's edge. He reached over and pushed a tiny button on what was now obviously the front lid and the brass top began to open delicately on its hinges, revealing that it was a portable ashtray. The man daintily put his cigarette out, closed the brass lid, and placed the antique contraption back into his backpack just as Father Caspian approached the front door.

"Hello, my son," the man said to Caspian.

"Good morning," Caspian responded with a slight chuckle as that wasn't a customary greeting to give a priest; it was usually the other way around. "I've not seen you around before. Are you new here?"

"No, you are new here," the man responded. "I am quite old; I've just returned from a bout of forty days in the wilderness."

"That is nice," Caspian said half-heartedly as he couldn't seem to get the key to work.

"It was Hell," the unidentified stranger said. "Quite literally, Hell. The devil tempted me, you know. Of course, it wasn't my first rodeo or anything; I've been quite the professional at being tempted by the devil at this point. Doesn't make it any less annoying, mind you."

"I see." The good father was not in the mood this morning, but the key was still not working. He wondered if he'd left with the wrong keys.

"I'm not rightfully sure you do; this temptation was a mighty one for sure. The devil came at me with hard drink, drugs, and more whores than you could shake a stick at."

"We don't open until 4:00 PM," Caspian responded, but this time the door popped open. *Eureka,* he thought to himself.

"Wouldn't be the first time there hasn't been room at the inn for me, Father," the man said with equal measures of amusement and disdain.

"I see," Caspian uttered a second time. "I'm Father Caspian."

"Jesus Christ." As he extended his hand to Caspian, the man said, "I am the second coming of the Lord here on Earth; I am pleased to meet you."

"Well, it's nice to meet you too; we are going to have to talk about my dental plan," Caspian quipped. "But even for the Almighty, we don't open until 4:00 PM."

With that, Caspian made his way inside but did not turn around to close the door fast enough and Jesus Christ followed him inside. Before Caspian could think of the words to try to adios the Lord back outside, Jesus Christ was making himself quite comfortable on his own, giving himself a tour of the facility. He walked into the kitchen first and had a good look before helping himself to a cold cup of coffee. He was sipping the coffee when his eyes caught the television set and he walked over in that direction for a while. He looked the device up and down for a few moments before quickly being distracted by a bookshelf that lay along the wall where the doors to the bathroom and shower facilities were. He placed his face very close to the bookshelves' side panels, running his hands sensually up and down the grain.

"Absolutely fucking awful craftsmanship," Jesus Christ finally exclaimed.

"Excuse me?"

"Just goddamn horrible. I tell you what"—he shook his head vigorously—"I am completely shocked this fucking thing hasn't fallen over. These joints here, they don't fit right. Back in my day, I would have gotten these as tight as a cunt hair; I tell you what."

Caspian stood there with his mouth partially ajar in complete shock over the situation he now found himself in. Detecting the confusion, Jesus Christ looked over at Father Caspian with a shrug and then pointed toward himself with an explanatory motion, simply saying, "Carpenter."

Had he more time, Caspian would have likely taken the bait and debated this man on the fact that it was unlikely that Jesus was a carpenter. It was Joseph who was the carpenter, and even then, it was probably a translation error and he could have been any level of tradesman, most likely a mason of some persuasion. Jesus, on the other hand, had made it very clear that he was going about his Father's business and all accounts seemed to lead to the idea that Jesus followed into some level of rabbinical studies. There was no evidence he ever lifted a hammer. These would have all been fine points to debate, but, sadly, he didn't have the time or the constitution for it that morning. Instead, he placed his hand out gently toward Jesus' back, motioning him toward the door.

"Should we need your services in the future, I am sure we will call on you." He then considered ending this statement with, "Do you have a number where I can call since you don't seem to be answering any of my prayers?" But he decided against it, instead walking him the rest of the way to the door where he thanked him again for stopping by and again reminded him that they would be open at 4:00 PM. With that, he locked the door and turned back toward the office space.

In the solitude of this broom closet turned office, the intrusive thought of how royally fucked he was began to ring and echo through his mind. On his desk was a list of assignments for the day. He was to call the volunteers for the evening to ensure they would be in attendance. The Unitarian Universalist Church that was supposed to be preparing the meal tonight was back on a brief lockdown after the pastor had a breakthrough COVID case. He would now need to call the folks over at the country buffet to see if they could pull through on that last-minute meal they promised they could provide once a month for just such occasions. Should they not be able to on such short notice, it would be pizza again tonight. It would then be time to reach out to the receptionist at St. Raphael's to see if the flyers had been made for the upcoming donors' tour so they could see the improvements made at the facility. There was also a missing sticky note that contained some other function he was supposed to be doing. He couldn't remember it, of course, and that was why he had placed it on the sticky note to begin with.

This will be the rest of my life, he thought. Many people would have felt it a pretty remarkable life; I suppose many others would have shared in Father Caspian's opinion that it was a mundane life. Whichever way you observe it, it certainly wasn't the life he had envisioned when he was in seminary. He knew it wouldn't always be pea soup and other such adventures, but this seemed painfully demeaning. It was not what he had planned. He had hoped to continue his studies at the Vatican and eventually become a very learned person. Maybe someday he would have grown up to be a custodian of the Vatican Library or eventually ascend to some important distinction like sitting on the Congregation of the Doctrine of the Faith. Something interesting, something grand, something other than this. Instead, he was the administrator of a facility he knew nothing about, cared nothing about, and the entire thing felt like such a letdown to the life he had hoped to one day live.

He picked up the phone and said, "Yes, this is Father Caspian and I would like to talk with someone about getting a meal delivered for tonight at The Mission." He paused for a moment to listen. "Yes, I'll hold."

CHAPTER TWO

If what Father Caspian had feared that day was that his life was going to be a boring one, he was now suddenly missing the mundane. He was correct in his internal assessment that he was woefully ill-prepared for this position. Not only did he lack any personal desire to help the poor, but he also had no experience or training to deal with the myriad of difficulties that shelter clients faced in their daily lives. Before this experience, like many other members of society, Caspian had assumed this would be a relatively easy job. How difficult could it be to operate a program that volunteers essentially ran? He quickly learned it was quite difficult and it would be a profound understatement to say things were going badly. However, he was also quickly learning that this was the type of position where one was allowed to fuck up a lot and no one would really notice.

Unlike when he worked as a parish priest, where even the slightest word being out of place could result in a parishioner calling the bishop's office to complain, there was no such thing within The Mission. The expectations of success for a program like this were set low. As long as there was somewhere for people to go and volunteer and the clients were fed each day there would be no complaints from anyone. Accomplishing these two elementary tasks, making the volunteers happy and ensuring the clients had food, was all it took for folks to call his mediocrity success. He began to realize that the bar was set so low because society didn't expect much good for those in the care of The Mission. There was no requirement for him to ensure that clients were placed in housing, found jobs, or improved their lives. They would rotate people out, make sure the cots were filled, and keep the violence to a minimum. This was a relatively easy task as most of the guests at the shelter were exceedingly grateful to have a warm and dry place to stay for the night.

Things were getting out of hand at the shelter and it seemed that Caspian, being neither a social worker nor a clinician, had no idea how to address the deeper needs of those in his care. This was evident in small ways like he was constantly referring clients to other agencies instead of helping them address any of their problems through the program he was operating. If someone needed anything outside the basic needs The Mission supplied, namely shelter and food, he considered it something he couldn't handle and sent them on their way. His inability to address the complexities of the human condition prevented him from stopping a crisis of biblical proportions from growing into a full-blown apocalyptic event.

Shortly after Jesus Christ had returned from his time in the desert, and by desert he meant a brief hospitalization for a staph infection, he met a prostitute by the name of Beth. She had been working on one of the streets not far from the shelter when Jesus Christ met her. He approached her to inquire about her profession and that was when things got interesting. Though he would not admit it now, Jesus Christ was approaching Beth to solicit her services when she happened to recognize him.

"Aren't you that guy they call Jesus Christ?" Beth asked, mostly unconcerned with the answer.

"It is you that say that I am," he responded with a terrible British accent that he often adopted when attempting to sound especially holy. "Do you say this because you have heard this about me or does it come from your heart?"

"The fuck is that supposed to mean?" Beth was indignant with the question. "I only know it because last week, at the feeding, the Chicken Man told me that I should be watching out because there is some whacko who says he is the second coming of Jesus and you kinda look like what he described, being as you are wearing a robe and sandals and the whole works like you are working down at Bible Adventureland or some shit."

"I am the I AM," he said in response to this. "Would you like to stop sucking dick and start being a fisher of men in a different way than you are currently?"

"The fuck is that supposed to mean?" she asked again.

"I am going to give you a new name." The British accent now sounded a bit more Australian. "You are Mary Magdalene and you shall be my first disciple."

"Sounds better than nothing, I guess; what's a disciple got to do?"

"You help me manage all the other disciples as I share my message, of course," Jesus Christ said matter of factly as if everyone knew this was the role of a disciple.

Considering that the police had recently been cracking down on prostitution since election season was around the corner, Beth thought this was a pretty good idea as far as career changes went. She and Jesus Christ shook hands on the arrangement. The two made an excellent team and, though they had not collected a perfect twelve just yet, their following was growing in droves. They had built up quite the little cult of about seven followers, nine in total if you included Mary, who used to be called Beth, and Jesus Christ himself. They were quite the gang and things became increasingly more troublesome after Jesus Christ performed his first miracle. Another homeless gentleman by the name of Black Jack had recently come down with a pretty high fever. At the request of some of his new disciples, Jesus Christ visited Black Jack at his campsite and gathered everyone around while he prayed for him to be healed.

"God!" Jesus Christ prayed, now with the gravitas of a street preacher and no trace of a British or Austrian accent; he then immediately responded to himself with, "Yes?"

The conversation went back and forth with himself like this for the better part of five minutes as he pleaded for the healing of Black Jack and then proceeded to go into all the reasons why Black Jack had ripped him off in the past and wasn't a very good person. The debate got intense for a while until Jesus Christ decided that it was the better and more honorable thing to go ahead and forgive Black Jack for all of his sins and past shortcomings. Once that was settled, he extended his hand to Black Jack and said, "You are healed, but if you fuck up again, so help me, I won't heal you again and you are fucking dead. You got that?" Jack nodded in agreement, which was the end of it. It would have been an uninteresting exchange, except that Black Jack was completely well the following day. His fever broke shortly after the whole healing ordeal and not only did Jesus Christ declare this a legitimate miracle, but so did a bunch of other folks.

Everyone staying at the shelter considered the impromptu Sermon on the Dinner Table that Jesus Christ would give each evening to be either legitimate or, at the very least, more entertaining than watching the same six movies on repeat. It was during one such event that Father Caspian tried to quell the coup, right in the middle of a rousing sermon on, "Why women shouldn't be talking back to a man if they know what's good for them because they ain't no smarter than a common snake. No man would be tricked by a stupid fucking viper. As a matter of fact, if it were me in the Garden of Eden, I would have grabbed that snake straight around its neck and then…." Jesus Christ trailed off because he suddenly got distracted by his uncertainty as to whether snakes had necks or if the whole body of a snake is one big neck. It was during this lull in his sermon that Father Caspian decided to jump in and ask Jesus Christ to meet him in his office.

Jesus Christ decided this was an excellent opportunity to stop for a brief moment and regroup his thoughts before continuing. He told everyone at the table to wait and think about what he had said and followed Caspian to the office.

"You can't continue on with these sermons," Father Caspian told Jesus Christ frankly.

"And who the fuck do you think you are to tell the Son of God what to fucking do?"

Ignoring the blatant blasphemy, Caspian continued, "Well, I am the administrator of this facility and we are having some complaints."

"From who?" Jesus Christ demanded sternly. "I'll smite the shit out of them. I'll smite them like no motherfucker has been smote before. Was it Charlie? I fucking hate that guy. He's been due for a good fucking smiting for a while, if I am being honest."

"No, it wasn't Charlie!" Caspian blurted out. The last thing he needed was the Lord and Charlie getting into a fistfight over dinner.

"If you can't provide me with a name, I'll pray on it. But last I checked, I have a Seventeenth Amendment right to know the name of my accusers."

The 17th Amendment of the Constitution does not promise any such protection. The 17th Amendment of the Constitution of the United States has to do with the number of senators from each state and how to fill their vacancies in the absence of a senator. It turns out there is no such amendment at all that would bind Father Caspian from divulging who it was that complained about Jesus Christ giving these sermons. This fact did not stop Jesus Christ from demanding that Father Caspian ensured that his constitutional rights were not being violated. Even after Caspian read the entire text of the 17th Amendment out loud, Jesus Christ was still sure that, even if he got the number of the amendment wrong, there was some amendment that demanded that Caspian cough up the names of his accusers. Father Caspian said at this point, "If this continues, I am going to have to ask you not to return for a while."

Jesus Christ stood up to his feet and walked back out into the dining room. Caspian quickly followed just as Jesus Christ began going into another robust sermon. "This man, who works for the very Whore of Babylon, is attempting to kick the Son of Man out!"

There was a figure hovering over in the corner near the entrance door. He had slipped in during the commotion and was accompanied by none other than Black Jack himself, the man at the center of the first known miracle of Jesus Christ of Mobile. The two men were standing there listening to Jesus Christ's profanity-laced railing against the Catholic Church and how he would destroy the Catholic Church and, in three days, rebuild it. He was just about to declare Mary Magdalene, formerly known as Beth the Prostitute, as the first female pope when he noticed that this stranger and Black Jack were both staring at him. This triggered a deep paranoia in him and he started to trip over his words.

Father Caspian was stuck in his mind after Jesus Christ said something to the effect of, "If it is my desire to take a whore like Mary Magdelene and make her pope, what is to stop me?" Caspian was now articulating the debate in his mind that Mary Magdalene was not a sex worker at all and was likely a well-respected businesswoman and benefactor of the disciples and that the whole confusion came from a mistake a pope made during a homily. Whenever Caspian didn't know what to do, he often liked to carry on these debates in his head of all the things he would like to say but rarely ever said. As Father Caspian was distracted with his own escapist thoughts, Jesus Christ couldn't handle it anymore with all the staring coming from Black Jack and the stranger and he finally snapped. He began yelling at the two of them. "The fuck do you two want?"

"I am just looking for a room," the stranger said.

"Sit down!" Caspian demanded of Jesus Christ. "Or you'll be out without even a meal!"

"I'll sit down but only because I choose to do so. You don't have any power over me other than what is given from above." And with that, Jesus Christ sat down and continued eating his meal.

Father Caspian walked to the front door and extended his hand to the new stranger. Black Jack did most of the talking.

"This here is John Doe, Father." Black Jack made the introduction relatively formally. "He won't give anyone his real name on account of him being a Russian spy, I suppose. But he needs a place to stay for the evening nonetheless, so I figured I would bring him here."

Father Caspian almost said, "We are all full up on crazy for the evening," but he thought better of it and introduced himself instead.

"I am not a Russian spy," John Doe protested.

"Oh, well, that is a relief." Caspian was quite relieved. "Where did that rumor come from?"

"On account of him speaking fluent Russian from his tent all night long," Black Jack interjected.

"I promise not to be any trouble," the stranger promised, "I just need a place to stay for a few days while I sort out a couple of things. I assure you I will not stay long and I am a very tidy person. I do not have any identification, I am afraid."

"Do you really speak fluent Russian?" Caspian was genuinely curious.

"I do not wish to entangle myself any more than I already have; if you don't mind, I would just like to straighten up my affairs and get going." John Doe was extremely polite. "As I said, it shouldn't be more than a few days."

"Well, we only allow people to stay night by night," Caspian explained, "but you can stay up to seven days in a row. So that shouldn't be a problem. We do not require you to have a state ID or anything like that. We are full this evening, but go help yourself to a meal and let me see if we can make some extra room just for tonight."

As John Doe was quietly attempting to find a place to sit, it seemed that Jesus Christ had decided to calm down a bit as well. This seemed like a good opportunity for Father Caspian to slip into the kitchen to check on some of the volunteers. Tonight, they had a group from the Society of Saint Vincent de Paul, so he needed to make an especially good impression since they were other

Catholics and could end up reporting how he was doing to the bishop. Everything seemed in order, and after sharing some pleasantries and blessings with the faithful who had come to serve, he walked the ladies out to their cars and went back into the shelter. The second shift volunteers had shown up, so Caspian spent a few minutes with them, letting them know about the new arrival, that they needed to find a space to put another cot, and that Jesus Christ was attempting another uprising, but he seemed in good spirits now. With that, he opened his phone and called for an Uber.

Though it had been a long time since Sister Mary Margaret had lost her life, the memory of it was not far from anyone's mind. Even though Caspian walked to work every morning, he used a ride share late at night. This wasn't due to fear; he had walked through far worse neighborhoods in his life. Instead, he had to do this because of a policy the board of directors of The Mission had put together. When they reopened, several changes were made; the shelter procedures were updated and they even brought in a consultant to help them design everything. Part of the safety protocol demanded that members of staff were not to go out at night alone under any circumstances whatsoever. If a client went missing, that was a job for the police, not shelter staff or volunteers.

His phone pinged to let him know his ride was just around the corner and he stepped outside; it had just started to rain. Before closing the shelter door, he looked back into the main hall; Jesus Christ was sitting at the table with his disciples and Caspian couldn't help but notice that it sort of looked like the *Last Supper* painting. The door finally finished closing just as his ride arrived and he walked over to the car, checked the license plate, and then stepped in.

"Getting ready for a part in *The Exorcist*?" the driver joked.

"More like *One Flew Over the Cuckoo's Nest*," Caspian replied.

"Never seen it." The driver shrugged.

"I'm living it." And with that, Caspian watched as the rain trickled down the car's windows and imagined that he was anywhere other than here.

CHAPTER THREE

It is often said, "rules are meant to be broken," but it is seldom meant. An argument could be made that much of the suffering in this world comes from the fact that society doesn't believe that rules are meant to be broken at all, no matter how many folks use it as a throwaway phrase during moments of inconvenience. Every day we see injustices happen all around us that could be resolved by breaking a rule and we collectively do nothing. Wars rage and famines starve, children are slaughtered, and we remain silent. We fear consequences or the crosshairs moving away from the oppressed and toward us, so we let terror win and choke out our voice. Then, when someone does stand up and say, "These rules are fucked," we bury them in the back of the graveyard of history and then name a road after them. We know that rules aren't meant to be broken and that there will be harsh consequences when we do break them. So we say, "Rules are meant to be broken," as we steal two coins from the take-a-penny cup at the convenience store and place them on the eyes of a dead kindergartner. God bless America.

Father Caspian was the kind of person who did not break the rules, at least not on purpose. In his previous station, as the pastor of a small congregation, he did break the rules frequently but not because he was attempting to do something bold or courageous. He broke the rules because he did not understand them, he forgot them, or, more often than not, he violated some unspoken rule that someone else had created in their mind. A great deal of offense happens in this world because someone has violated an invisible rule we have curated for ourselves and then attempted to impose on everyone else. These were the types of invisible social constructs that Caspian was frequently guilty of infringing. On an average day, one could not accuse him of being politically minded or socially aware. He was not particularly concerned with these matters in the slightest, outside of the norm that any other human being might be tacitly conscious of because we are all inundated with them through our phones and social media.

Many heroes in the world have become such because they care deeply about a thing and choose to act upon that thing, whatever the thing might be. Some doctors provide abortions despite the daily fear of arrest or even death for the cause. In times of war, we often read stories about common folks who pick up rocks and sticks to defend their homes and homeland from destruction, often to their peril. They are silent warriors who die silent deaths and will likely never have great monuments dedicated to them.

It would be accurate and not an unkind thing to say that Father Caspian had never done a brave or impressive thing in his entire life. For example, during the pandemic, there were plenty of news stories about priests who risked it all to go into hospitals to administer last rites to those in distress. Of all these remarkable people who did such things to relieve the suffering of those around the globe Caspian was not numbered amongst them. That is not to say that a person should have to put themselves in harm's way to be considered a good person. Plenty of good people did nothing more than quarantine in their homes during the global crisis; for them, this was a great act of sacrifice. I could not say that Caspian was courageous even in this way. There were plenty of times during lockdown when he went out into the world when he certainly didn't need to.

It is essential to understand this to better paint a picture of how uncourageous Father Caspian truly was. Caspian was an academic, someone who wanted to learn and read books. There is nothing wrong with that at all. There is a great honor, in its way, about hoping to continue to educate oneself on any number of topics.

Unfortunately for Father Caspian, he had no particular interest that piqued him more than another. He bounced from one type of thing to another and never settled on any one thing. This made the wealth of knowledge he had in his brain seem rather useless unless he were your partner at trivia night at the bar. In these cases, he was pretty helpful. Otherwise, he was not helpful at all.

Understanding what an uncourageous person he was is paramount for anything that happens next to have any significance whatsoever. It wouldn't be fair to say he was a coward, but if you were to pick anyone out of the whole world who would be most unlikely to break a rule, even for a just cause, it would be Father Caspian.

In his defense, it was not as if he had been given many opportunities to be courageous. Significant impacts have been made on the world by people who also did not have opportunities to be courageous until it was suddenly thrust upon them to do so and they happened to rise to the occasion. It was just one of those occasions that Caspian was about to wake up to and he had absolutely no idea. As he woke up, he stretched his arms out, but not in the way people do in the movies; he just stretched them deep underneath the pillows and restlessly moved about in his bed before reaching over to his nightstand, where his phone was lying across a charging pad. He picked it up and saw he had multiple social media notifications and a few word games he liked to play. One particular notification stuck out to him because it was from the bishop. He had been mostly still in a state of sleepiness, but seeing this text jolted him awake in a way that only correspondence from your superior can do.

The message read, "Busy today. Can't talk. Please call my office and set up a meeting. ASAP."

Caspian spent a few minutes trying to decide if he was supposed to respond to the text then spent another grueling forty-five minutes waiting for the diocesan office to open before he could call and speak with the bishop's receptionist to attempt to schedule the meeting. Even though he and the bishop had been classmates during seminary, it was clear to him that the bishop was now taking himself very seriously and must now treat him as he would any other hierarch within the Church. Pamela, the bishop's receptionist, let Caspian know that his next available appointment would be a week away.

"Fucking great," Caspian whispered aloud as he hung up the phone.

Now he found himself in an even worse situation, not only because he had to make himself busy for the next week to try not to think about whatever trouble he may have found himself in this time, but also because he was now late for his first appointment for the day at The Mission. They operated almost exclusively on a volunteer staff and did not have anyone there that day to do any office duties. That meant no one was there to greet his appointment and let the person know he would be running late. He quickly dressed, skipped his morning prayers, and ordered an Uber to cut his time down from the thirty-minute walk he usually enjoyed in the morning to a five-minute commute. This would have been a brilliant plan if it weren't for the fact that the city was doing some scheduled maintenance on some of the roads, which resulted in his five-minute Uber drive being closer to fifteen minutes.

When he finally arrived, he was glad to see that his appointment was still outside, waiting for him to arrive. The day before last, John Doe had asked him if he would meet with him to discuss the possibility of getting a bus ticket out of town. This was not something the shelter typically provided, but Father Caspian did not know that was what John Doe wanted to discuss with him. He was quite curious about this new character who had found himself in the care of The Mission, so he was eager to take the meeting. Unfortunately, it appeared that John was now being harassed by Jesus Christ, Mary Magdalene, and the other seven disciples. All of the cool names like Bartholomew and Thaddeus had already been taken by earlier adherents to the new street cult and they were severely lacking in Johns, Jameses, and Judases. It appeared no one was particularly interested in being a Judas. However, Caspian had already personally pegged a few followers of Jesus Christ of Mobile that could be rising to the occasion, if not in name then indeed with intent and malice. Their group desperately needed a John to help them round out the twelve groupies they were going for and Jesus Christ was currently attempting to convince John Doe that this was his divine purpose in the world. It was the divine purpose for which he was born and the reason he had been named John in the first place. The only real problem was that John was not his actual name, a point that Jesus Christ and the other disciples were attempting to drive home to John when Father Caspian arrived.

"For the last time, you don't have to be named John from birth to be John; how many fucking ways does a man have to explain this? Am I explaining this in a way that doesn't make any sense, Mary?" Jesus looked directly at Mary Magdalene as he asked the question, making an exacerbated hand motion as he asked it.

"Nope," she said, shaking her head at John. "Makes perfect sense to me."

"How about you, Thaddeus?" Jesus Christ was looking for a consensus.

"My name was Jackson before I became Thaddeus," Jackson, now known as Thaddeus, said in agreement with Jesus Christ.

"See!" Jesus said, poking John Doe in the chest. "It's pretty fucking simple to everyone except you, unless you are denying your true calling and aren't interested in eternal salvation. In which case, go to Hell for all I fucking care. It's your choice."

"What's going on here?" Caspian interrupted.

"I am just trying to explain that John here is missing the purpose for which he was born on Earth, and if he doesn't watch it, he is going to end up in the belly of a whale as Moses did," Jesus Christ explained matter-of-factly.

"That was Jonah whom the whale swallowed." As soon as the words escaped Father Caspian's lips, he regretted them. He had finally gotten up the courage to question Jesus Christ's theological prowess a few times over the last month and it had not gone well.

"Caspian, you little pimp of the Whore of Babylon, how many goddamn times do I have to explain to you that if I say something that doesn't fit in with your little agenda it means the Bible was wrong? They mixed up all kinds of names and such. They weren't so smart back then." Mary Magdalene snorted out an agreeable snort that reminded Caspian of Miss Piggy. The agreement did not interrupt Jesus enough to stop his tirade. "Sometimes I wonder if you ever went to a real seminary. You don't seem too smart to me."

Whenever Jesus Christ got into these moods, Caspian knew it meant that he had fallen back off the wagon and was drinking or using again. On an average day, Jesus Christ was already really special, but on days like this, when he had a bit of additional courage embedded into his veins or belly, it made him all the more intolerable. This was going to be even more troublesome because the only reason why Father Caspian was willing to meet so early in the morning with one of the guests was that today was Tuesday and that meant it was shower and brown bag day. The clients could always use the showers and laundry facility when they stayed the night, but every Tuesday and Thursday they had showers and bagged lunches that the volunteers provided. This was one such morning and the volunteers would be there in about an hour. With Jesus Christ being as wound up as he was, it would make for a lively morning.

"How about I get y'all some coffee," Caspian said as a statement, not a question. He was also surprised with how quickly he had adopted y'all into his vocabulary. It rolled quite nicely off the tongue and worked in all kinds of situations. Even better, it was acceptable in all social circles within the South and he just adored the word. He quickly apologized to John Doe for holding him up and went inside to start a pot of coffee. He ushered John inside with him to save him from the rabid disciples and their attempts to evangelize him.

"I will just be a moment!" Caspian shouted from the kitchen.

"Take your time; no rush," John shout-whispered back.

After the coffee finished percolating, Caspian placed it in a disposable thermal he used for just such occasions. He took the coffee, some creamer packets, sugars, and styrofoam cups out to the stoop where the disciples and Jesus Christ eagerly awaited. He hoped this would help sober Jesus Christ up enough before the volunteers arrived within the hour. He then invited John Doe to join him in his office, so they wouldn't be interrupted once the volunteers arrived, and they took their respective seats.

"I am sorry this was so hectic and for my tardiness," Father Caspian said, exhausted, as he sat in his swiveling office chair.

"It's quite all right," John Doe said.

"What can I help you with today?"

"Well, I need a bus ticket out of here," John Doe said, looking at his feet. "I am trying to get back to Kentucky."

Father Caspian sighed. "That is something we might not be able to help with. Do you have family up there?"

"Not exactly," John Doe said.

"Well, what is there for you in Kentucky?" Caspian inquired.

"Rather not say."

Caspian leaned back and then rocked himself in the swivel chair for a few moments. It was unbelievably comfortable for such a shoddy thing. The pleather was beginning to peel at the high impact points and sometimes the screw that held it to the base came loose and its occupant would be propelled from it like in the cartoons when they would push the evacuation button. Caspian kept a screwdriver in the desk so he could tighten it weekly so he didn't fall like he did when he discovered that the screw had come loose. He often made this rocking motion when trying to think of something to say, which was the case now.

"You are kind of an enigma, John. I don't know what to make of you." He rocked a final time before settling back into the chair and leaning in toward the desk. "We don't offer bus tickets here and at the Homeless Coalition meeting last week the other agencies said they were tapped on those funds at the moment. And without you having an ID, a real name, or family that you are returning to, it would make it all the more difficult to accomplish, if not impossible."

"I understand," John said, standing up to leave.

"Don't rush out so fast, John," Caspian protested. "I do want to help you. We haven't found a solution yet; that doesn't mean there isn't one."

John Doe wasn't sure if it was the tone of Caspian's voice or if he had just found himself in a particularly impossible situation, but something about how Father Caspian said those words made him realize that Caspian truly meant them. Even though he was utterly unprepared for this job, he was finding a way to make it work. Slowly, he even started to find himself thinking about the clients when he was off work. He began to wonder how they were doing and thought about ways he could do more to help. That was one of the reasons he had started taking meetings like this on Tuesdays and Thursdays. I am not sure that Caspian would have put it in those terms yet, but something was awakening inside him, and even though it was only a slight glimmer of light, he might have started to find his purpose. That truth, hidden deep under the ground that John Doe heard in Caspian's voice, made him do what he did next. He turned around, closed the door, and then faced Caspian again, placing both hands on the desk and leaning in close to Caspian's face.

"Turn on some music. Loud," John whispered.

"Excuse me?" Caspian seemed confused, but then something about the sternness of John Doe's face made him comply. He turned to his computer and opened his music player. He selected some music but must not have made it loud enough because John Doe pointed his thumb up and down to indicate it must be louder. As soon as the music reached an adequate sound level, John Doe leaned in closer and began talking directly into Caspian's ear. He was so close it tickled.

"My name is Stephen Michael Jenks. I have been working as a contractor for the CIA within a division that monitors cyber terrorism. Most especially, my assignment is to monitor Russian cyber-attacks on high-profile institutions. I was recently given a new assignment to track information moving from a potential Russian sleeper cell within the United States. While working on this project, I uncovered disturbing and classified information. I knew I could not transfer that information electronically, so I flew to Tallahassee to meet with a counterpart there to bring them a microdrive with the intelligence. Our meeting was intercepted and my counterpart was killed. I have spent the last few weeks hiding on the streets as a homeless person, but this intelligence is more important than ever and I must get to Kentucky, where I have a hideout location where I can get this information to those who can do something with it." Stephen Jenks paused to allow Caspian time to digest the information. "Do you understand?"

Inside his mind, Caspian was shaking his head, but he sat there stoically. Mainly because he was shocked at the profound luck he was having; first, he had Jesus Christ's second coming happening right here on his doorstep. He was going to be in the second Bible! How grand. And now he had found himself smack dap in the middle of a Russian spy movie. What luck! What had he done to deserve so much prestige? He had not yet turned down the music when he heard a deafening noise that was not coming from the computer. He quickly shut it off and the sound became more evident.

"Father Caspian! Father Caspian!" Someone was banging on the door. "Come at once!"

He quickly ran around his desk and made his way to the hallway, momentarily tripping over Stephen, John, or whoever he was. He looked down the hallway to the main hall and saw Jesus Christ lying down on the ground, convulsing. He ran back to his desk, opened a drawer, and pulled out a small box with Narcan. He started to make his way back toward the door but Stephen stood up, blocking the way, and slapped an envelope against Father Caspian's chest. "If anything happens to me, open this."

Caspian shoved Stephen out of the way and ran down the hallway. The blood was rushing to his head and it felt almost like a dream. He was nearly certain the hallway was getting longer as he ran like he was stuck in a Kubrick film. An altogether odd thing was happening at this moment: he was not finding himself worried at all about his well-being. Thoughts of his upcoming meeting with the bishop were nowhere to be found in his mind. He wasn't thinking about newspapers or social media statuses. He did not fear for himself but singularly for the victim of circumstance that lay on the floor. When he finally made his way to Jesus Christ, he was turning blue. He read the instructions on the side of the Narcan again quickly as a refresher and then shoved the dispenser up Jesus' nose and depressed the button.

"Fuck," Caspian screamed, a single tear rolling down his cheek.

A volunteer had already called 911 and the room was soon flooded with EMTs, firefighters, and police officers. It was a chaotic scene and Mary Magdalene and the newly appointed James were standing on either side of Caspian as he cradled Jesus Christ in his arms.

They took Jesus Christ out on a stretcher and took him to the Baptist Hospital. Father Caspian followed. He waited in the room where you wait during times like this. Eventually, a doctor came out and called him back. He explained that the trauma was just too great, and even though the Narcan was undoubtedly a good idea, nothing could be done and he had been lost. Jesus Christ of Mobile had died of a heart attack brought on by mixing a liter of 100-proof vodka with cocaine laced with fentanyl.

It is finished, Caspian thought.

CHAPTER FOUR

The inside of Kyle's car smelled of lingering cigarette smoke and fried food congealing together, an aroma similar to a dive bar after closing time. The small pillow he stole from a couch in a motel lobby had fallen to the floorboard as he slept. This caused him to wake with a crick in his neck. The windows were covered in condensation from his breath as he slept. He sat up in the backseat and tried to rub away the pain in the back of his neck and shoulder. He was far too young for his body to feel this old, but he had put many miles on his flesh and bones in a short amount of time. He was suffering for it now. He had considered just climbing over the center console to make his way to the front but decided he was far too stiff for such a maneuver, instead choosing to exit from the passenger-side rear door. He was instantly struck by how bitterly cold it was and wished to retreat into the car quickly.

The early morning hour gave way to an eerie blue hue that cast across everything in sight. The mythical light and odd silence caused Kyle to look over his shoulder into the backseat. Nothing was there except for the trash that was beginning to build up with his collection of empty to-go cups and fry containers. He hated living in his car, but it was a necessary evil. His family and friends had abandoned him along the way and he had searched for a new community. One where he would be accepted and his brilliance would be appreciated. He did not begrudge living in his vehicle; it was from these ashes that he would rise and build a better America for himself.

First, he needed some breakfast. He began digging through his duffle bag pockets to see if he had enough money for gas and food. As he was rummaging, he heard a noise coming from behind his car. His head shot back again towards the backseat. Suddenly, the blue of the morning was neon bright and he instantly covered his eyes from the pulsating light.

"Fuck," Kyle said as he slumped into his seat.

He watched through the icy tent of the condensation on the windows as a silhouetted figure approached his car. He watched as this figure moved from behind his car to the passenger-side window. He quickly turned on a dashboard camera just as a shadowy hand knocked the window, shaking some condensation down into little dripped lines across the panes. Kyle slightly cracked the window about an inch, just enough that the officer could hear him but not enough to expose himself.

"Everything all right?" the officer asked.

"Am I being detained?" Kyle asked robotically.

"This is a private business," the officer responded. "There is no overnight parking."

"I'll be on my way then unless I am being detained." Kyle was facing forward as he said this, both hands on the steering wheel so that the camera could see his face.

"Kid, I don't have time for this today." The officer was leaning down toward the car to peek in through the window crack. "I just wanted to make sure—"

"Am I being detained?" Kyle cut the officer off. "And you should always have time to protect the rights of citizens."

Officer Davis did not want to be dealing with this. He abhorred sovereign citizens more than any other interaction he routinely encountered as a cop. Today was an especially unfortunate day for him as he had only half an hour left on his shift and the next day he began a two-week vacation with his wife. They were going to the Bahamas and would drink alcoholic drinks out of weird-shaped glasses with little umbrellas. He had never had one of those little umbrellas and planned to add it to his collection of vacation trinkets. This was their twenty-third vacation together since their wedding. So far, he had collected several little oddities like a clover from Ireland that had been preserved in a heart-shaped resin and some dirt from the catacombs in Rome. The umbrella would be the pinnacle of all his treasures.

The reason he hated sovereign citizens so much, aside from the fact that he thought their entire ideology was absurd, was that they took up so much time. That was their point, to wear law enforcement down in circular conversations and paperwork so that you would just let them get away with anything so you wouldn't have to deal with their particular brand of silliness. The problem was that they were almost always committing some crime and should have been in trouble. This left an officer with two choices: just let them go or get stuck in an unbearably long confrontation and then be bogged down with endless paperwork and court cases.

Officer Davis decided he would give this kid one more chance to get this right before he called for backup and handed this situation off to someone else who wasn't about to go on vacation.

"Can I see your license and registration, please?" Davis gritted, bracing for the worst.

"You know I am not required to give you anything unless I am being detained to investigate an alleged crime," Kyle said, still staring at the steering wheel. "You pigs never know the law."

"I really don't want to have to escalate this situation." The officer was as calm as he could muster. "Can we just move this along smoothly?"

Kyle slipped his license and registration through the tiny crack in the window and Officer Davis removed them gently. He explained that he would be right back and walked to his patrol car to look up the information. It was no surprise, but to Officer Davis's great dismay, Kyle had an active warrant and a suspended license. However, it was an out-of-state warrant, so he could technically give Kyle a warning. As the officer debated how he wanted the last ten minutes of his work day to go, Kyle was inside, fumbling again through his duffle bag, looking for change. The hunger was getting the best of him, so he leaned back over the center console to the back seat to see if his money slipped out of his pocket while he slept. While doing this, he lifted his knee to allow him to reach just a bit further. This motion caused his knee to hit the lever that opened his trunk. This happened just as Officer Davis stepped back out of his patrol car, and as he lifted himself out of the vehicle, his eyes met with the contents of Kyle's trunk.

The contents of the trunk of Kyle's vehicle were as follows:

One bulletproof vest
Three tactical style vests
One first aid kit
One motorcycle helmet with a face screen
Six-packs of pepper spray
Two AR-15 style guns

Thirteen magazines
Two hundred and thirty-seven .226 rounds
One hundred and seventy-two 9MM rounds
Two military wool blend blankets

Those two blankets caught Officer Davis's eye as they covered all of the other contents within the vehicle. They were a rough gray fabric with little red and white speckles throughout them. They looked just enough like the liners within a trunk that he didn't think much of at first and assumed that Kyle had just opened the back of the vehicle to show him that nothing was inside. Believing this assumption to be fact and this fact annoying him, Officer Davis walked over to the trunk to close the door. As he did this, he could see the butt of a gun sticking out from under the blanket, along with some loose ammunition. He lifted the edge of the blanket slightly and, though he could not see all of the contents, he saw enough to get the gist of what was going on under there.

Kyle was watching Officer Davis's motions from his rearview mirror. He slowly reached into the compartment in his door, lifted his 9MM, and pressed it against the paneling as the officer walked back up to his window. Officer Davis slowly slipped the driver's license and registration back in through the slit of the window, unaware of the danger he was now in.

"You've got some interesting, uh—" Officer Davis paused for a moment waiting for the right word to come to him "—equipment in your trunk."

"Are you violating my Fourth Amendment rights, officer?" Kyle asked sternly.

"It's not a violation for me to look inside an open trunk," Officer Davis responded cautiously. "You mind telling me what all that is for?"

"Hunting," Kyle responded glibly.

"Hunting what?" Officer Davis was pushing his luck.

"I'm a bounty hunter." Kyle shrugged. "I'm looking for someone."

"Can I see some identification?"

Kyle slowly reached with his free hand and opened the glove compartment. In the glove compartment was a printout of the man he was looking for as well as an authorization letter from a bondsman. After shuffling through some papers, he found the authorization letter and a piece of paper with a mug shot and description. He turned slowly and placed it through the window. Officer Davis examined the documents for a few moments. He had yet to mention the out-of-state warrant or the expired license to Kyle.

"Stephen Michael Jenks?" Officer Davis said out loud.

"That's the guy." Kyle smiled.

"What's he wanted for?" the officer inquired.

"Oh, he's just some local whack job. He's always in and out of trouble back home for loitering, stalking, disturbing the peace, shit like that." Kyle's hand was beginning to sweat and tremble as he held the gun against the door. "I just know he skipped bail; I do mercenary work for one of the bondsmen. That's about all I can tell you. Just a messed-up guy, out of his mind with delusions."

"Right." Davis wasn't so sure. "You think he's here?"

"Have you seen someone like him?" Kyle asked.

Officer Davis shook his head to indicate he had not. He was just about to ask Kyle if bounty hunters often had open warrants. He looked down at the paperwork and wasn't sure what to make of it. In all his years on the force he had never encountered something like this. He was confident that this kid wasn't telling him everything. Maybe it was his intuition from his years of service or just the vibe that Kyle was giving off, but something just didn't fit.

Kyle was not telling him everything. He would rather have been telling him nothing and was becoming increasingly jittery. In his mind, he had already shot Officer Davis four times. He was playing it out in numerous scenarios with varying levels of success. Cerebrally, he knew that shooting a cop would not help him in his endeavors. It also wouldn't be his first time harming a police officer. His active warrant was for trespassing, but he had done much more than just trespass that day.

Neither of these men was enjoying the situation they had found themselves in. However, Kyle had something going in his favor. It was now shift change and as he had been playing out numerous fantasies of blowing Officer Davis to kingdom come, Officer Davis had imagined that piña colada with the little umbrella. He could not decide if he wanted a pink, blue, or yellow one. He wondered if he was allowed to pick the umbrella or if that was chosen at random by the bartender. The only way to find out for sure would be to get on with his day and make it to that vacation.

"This Jenks guy, pretty dangerous?" Officer Davis asked.

"Just some street bum," Kyle responded through the crack in the window, "A crazy, no account nobody. He happens to owe my boss bail money. Open and shut, really."

Maybe this kid was lying to him and perhaps he was planning to blast away some homeless guy. He didn't know. But this warrant, the suspended license, the bail-jumping bum, none of these were his problem. It would be a problem for someone else to figure out on another day while he was off getting that umbrella.

"Listen, kid, you've got a suspended license," Officer Davis offered in a tired tone. "You need to get that taken care of and you've got a misdemeanor warrant in Washington, DC. Probably want to figure that out too."

"Am I being detained?" Kyle asked again.

"For fuck's sake, you aren't being detained." Officer Davis rolled his eyes. "I just hope for you that this fellow you are looking for is as much fun for you as you've been for me."

With that, Officer Davis handed the remaining paperwork back to Kyle through the window and walked back to his cruiser. He opened his laptop on the dashboard, which had an image of some beach in the Bahamas on the screen. He flicked the dangling donut air freshener on his rearview mirror and chuckled. He was officially on vacation.

Kyle watched as the cop drove away, ready to get out of there himself. That was a pretty close call. If he'd had any sense about himself, he would know that he had no one else to blame but himself for how poorly that all could have gone. He would learn absolutely nothing from this experience. He rolled his window down the rest of the way, lit a cigarette, and put the nearest breakfast place on his GPS.

"You better be fucking worth it," he said, looking down at the photo of Stephen Jenks lying on his passenger seat. With that, he set off for breakfast.

CHAPTER FIVE

The waiting room for the bishop's office looked very unlike what someone might imagine the bishop's office waiting room would look like. If you were designing such a room for a movie set, I suppose the set designer would look for stone walls and burgundy curtains covering stained-glass windows. The walls would be covered with well-crafted bookshelves containing ancient-looking books placed in an intentionally haphazard kind of way. There would maybe even be an enormous crucifix and reliquaries lining the top of these bookshelves. In the corner, there would be a coat rack with vestments hanging from it and maybe some fancy bishop hat; whatever part of the walls that were not covered by bookshelves and relics would have large and intimidating icons of the Virgin Mary sadly peering down at you. Then, whoever was waiting for the bishop would be sitting on costly-looking chairs. Finally, a young priest or maybe a guard would open the door and say something like, "The bishop will see you now." Then you would walk into a vast room with Spielberg lighting emitting from the even larger window as the bishop overlooked the city below. He would be wearing a long black cassock with purple trim and cincture. He would turn toward the visitor, cut through the dust floating in the air that was giving the appearance of divine light coming from the window, and usher you to sit.

"The bishop will see you now," Pamela said, smiling.

The small room where Caspian was sitting looked much like a doctor's waiting room but smaller. Pamela had been rustling around with some papers on her desk before an instant message on her screen let her know the bishop was now available. It was an archaic system, but the diocese had paid a lot of money for it back in the day, so they still used it as it functioned well enough. The only thing that made any distinction between this waiting area and that of your local primary care physician was that there was a small picture of the Virgin Mary near the door of the bishop's office. No one came out to greet Father Caspian; he just walked right over and opened the door. The bishop was sitting at his desk and had just completed a call or was at least making himself look busy. The entire room was one big clear glass window that looked out over the highway. There was an empty lot beyond that where people parked their RVs and oversized trucks for a fee.

"Caspian," the bishop said with a smile and walked around his desk with his arms extended.

"Your Excellency," Father Caspian said with a bit of a bow.

"Absolutely not, old sport! Call me Nick, please." The bishop smiled again.

With that, they embraced, "Old sport, eh, Nick? I see you haven't forgotten."

"I'll never watch *The Great Gatsby* without thinking of those times back in NOLA with the Men in Black. What a grand experience." Nick chuckled and pointed with an open palm towards a seat.

Caspian took his seat and couldn't help but think about how much more comfortable his old swivel chair at The Mission was. This was genuine leather and was exceedingly hot because it was in the sunlight. It almost burnt his back, making an already uncomfortable situation much worse, considering he was sweating, beginning with the anxiety looming over him concerning the meeting. The familiarity with which Nick had greeted him was reassuring but not entirely comforting. To look at the two of them, wearing matching black clerical attire, you couldn't tell they were different in rank: black slacks, a crisp clerical shirt, and a jacket. The only thing that could have given it away was that Nicholas wore a gold and purple amethyst-encrusted crucifix. For a few moments, the familiarity felt nice. They talked about old times and some adventures that would have made Pamela in the other room blush if she had known that the bishop was capable of such naughtiness while in seminary. Eventually, as all conversations do, it reached a natural lull, and this was the moment the bishop had been waiting for to interject his real intent for this gathering.

"A lot has changed since I originally asked you for this meeting, sadly," Nick said with a consoling tone, but his face had a strange look of relief about it. "How are you holding up after this loss?"

"It has certainly been a week, your"—he meant to say excellency and then remembered he was supposed to call the bishop Nick, and instead, the words merged into—"your Nickelency."

"Well, I certainly hope you are getting your rest and making regular Communion. There is nothing more healing for the body and soul than the Eucharist," the bishop admonished, knowing full well that Father Caspian had not been making it to daily Mass.

"Yes, of course," Caspian lied.

"I had originally hoped we could meet to discuss this Jesus problem of yours, but it appears that the natural course of sin has resolved that problem by itself." Caspian squirmed in his seat as the bishop said these words, but he didn't have time to say anything before he continued. "Regrettable circumstances all around. Some folks from Saint Vincent's had sent an email concerned about what was going on over there. I do have to ask you, how did this possibly get so out of hand?"

Father Caspian looked around in the air for an answer before finally responding, "I'm not really sure. It's clear that the man had some deep issues we couldn't resolve at the shelter. But there isn't much more we could do, I'm afraid."

"You could have just told him not to come by anymore." Like he had resolved the whole thing, the bishop said, "People like that just stir up trouble and we do not need trouble at the Sister Mary Margaret Mission for Those Experiencing Homelessness. We need this to work, Caspian, very badly. We need this not to have any more issues."

Caspian nodded.

"That is why I knew I could trust you with something like this because we understand each other. We've known each other such a long time"—the bishop was beginning to talk like he was much older than he was—"and for this reason, I need you to keep those that are … what is the right word? Those who are beyond help away for the time being."

"I am not sure I know what you mean, Nick." Caspian looked concerned.

"Oh, come on, Caspian, you know the type. The drunks or addicts: the ones talking to themselves. Like that guy down at Jackson Square that smeared his own mess all over the walls of that tourist trap shrimp place. Folks like that; we don't need folks like that at the shelter for now. Just no one weird."

"They are all weird." I am not sure that anyone was more surprised than Father Caspian at the defiance in his voice.

"I'm sure; just be discerning, please." The bishop seemed suddenly over the conversation. "Is there anything else I can help you within your endeavors, Caspian?"

"There is." Caspian set up straight in his chair. "There is the issue of the funeral."

"Funeral?" The bishop seemed indignantly confused.

"Well, yes, some of the volunteers would like to do something special for him. Especially since his disciples are so distressed that he didn't rise from the dead," Caspian paused for a laugh but didn't get one, so he continued, "So, yes, we would like to have a funeral. I mean the corpse won't be there. Without the next of kin being found, we can't obtain the body or anything. Just more of a memorial than a funeral, just the volunteers and some people from the streets. It won't be anything spectacular or anything like that. But we would love to have you present, of course, and it will be at The Mission—"

"Sister Mary Margaret Mission for Those Experiencing Homelessness," the bishop interrupted.

"Yes, the Sister Mary Margaret Mission for Those Experiencing Homelessness," Caspian echoed back.

"That is, of course, out of the question, I'm afraid," the bishop said.

"You can't make it?" Caspian asked.

"You can't do it," the bishop responded. Before Caspian could ask questions, the bishop explained, "This man was not a Catholic, I am sure you know. Even if he was, it's not as if he had been attached to any church. There is a vast difference between giving last rites to a stranger on the streets in a time of uncertainty over their soul and performing a funeral for someone not of the faith. I think this would send the wrong message, not to mention that it is against canon law. It is simply out of the question, I am afraid. Honestly, you should know better, old sport."

The second time the bishop said it, it didn't feel as nice. The bishop was saying it in some hope of eliciting that feeling of familiarity with Caspian, but it came across with the same level of condescension that Gatsby meant when he used the phrase. Caspian was unsure where this anger was coming from, but it bubbled up inside him. He had never felt anything like it before. He wasn't even sure if anger was the right word for what he was feeling. He nodded in agreement, but he didn't agree to anything, not really. He and the bishop embraced and said their pleasantries. Caspian walked out of the office and past Pamela, who was still smiling. He made his way down the stairs and out the front door; still, this feeling of anger was churning around in his belly until he reached the Uber waiting for him. He got inside and it seemed the feeling had exited his stomach and moved up his throat and then it rattled around in his brain like a bullet. By the time the pressure had reached his ears, turning bright red, he had finally found a word for this feeling: rebellion.

He had never had the feeling before, and he certainly didn't know what the fuck he was supposed to do with it now that he was feeling it, but it was a persistent devil that was now possessing his consciousness.

With this new friend of rebellion now living inside of him, he made many decisions that the previously uncourageous Father Caspian would never have done. For example, when he arrived at The Mission, some of the volunteers were having a planning meeting for the funeral of Jesus Christ. He did not stop them. He did not report to them what the bishop had told him to do. He didn't disband anything. He went into his office, cracked open his Bible for the first time in a long time, and began writing his eulogy. One of the volunteers knocked on the door and he offered for them to come in.

"Sorry to interrupt you, Father," she said.

"It's fine, Caroline," he said, smiling. "What can I do?"

"Well, Beth—"

Father Caspian interrupted her. "You mean Mary Magdalene?"

"Uh, yes." The volunteer corrected herself and continued, "Well, Mary Magdalene found Jesus' mom. She's rather old and can't make it to the funeral, but she wanted to know if she could Zoom in. Is that allowed?"

Caspian was sure there must be some canon against such a thing, but at this point he didn't rightfully give a flying fuck, so he gave his blessing. With that, the volunteer left with gratitude all over her face and reported to the others that the mother could attend the funeral virtually.

When the day finally arrived, far more people were present than Father Caspian had expected. If they were going to do a count of the homeless in their town, today should have been the day. It seemed that everyone in the community had come out of the woodwork to be present for the funeral of Jesus Christ of Mobile. It was quite the ecumenical affair as clergy from the Unitarian Universalists, Baptists, Methodists, Anglicans, and Church of Christ were all present, along with the volunteer groups for their respective churches. Eight seats had been reserved at the front of the aisle for Mary Magdalene and the other seven. On the opposite side sat several volunteers.

Caroline had a computer sitting in her lap that had been turned around towards the stage where the altar was set. On the screen was the mother of Jesus Christ. Father Caspian walked up toward where Caroline was sitting, with the computer in her lap, and he knelt in front of it. The woman was very old and frail looking. She had a shawl over her head and she had been crying.

"Good evening, Mother," Caspian said, "I am so sorry for your loss."

"I appreciate it, Father, I truly do," she said, wiping away a tear, "but I knew he would die like this. A mother always knows. It was how it was meant to be, I suppose. We can't ever question God's plan."

Caspian nodded at her. "I suppose we can't. I hope I do him justice today."

With that, Caspian pushed himself back off the ground and couldn't help but think about how much it hurt to get up. *Things didn't used to hurt like that,* he thought. He walked back toward his office and then announced that he was going to get prepared for the service and asked everyone to take their seats. He entered his office and placed his vestments on, saying the appropriate prayer for each. He picked up his eulogy off his desk and exited the room. As he walked down the aisle of folding chairs and his vagabond congregation, he couldn't help but smile. He missed this. Yes, he got to go up to the altar and concelebrate each Sunday with Father Kilpatrick, but it wasn't the same as this. As he made it up to the lectern, he placed his eulogy upon it, turned to the congregation, and greeted them with, "The Lord be with you."

A half grumbled, "And also with you," came back toward him, not because people didn't feel the words but because more than half of those in attendance didn't know how the liturgy was supposed to go.

He went delicately through the rest of the motions and, after reading the Gospel, invited a few of Jesus Christ's friends to share their stories. They were as colorful as he was. Mary Magdalene told about when some man had run up behind her as she walked down an alleyway near the liquor store. She was certain the man would assault her in some way, and, "Right out of nowhere, there was Jesus Christ, and he stabbed that man right in the side. Not enough to kill him, mind you, but just enough to startle him off. That was just the kind of guy he was."

Some of the volunteers seemed less comfortable than others about the whole situation. Father Caspian could feel the eyes of the Baptist minister especially burning a hole into the back of his head that he didn't demand that others use Jesus Christ's given name. But, on the contrary, Father Caspian had given direct orders that no one was to mention his given name at all. After Thaddeus had given a rousing rendition of "Amazing Grace", right after telling about the time he was pretty sure that Jesus had turned his Sprite into vodka and, "If that ain't a miracle, I don't fucking know what is," it was now Father Caspian's turn to find the right words to say. He stood up and made his way up to the pulpit and looked out into his congregation and then looked down at his pages of notes.

"You know, I've done a lot of thinking about what I am supposed to say today. I have to admit I don't think I've done many funerals during my time as a priest, at least not where I was the person in charge. I think that, in a way, that is good." He paused briefly. "I can't remember where I was going with that. I better stick to my notes. Okay, here we go.

"Jesus Christ was a strange character. I must admit to you, especially to those of you here in the front who were his devoted followers, that when I met him, I had my doubts about him. I am not sure that he was exactly what I was expecting regarding what Jesus was supposed to look or act like. For example, I'm not sure I was expecting that in my first conversation with the Lord in person he would say the phrase 'cunt hair'."

A woman in the congregation gasped so loudly that Caspian paused for a second, lost his place in his notes, and stumbled around to find them. "Well, I just didn't expect it; that is all I'm saying, so I had my doubts about his divinity. That was until this week when I had a conversation with a priest I once knew. He certainly didn't believe in Jesus Christ at all. His doubts sounded very different than the ones I had, so I opened my Bible for the first time in a long time. Well, I read something from the Gospel of Matthew."

Matthew in the front row shouted about how he would write it better the second time and the congregation chuckled.

"I hope you do." Father Caspian joined them in the laughter. "Well, in the original Gospel of Matthew, he says something about how, 'Whatever you do for the least of these, it's as if you did it to Me.' And I've thought about that a lot this week. About how whenever we care for our neighbor or when those EMTs picked up the body of Jesus Christ and tried to save him, whenever we help each other find food, I guess we are all doing that for Jesus Christ. At least we are supposed to be. So that is my sermon for today, I suppose, that I do believe in Jesus Christ of Mobile. I think he is the closest any one of us will ever get to seeing Jesus in the flesh. And, well, I guess that's what I wanted to tell you today. I sometimes have doubts about my faith if I am honest—about the institutions, the leadership, the Church—but I don't doubt Jesus Christ."

A couple of people in the congregation tried to start a slow clap but it fizzled out pretty quickly. Father Caspian walked back toward the altar and continued forward with the funeral. When it was all done, he joined everyone for coffee and cake. Some volunteers had ordered some incredible food, but it hadn't yet arrived. Black Jack approached Father Caspian with a hug. He was a burly man, but tears rolled down his cheeks and into his thick black beard.

"I am going to miss him," Black Jack said through sniffles.

"Me too," Caspian agreed. "You reckon that everyone in town came out for the funeral today?"

"Just 'bout," Black Jack said, looking around. "Just 'bout. The only one I can't account for is John Doe."

"Maybe he made his way back to Kentucky?" Caspian inquired.

"No, sir, Father, sir." Black Jack shook his head. "He got picked up that day in all the commotion when Jesus Christ died. The officers were going through people's things after you left to check on Jesus at the hospital and I don't know what John Doe had in his bag, but one of the officers gave him a pretty good roughing up. I imagine he is still in jail since he would be a flight risk as a transient."

"I'm sorry to hear that," Father Caspian said. "I'll check Jail View later today, and if I find out anything, I'll be sure to let you know."

Just then, the food finally arrived and everyone sat down. Bartholomew led the prayer and everyone bowed their heads. "Jesus Christ, if you are listening up there, I hope you know what a motherfucking asshole you are to leave us here like this. But every time I have a vodka, I'll remember you, just like you said. You don't worry about that. Amen." Everyone said amen and enjoyed the meal together in his memory.

I'm not sure that anyone enjoyed that meal quite as much as Father Caspian because it was probably a last supper as well for him. No amount of friendship with the bishop was going to save him from this level of defiance. But oddly, his new friend rebellion made him not feel so bad about it. He knew he had done the right thing and was content with that. As the day wound down, he stayed to help everyone pack up the food into little doggy bags so people could take seconds with them. Then they folded up the extra tables and chairs to make room for the cots to be put back where they belonged. In just a few more hours, the place would be back to just being a shelter from the elements, not the fellowship it felt like earlier in the day. Finally, the last of everyone made their way outside and Father Caspian gave the place one more good look over before heading back into the office to pack a few personal items up, just in case the axe finally did drop on him.

As he was about to leave, he swiveled back around in his chair and turned his computer back on. He pulled up the website for Jail View. At first, he realized he didn't know John Doe's name. He couldn't very well just type "John Doe" into Jail View and hope that someone would pop up. Then he remembered that he had given him a name he claimed was his own. He tried several different spellings of Stephen and then tried searching using just his last name. Nothing. Finally, he searched the whole site, starting with the most recently booked, and scrolled up to the date when he would have been arrested—still nothing. Caspian was just about to give up and go home when he remembered that Stephen had given him an envelope right before everything happened with Jesus Christ. He looked around on his desk and found it under a few newspapers. He was starting to wonder if he was being pulled into the delusions with the rest of them and then took a big sigh and opened the envelope. Inside was a single card stock-sized piece of paper with a telephone number and the word RASPUTIN written under it.

"I'm in it now," Caspian said out loud. "And now I am talking to myself. Fuck."

He reached over to the office phone, put the receiver to his ear, and began dialing the number as he mumbled, "This is fucking stupid." The number started ringing. He heard a click and then silence.

"Rasputin?" Caspian said, almost as a question.

"Jenks, thank God you are alive!" said the voice on the other end of the line.

"I'm sorry, this isn't Jenks."

"Who is this?"

"My name is Father Caspian and he gave me this little envelope and told me to open it if I hadn't seen him in a while. So I just thought I would call and—"

"Listen to me now; my name is Nadya. Are you calling from a landline?" she asked.

"Yes." Caspian was kind of nervous.

"Then you have even less time than I thought. I need your full name immediately."

"What is this?" Caspian demanded.

"We don't have time for twenty questions. If you want to stay alive, you better give me your full goddamn name right now." Nadya was not playing around.

"Caspian Eugene Castellanos."

"All right, Caspian, you have a flight at the Mobile regional airport departing in one hour and thirteen minutes. This will be the only time I will help you. This number will not be reachable again. And you better have some fucking answers about Jenks when I see you."

She immediately hung up.

"Well, that was the second craziest part about today." With that, Caspian picked up his briefcase and headed toward the front door. He opened his phone and called an Uber. He stood outside waiting and wondered if this would be his last night at The Mission. He could not wait until he was able to lie down in his bed and let this entire thing be over and just drift off to sleep. The car pulled up and he stepped inside. After buckling in and setting his briefcase down on the ground between his feet so he would not forget it, he looked up at the driver to ask how his evening was going. His eyes tried to focus on the black object obscuring his view of the driver.

"Don't say a word," the voice behind the gun said.

CHAPTER SIX

We have all been guilty of not believing people when we should have. Sometimes, that lack of belief in a person has caused us to have differing levels of consequences. Maybe there was a time we didn't believe a friend when they told us about an experience they had or we thought a co-worker was fluffing their resume. Perhaps someone told us about a pain they were having but we didn't think much of it, instead thinking they might be exaggerating a circumstance because they always complained about their discomfort, only for them to report back that they had gone to the doctor. The pain in their back was, in fact, cancer. In the world of misinformation and disinformation that we all now live in, we almost have to be more cautious about the things we believe than maybe at any other time in modern history. Tomorrow, we might open our favorite social media app to the sad news of a beloved celebrity dying, only later that day to find out that they are resurrected from the dead: just another viral hoax. Then there are times when people choose not to believe something true and that can also have devastating consequences that can lead to things like a global pandemic only getting worse because enough people believe a lie about vaccines, or maybe it will lead to an insurrection because so many people refuse to accept the legitimate outcome of an election. Whatever the case, we've all been guilty of not believing a truth that was right in front of us because our own presumption and prejudice caused us to doubt. That doubt does have consequences, sometimes good ones and sometimes negative ones. In the case of Father Caspian, this doubt had led him not to believe Stephen Jenks when he had told him that he was an operative working for the CIA and the consequence of that decision was that he now had a gun pointed directly at his face.

Now, we should take a moment to absolve Father Caspian a bit because I doubt anyone would believe what was happening if they had found themselves in this situation. In the short time that Caspian had been the administrator of The Mission, he had already met Jesus Christ and his disciples, a woman who believed that her cat could prophesy the end of the world, and someone certain that all of the songs of Kylie Minogue were about her and who was currently writing a handwritten copyright infringement case to be delivered to a federal court. Of course, logically, none of those things could possibly be true, so is it any surprise that the situation of Stephen Jenks would also have been equally categorized under the file of "batshit crazy" like everything else? And it was this space of disbelief that Father Caspian was still living in as he looked down that barrel of the gun because his first thought was not, *Holy shit, this is all true!* His first thought was that he was being robbed. For that reason, he leaned over and opened his briefcase while screaming, "Don't shoot! I have some money!"

"I don't want your fucking money!" the man with the gun shouted.

"Okay, okay," Father Caspian said with his hand still inside the briefcase.

"Don't look at me!" the man yelled and then he said, "Don't look at me if you want to make it out of this alive."

Caspian looked down, his entire body slouching toward the ground as he yelled back, "I'm not looking!"

"Where is the drive?" the man demanded.

"I don't have any drive; I promise." Caspian was almost crying; he had never been so scared before in his entire life. He wasn't even sure he had ever seen a gun before in real life and he certainly didn't know how they operated. He was convinced that at any moment, the thing could go off.

"Don't look up!" the man shouted again. "If you had that number, then you have to know where the drive is. I am going to give you about five goddamn seconds to tell me where it is before I blow you right back up to your God. Do you understand what I am saying?"

"Yes, yes." Caspian's right hand shook with fear. He could feel the large crucifix he had used for the funeral in his briefcase. He gripped it around the base and silently prayed.

"Do you know what time it is?" Caspian asked the man with the gun.

"The fuck?" the man said, but at the question, he instinctively looked at the clock on his dashboard, just like anyone else would if they were asked the time and looked at their wrist even if they weren't wearing a watch. In this very brief fraction of a second, Father Caspian grabbed the crucifix out of his briefcase and, in one swift motion, smashed the man with the gun over the head. Unlike in the movies, the man did not instantly pass out. This startled Father Caspian because he falsely believed that just one knock to the head would do the trick. The man attempted to reposition himself and point the gun back at Caspian. Realizing he was now in danger again, he smashed the man on the hand and he lost control of the gun, which fell to the floorboard. Caspian struck the man a second and third time on the head. With the third blow, the man slumped over in his chair. He had a substantial wound on his head from the base of the crucifix. Caspian reached for the door and attempted to open it, but nothing happened. The man with the gun had put on the child safety locks. At first, he thought he could smash the window with the crucifix, but then he was afraid that this might wake his sleeping assailant. Then he looked up at the dashboard and realized how much time he had already wasted. He now only had about forty-five minutes to make it to the airport.

See, in the time it took for him to answer all the questions the man with the gun had asked, and then to fight off his would-be killer with a crucifix, he had concluded that everything that Stephen Jenks had told him must be true. That was a very short amount of time to become a true believer in anything; however, sometimes it just takes a moment for us to find faith again. Though Caspian still had many doubts about many other things in this life, he was certain that Stephen Jenks had gotten himself into some kind of a mess. Now he was stuck in the same mess with him.

This situation left Father Caspian in a position with few good options. His first thought was to smash the window in with the crucifix and risk waking up the potential murderer. There was also the possibility that he had killed the killer with his crucifix, but to find out, he would have to check his pulse, which would mean he must touch him, which could also lead to him waking up. He could crawl into the front seat and hope to sneak out the door before he woke up. There was also the option to reach over the man with the gun, attempt to hit the child safety lock button, and then rush out the back door. Then he realized that this man was no longer a man with a gun; he was very much a man without a gun. His final thought on the subject of escaping made him shudder that it even entered his mind, but he could pick the gun up off the floorboard of the backseat and shoot the man in the head with it, and then he certainly wouldn't have to worry about him waking up at all. After what seemed like an eternity, Caspian decided that his best option was to crawl into the car's front seat to try to make it out the passenger side.

Caspian was not a particularly large fellow. He was not very tall or round, but he certainly wasn't as agile as he had once been. It is also challenging to crawl through the front of a seat when you are afraid you might wake up someone who wants you dead. That is very troublesome. He had also decided to combine some of his options into a new plan. First, he checked the man's pulse and determined he was alive. He had never checked someone's pulse before, so he wasn't sure he knew exactly what he was supposed to be looking for or where to find it. He eventually felt blood pumping below a tattoo of a cross the man had on his neck. It was a symbol of the three-bar cross, but blood was covering most of it. The man was undoubtedly still alive, but he did not wake up from Caspian fondling his neck. He felt a bit more confident about the escape knowing that. The other decision that Caspian made was that he put the gun in his waistband. He used to think it was foolish when people did that in movies because what if the gun discharged and shot your dick off? But at this moment, it suddenly made sense because he couldn't very well hold the gun in his hands when he was trying to make it through an already difficult situation.

After some very unorthodox maneuvering, he made it almost into the front seat, and suddenly, another option hit his mind. His legs were still in the back, but he could reach the door, so he tried to open it. But when he did this, the alarm to the car started to go off and he suddenly felt someone gripping his legs. He wiggled free for a second and then the man took his left leg into his hand and bit him. Father Caspian was the middle child of seven, so this was certainly not the first time he had ever been bitten in his life. However, it was the first time in a long time that he had been bitten and he had forgotten how effective it was at being painful and disempowering a person. The struggle lasted for a few moments and then Caspian kicked the man in the head with his free leg. He could feel the door behind him wiggling because it was partially ajar but still attached to the locking mechanism just enough that it wouldn't open. He saw the man reach for something and he began to be very concerned that the man who once had the gun might be the man with multiple guns, and it was at that moment that he remembered that he was now a man with a gun. He reached for the weapon and pointed it at the man. Again, unlike in the movies, this did not stop the man from attacking him. He did not freeze when Father Caspian demanded that he freeze; he just attempted to harm Caspian in any way he could and was also now scrambling to get the gun from him. At this moment, Caspian shot the gun at the man and the grip around his leg went limp.

Caspian was now free to escape the vehicle but was suddenly gripped with almost immediate guilt for having shot the man. He was unsure if the man was dead or just wounded and part of him wanted to open the door to the vehicle to check on his attacker, but then he realized that he was now even shorter on time. He then thought about waiting for the police to arrive so he could explain what had happened but remembered that, according to Black Jack, Jenks had been arrested and someone who came with the police was also working with the man with the gun. Father Caspian then made the next most logical decision and ran as fast as he could in what he assumed was the direction of the airport.

As he ran, he felt awful for the volunteers who might find this man's body and all the questions they would have. Eventually, the police would arrive and they would have a look at the security footage. They would see Father

Caspian emerging from the vehicle and then running and everyone would have many questions about that too. But he didn't have any time for any of those worries at the moment, so he kept running.

He turned a corner and heard a loud engine noise coming up behind him. He looked behind him and saw a large figure on a motorcycle following him. He was wearing a leather jacket with several patches on it and a massive helmet with metal spikes going up and down the center, almost like a Mohawk. Caspian began to run and the motorcycle continued to gain on him. He turned left down an alleyway only to realize too late that it was a dead end. He started to make his way towards a dumpster that was at the far end of the alley and thought that if he could reach it quickly enough, he might be able to jump over the brick wall that the dumpster was up against. He was unsure what was on the other side of that brick wall, but he was certain that the man on the motorcycle wasn't, which was good enough for now. As he ran, he realized that the man with the gun had broken his skin when he bit him. He was bleeding and limping. Before he reached the dumpster, the motorcycle was right upon him and Caspian fell.

The man removed his helmet, placed it under his arm, and then extended his hand to Caspian.

"Black Jack?" Caspian said in absolute shock.

"Yes, sir, Father, sir," Black Jack replied.

"I didn't know you had a motorcycle!" Caspian exclaimed.

"You never asked!" Black Jack reached down. "Mary called me and said you were in trouble, so we all came running. Now get on! We have to get out of here. Where do we need to take you?"

"The airport!" Caspian said as he jumped on the back of the motorcycle.

"Helmet," Black Jack roared and pointed to a pink helmet hanging from his side saddle, and Caspian put it on as they drove off.

They weaved in and out of the alleyways toward the airport; one of the cop cars that was making its way toward the crime scene saw the illegal maneuver and the officer made a U-turn in pursuit of the motorcycle that was carrying Black Jack and Father Caspian.

"What do you do now?" Caspian screamed over the roar of the motor.

"Hold on, sir!" Black Jack shouted as he took a sharp turn down a smaller alley and lost the cop. The alleyway connected right onto the highway near where the interstate went right over the bay. The sun was just on the verge of setting and Caspian couldn't help but think about how beautiful it looked amid the chaos he had suddenly found himself in. Time was ticking against them and now Caspian's mind had gone to the fact that he certainly didn't have enough time to get through TSA and still make his flight. There was also the issue of him not knowing which flight he was supposed to be on or where he was going. None of these worries he had internally had any sway on Black Jack from charging forward like a knight on a noble metal steed. They had made it to the airport within a few minutes and Caspian dismounted the motorcycle and turned to Black Jack to hand him back his helmet.

"I don't know what shit you've gotten yourself into, sir," Black Jack said with a smile, "but whatever it is, you've got the streets on your side."

With that, they clasped hands and Black Jack kissed the priest's ring. "Now go!"

Caspian rushed into the airport so quickly that he almost crashed into a man holding a small piece of paper that said, "Caspian Castellanos." When the priest declared himself to be the man on the piece of paper, the gentleman holding the paper asked to see some identification. Caspian pulled out his ID and the man examined it; he simply said, "Follow me," and took Caspian away from the ticketing counters, out towards a back door and onto the tarmac. In all of his life, Caspian had never stood on a tarmac. All of his concerns about TSA and tickets and gate numbers appeared useless. The man walked him toward a small plane that was waiting for him. He was ushered onto the plane and realized he was the only person inside other than the pilot. The aircraft was extremely loud.

"Cutting it close, Padre?" the pilot said.

"Where are we going?" Caspian shouted.

"Kentucky!" the pilot shouted back. "Now please sit down!"

For the hour and thirteen minutes of his flight, Caspian had time to think about what was going on and what he would do about it. The man with the piece of paper with his name on it had taken his phone, credit cards, and everything else he still had on him. Caspian wasn't even really sure why he had given it all to this man or why he was suddenly so willingly doing any of this. Then again, it wasn't much like he had a choice in the matter. This was happening to him; it wasn't something he had any choice over. He was rolling with it. Without any access to technology, he couldn't do the things he had hoped to, like google the symbol he had seen on the neck tattoo of the man who tried to kill him. He couldn't call the bishop and explain that he didn't murder anyone, that it was all in self-defense, or that he was choosing to run from the police. He believed he might now be working with the CIA to help them find a lost agent living as a homeless man because he had uncovered something to do with the Russians.

With each passing minute, doubt began to creep back in. There are few feelings as awful as when you start to gaslight yourself. Had he actually lost it? Caspian began to wonder. Was this all a mistake? A delusion? What was the separation between this insanity he was now experiencing and that of Jesus Christ believing that he was the second coming of a mythical God/Man from two thousand years ago? He wasn't sure that he liked any of the answers to those questions he was asking. Then he looked around himself and he was on a plane that someone had produced, and there had been a man with a piece of paper waiting for him, and that meant someone had to be orchestrating all of this. But who?

They were landing and soon enough Caspian would be walking off of this private plane and landing in some town he did not know in what he assumed must be Kentucky, a place he had never even thought about visiting, and he had no idea what was going to happen next. He had foolishly thought he had never been more scared in his whole life earlier when he had the gun pointed at his face in the car, but that was incorrect. This was the moment he was most scared as he was about to step off of this plane and face whatever reality he was about to face. As the door opened, a woman was waiting on the tarmac for him. She was taller than him and wearing a long grey coat. He realized he was pretty disheveled and tucked his shirt in before walking down the few steps on the door that doubled as stairs. The woman approached him as he finally reached the bottom.

"Hello, Caspian. I am Nadya. I am glad you made it. I wasn't sure you would come. Now, we have a lot of work to do to find out where Jenks is. Please, get in." She pointed to a car.

For a moment, Caspian wasn't so sure he wanted to get in the car. He wanted to pull the escape button and start over. He wanted to go back in time a couple of hours and handle this all differently. He didn't want to kill anyone, he didn't want to be here right now, and he just wanted to run in any direction except toward that car. Then he realized that the alternative, if he could pull that lever and go back in time, was that he was in a lot of trouble with his old classmate turned bishop, who was likely going to fire him at best and defrock him at worst. The alternative was no better than the future that now lay before him. No matter how far he went, life would never be the same from here on out. And he suddenly laughed.

"What is so funny?" Nadya asked.

"A week ago, I thought my life was royally fucked because it was so boring."

"Well, it is certainly not boring now," Nadya said without emotion.

With that, Caspian ducked into the black car waiting for him on the tarmac of the Kentucky airport. He entered the vehicle with a person he must now presume was another CIA operative who was working with the other CIA operative who was pretending to be a homeless guy and living at the shelter he had been operating until earlier today when he decided to set his life on fire. At that moment, he started to wonder if Jesus Christ of Mobile might have been the second coming after all because, at this point, anything was possible.

Chapter Seven

As he sat in the vehicle with Nadya in silence, new and terrifying thoughts entered Father Caspian's mind. By this point, he had accepted that this was reality. He had now long moved past the idea that the man with the gun was attempting to rob him or that anything happening around him was some kind of accident. He had found himself caught up in something he couldn't explain. Stephen Jenks had been telling the truth to him that day in his office and he could not deny that anymore. He was even feeling tremendous guilt for not choosing to believe Jenks at face value. Three separate and dueling thoughts were happening in his brain during this silence.

The first was that he couldn't help but wish he could start back over at The Mission and do things differently. He shouldn't have judged Jenks based upon all of the other odd things happening around him but purely on the merits of what Jenks himself was saying. Of course, that's not what he had done; instead, he had lumped Jenks in with everyone else whom he had also discredited. It seemed easier to discredit someone claiming to be the second coming of Jesus or that the entire catalog of Kylie Minogue songs was actually about some woman in Mobile who had never traveled outside the city, much less the state. So, on the surface, all of these issues seemed utterly insane and easily discarded. But he also dismissed them immediately without ever investigating them further. Maybe there was something deeper going on that he was refusing to explore or, perhaps, just like with Jenks, he was discounting other realities around him that could, as bizarre as they seemed, have some truth to them. Moreover, even if there was no truth to these claims and they turned out to be simply delusions, shouldn't he have done more to help?

The second thought plaguing him was not necessarily a new thought to him, but now, with everything happening, it was given a new life of unease in his soul. What if Jesus was just an alcoholic from Nazareth who convinced twelve people that he was the Messiah? Was his entire faith based upon some delusion of an extraordinarily kind and well-meaning man who was deeply disturbed? Now billions of people across the globe commemorate him every Sunday because, for whatever reason, his delusion caught on where others had been discredited. Was there a difference between the claims of Jesus Christ of Nazareth and Jesus Christ of Mobile if you broke down their claims to the finest points? Yes, the Mobile version was a potty mouth with a checkered past, but what did we really know about the missing years of Jesus? Did he make a shit ton of mistakes that got expunged from his record? Were the gospels possibly nothing more than the Twitter rants of a few folks who bought into one man's self-aggrandized mental breakdown? If this was true, then that meant that the Jesus Christ who had been in his care at The Mission was just as legitimate a candidate for the Son of God as anyone else who had ever claimed that throne for themselves. Maybe two thousand years from now, people would be debating over his divinity and doctrines as he did with others about his faith. Worst of all, who did that make him in the narrative: Judas, Pilate, Peter?

The final intrusive thought rattling around in his mind was this: what was the difference between him believing the reality, as unbelievable as it might seem, that he was suddenly thrust into a modern-day Russian spy novel and the reality that was believed by Jesus Christ of Mobile? What if he was also living on the streets and firmly believing that he was a Catholic priest and that he was driving around in a car and yet he was really just standing on a street corner somewhere as strangers walked on the other side of the road to avoid him talking to himself. Could he be waiting outside a shelter somewhere waiting for his soup and bread and have no idea that he was the one being laughed at and mocked? Worst of all, he was now struggling with the question: how would he ever know the difference?

As the car came to an abrupt stop, he decided that there was nothing he could do to answer any of these questions and the only thing he could do was to continue in reality; he knew it and hoped for the fucking best. Nadya reached for the handle on the car as if she intended to exit.

"What are we doing?" Caspian asked her.

"Follow me," she said as she stepped out of the vehicle.

Having no option in his life other than following orders, he did precisely that. He exited the black sedan that had been waiting for them on the tarmac and then discovered that another car was waiting for them wherever it was that they now were. He got into this vehicle and the driver began heading forward. To say that Caspian was extremely confused would be an understatement and the curiosity was getting the better of him.

"Where are we going?" he finally asked Nadya. He felt like this was a fair question considering he hadn't asked anything of her over the last hour that they had driven together so far and he felt he was owed some explanation.

"In time," was her only response.

They sat there in silence, and by this point, Caspian was exhausted from his thoughts and wished he had his phone back. He would have done anything to be playing a word game or mindlessly scrolling through all his former high school friends on Instagram. He wouldn't have even minded if his feed was flooded with everyone posting pictures of their kids doing mundane things or trying to get their friends to sign up for a pyramid scheme. He would be thankful for any level of entertainment to numb his mind from the exhausting reality he was now grappling with. Instead, he just had to sit there in the silence, look out the window at all the passing trees, and wonder what was next for him. Finally, the second car came to a stop and they both exited this vehicle. Caspian was surprised to see two things. First, there was not a third vehicle waiting to take them anywhere; secondly, they were in the middle of nowhere.

"This way," Nadya said and she stepped off the road and into the darkness of the woods.

Caspian followed her about two hundred feet into the dense forest before he stopped to say, "Listen, I am tired, I am scared, I don't think I have ever been this thirsty in my entire life, and frankly, after six years without one, I could use a fucking cigarette. I don't know who you are; I don't know where we are going or if we are even the good guys! And now I am walking in the woods in the middle of God knows where. What the fuck is going on?"

"That's fair," Nadya said and she stopped walking and sat down on a fallen tree. Caspian sat down as well.

She tossed him a bottle of water from her backpack and a pack of cigarettes. Caspian chuckled and tossed the smokes back to her, but he did consume the bottle of water quickly.

"I appreciate that you have many questions," Nadya finally continued, "and to be honest, I have quite a few for you. How did you end up with that number?"

"That man you know as Jenks," Caspian explained, "we knew him as John Doe. He had been staying in the camps and eventually at the shelter I was operating. He told me one day that he was an operative working for the CIA and that if something happened, to open that envelope. Frankly, I didn't believe him. I figured he was just like many other people at the shelter living in some personal struggle of the mind."

Nadya nodded. "We both had an emergency number like that, me and Jenks."

"And Rasputin?" Caspian inquired.

"That was the code, so we would know it was legit in case someone called the number by accident or gave it out as a random number to some guy who was hitting on them at the bar," Nadya answered.

"That makes sense." Father Caspian was finally feeling himself a little but also partially regretting not taking that cigarette. "So are you, like, secret agents or something?"

"It's more complicated than that." Nadya extended her hand towards Caspian with a bag of chips, but he put his hands up in refusal; his stomach was churning from all the anxiety and drinking the water too fast. "Jenks and I were both hackers when we were kids. We developed a firm when we became grown-ups. We helped private businesses bolster their security from cyber-attacks. After the election, we were tapped by the government to be independent contractors to help track Russian spyware activity. We did a little bit of everything: tracking bot activity and monitoring dark web chatter. We are sort of digital mercenaries; we were being bounced around from agency to agency. But the checks kept cashing, so we kept working."

"Thank you for trusting me with this information," Father Caspian said with a reassuring half-smile.

"I don't trust you," Nadya said, smiling back. "I just know that I can kill you if I have to."

"You aren't Catholic then?" Caspian quipped.

"No, I am," Nadya hit back. "Or at least I was."

"Understood." Caspian firmly believed her about the killing thing. "So how did this all get started? Why was Jenks running?"

Nadya stood up and started walking back in the direction she had been initially heading and Caspian quickly got up to follow. She waved her hand from her hip for him to stand closer so she didn't have to yell. Once they were walking at pace with each other, she began to answer his question. "We were eventually sent to the CIA to help with a project investigating American fringe groups working directly with Russians sympathetic to their cause. Jenks and I would work both ends of a case, meaning we each wouldn't let the other know what we were finding. This way, if one of us was ever compromised in any way or found something too scary, the other wouldn't be in the shit with them."

"And you think that's what happened?"

"Yes." Nadya pointed to indicate they needed to shift slightly north. "But because of our system, I am not exactly sure what he found. I continued to work the case until I got your call. Now, both Jenks and I are off-grid. That means we've got two problems. Whatever he got himself into with whatever it is he found out there on the web, those people are after us, but now the government will be too. They will think we went all Snowden on them or something."

"Did you go Snowden on them?" Caspian wasn't sure.

"I guess that depends on what Jenks found." With that, she pointed the final time and Caspian could see they had made their way into a small clearing with a cabin in the center of it.

This was the first time it had started to feel like a movie to Caspian. As best he could tell, there wasn't a road leading up to the cabin. He did notice that no wires were going to the building and there were no lights on inside of it. As he looked around, he was becoming increasingly more confident that this cabin had been built out of the logs that had been cleared to make this little area where the house now lay. It was probably no bigger than a thousand square feet in total. It was a Lincoln log-style single-story building. It had grass or moss growing on the roof, but he couldn't make it out in the dark. It had a cute little porch and fur traps and other antique oddities hanging from the exterior walls under the porch's overhang. It had two rocking chairs with a whisky barrel checkerboard nuzzled between them, as you would see at a Cracker Barrel. The door seemed sturdy and the windows were newer than this place's aesthetic implied. You could have easily convinced anyone that this building was from the 1800s, but upon close inspection, it had been built much more recently primarily because it was not in disrepair. There were multiple deadbolts on the door and Nadya began unlocking it.

"I assumed you would have some high-tech thumbprint type lock," Caspian jabbed.

"Are you fucking kidding?" Nadya shook her head as she unlocked the last bolt. "Those are way easier to hack than a conventional lock like this to pick."

Once inside, she walked over to a breaker box and opened it, flipping on the master breaker, and suddenly the building lit up inside. It was not a harsh light like fluorescents but a beautiful soft light. As Caspian surveyed the interior of the building it was an odd mix of ancient and new technology. There were gas lanterns atop bookshelves and a cast iron stove over in the corner with a coffee percolator, ready to be used. The tables and chairs also looked like they had been crafted right off of the property as well. Herbs were drying from the rafters. It was only missing some decapitated animal heads and it would have been the quintessential cabin in the woods.

In contrast, there were two large battery packs against the wall that Caspian recognized as solar batteries. He had seen them before while touring some facility back home when the diocese looked into green energy alternatives. Computers and routers were in the opposite corner to the cast iron stove. Caspian thought it was strange that these two worlds didn't seem at odds with each other; somehow, they had designed it all to blend as a perfect little ecosystem. It appeared quite apocalyptic—the ideal place for the end of the world.

"Quite a place." Caspian looked up at the ceiling to see if it had an antler chandelier.

"We built it over a summer a few years ago." Nadya was leaning down at the stove, trying to light a match. "We knew a guy who could build cabins right out of the land. We used to watch his videos on YouTube. We offered him a cash job to do it and brought him out here blindfolded so he wouldn't know where the cabin was located and he built it over the course of about a month with his own hands and eating off the land. It was a wild thing to see. Then we slowly brought technology out here, set up our solar system, servers, etc. The land cost us hardly anything because it's in the middle of nowhere and doesn't have power or water. Still, we spent probably half a million outfitting the place."

"Jesus." Caspian was shocked. "That's a lot for such a humble place."

"It's expensive to make sure people don't ask questions." Nadya finally had the fire going.

"How did you afford it all? From the government contracts?"

"Fuck no." Nadya laughed. "They don't pay us nearly enough to pull any of this off. Jenks and I were early investors in crypto. We just do the government gigs to keep us sharp, not for the money. It also helps keep the government off our fucking backs all the time. We get away with a lot more when they need us."

The cabin was substantially bigger than Caspian had initially estimated. All the computers, cast iron stove, dining area, kitchen, and storage cabinets were in the front portion of the house. Then there was a doorway towards the center of the room that led to a hallway with four separate bedrooms and at the end of the hallway was a bathroom with a composting toilet. He was shocked to find out they had hot water. They had rigged up a rainwater collection system and also had someone come and dig a well. This was a completely self-sustaining compound. Nadya explained that they had also built a greenhouse in the back, an aquaponics system, and a chicken coup with an automatic door so the animals could live off the land.

"There is much more to see when the morning comes around." Nadya was almost giddy to show it all off to someone new.

They opened two packs of MREs for the evening dinner and Caspian was surprised by how good it tasted. He had a beef taco and it even had candy for dessert. When dinner was over, Nadya taught him how to use the incinerating disposal system and what to set aside for composting. They finished the evening around the fireplace with some moonshine from a mason jar while playing a game of chess. Midway through the game, a small piece of stained wood with numerous locks caught Caspian's eye. There were two door locks, one a deadbolt and another a regular lock. But there were also other types of locks attached to the board held on by being locked to little loops that had been screwed into the board. It was chaotic looking but beautiful in a way.

"What is that?" Caspian asked while pointing at the stained piece of wood.

"That is my old lock-picking kit," Nadya said without looking up from her turn at chess. She was pretty sure she was in check but wasn't so sure Caspian had figured that out yet.

"That's so cool!" Caspian had never seen anything like it. "Can I look at it?"

"Knock yourself out." Nadya removed her piece to safety.

"How does it work?"

"Well, you see that little bag on the back? It's full of tools you can use to pick a lock." Caspian turned the stained wood over and there was a small black bag with a zipper on it that had been velcroed onto the back. "Where did you find this thing?"

"I made it," Nadya said. "Checkmate?"

"Are you sure?"

"That I made it or that you are in checkmate?" Nadya smirked.

"That I'm in checkmate." Caspian laughed.

"Yes." Nadya pointed toward her winning position. "And I made it."

"That's amazing!"

"I was ten." Nadya shrugged.

"So you always wanted to live a life of crime?" Caspian asked it as a joke.

"I never wanted to be trapped," Nadya responded sincerely. "I figured if I always knew how the locks worked, no one could ever trap me. There was always an escape plan."

"It's very neat." Caspian meant the compliment genuinely.

"You can keep it if you'd like. I have no use for it."

"Are you sure?"

"Absolutely. I can get out of anything now."

After relenting that he had lost at chess, he snuggled into the chair and began to tinker away at the lock-picking kit. He was relatively unsuccessful at his endeavor, but he enjoyed it tremendously. He couldn't help but think how nice it was in the woods. He kept wanting to say the quiet was peaceful, but there was nothing quiet about it. Even through the thick wooden walls you could hear all manner of critters rustling around or making music with their cries, croaks, and legs and the splashing sound of toads leaping into the pond. He also heard a howling noise that made Caspian now sure coyotes existed somewhere out there, even though he had yet to see one and Nadya had yet to mention it. Even in the middle of all the chaos that this day had brought, he determined that if there was a Heaven on the other side of all this Hell they were now living, this was what he wanted his paradise to be like. And this was his final thought before the exhaustion finally took him and he passed out in the chair by the cast iron fire. Nadya laid a blanket over the sleeping priest before making her way over to the computers and clicking them on. They hummed back to life.

"All right, Jenks, where the fuck are you?" Nadya asked the screen.

Chapter Eight

The gates to the building were ornate wrought iron swirls that almost gave the impression that they were some vine that had slowly turned to black metal as time moved on. At random, there were flourishes of gold flowers attached to the vines. They grew about eight feet tall before there was a separation of space about another two feet until the actual top of the fence plumed to a point where a gold frame encircled an icon of the Theotokos; above her was the image of the three-barred cross and the gules. These gates diligently guarded a large brick three-story building that would have looked magnificent in stature if it were not made minuscule by the towering skyscrapers on either side. The structure looked like it was entirely out of place as if it was a small embassy ready to welcome back another time. If one were to look at the building alone, to remove the towering buildings on either side, if the sounds of the streets were silenced and the flashing neon of a changing world all disappeared, you could easily have believed that you had been taken back to pre-Revolutionary Russia and this massive mansion could just as easily have been a summer palace awaiting the happily welcome pattering feet of the grand duchesses and their fragile future tsar of a little brother.

This building was far from its own land, instead acting as a safe haven for those of the Holy Synod of the Russian Orthodox Church of the Diaspora. Even though over a hundred years had passed since the fall of the tsar, once you made it to the other side of these gates time stood still and immediately it felt as if everyone inside was patiently waiting for the rabble to stop rousing in Petrograd and soon all would be well once again.

The opulence of it all made the appearance of the busted black car at the royal gates seem much more out of place. The glass in the front window was cracked right down the center and it looked like it could just snap in half at any moment. The driver's side window was completely missing, making it all the easier for the driver to lean over to the only piece of visible modernity in the entire palace. There was a small speaker box with a buzzer to announce your arrival. The driver leaned out of the window and then groaned as he realized his doing so caused his wounded arm to press up against the steering wheel.

"Greetings." The voice coming from the speaker sounded annoyed. "How may I help you at this late hour?"

"Tell the boss I'm here," the driver said.

"I am sure I do not know what you mean," the speaker responded.

"Tell his excellency, the Metropolitan, that Kyle is here."

A few moments passed before the gate finally opened without any further announcement. The seemingly ancient iron gate opened by the magic of technology but made a grinding noise against the cement under its weight as if to show that the two worlds could not properly function in unison, try as they might. Kyle nearly hit the edge of the left side of the gate as he moved his tattered vehicle forward, unaccustomed to driving with only his left hand while his dominant arm was in a makeshift sling. With difficulty, he parked his car, exited, made his way up two flights of stairs, and waited outside two large wooden doors until he was greeted by the man who had been on the speaker.

"The Metropolitan will be with you shortly," he said and then disappeared down a hallway.

Kyle stood in the foyer, which seemed exceptionally bright against the backdrop of the dark night he had just escaped from. Lining the wall were images of previous bishops and metropolitans. These images of now late clerics gave way to pictures of the current synod and above them was the official portrait of Patriarch Kirill. As he paced up and down, looking at each picture intently, he fingered his beard, feeling rather inadequate at its length in comparison to those of the hierarchs. As he tried to imagine his fur reaching such lengths, the echoing noise of footsteps reverberated down the marbled floor of the same hallway where the man over the speaker had disappeared. This time, it was the Metropolitan heading towards him. The hierarch had clearly been asleep, as his usually well-combed hair was disheveled. He was not wearing his usual pectoral icon or any other ornaments, just a simple black riassa. As he reached Kyle, the sternness of his face met the oddity of the hour in which he was being disturbed.

"You should not be here," was the Metropolitan's curt greeting before he extended his hand to the visitor. Kyle always forgot this part and then he placed his only good hand out and the bishop made the sign of the cross over it, placed his hand in Kyle's, and then Kyle lifted the bishop's hand to his face to kiss it. He hated this bizarre custom, but he thought to himself, *When in Moscow.*

"I apologize; it was necessary," was his only response.

"This way." The bishop ushered him down the opposite side of the dueling hallways.

When the Metropolitan opened the door to the cathedral, Kyle was struck with a sense of awe. For him, it was like peering into history, one he hoped to bring as a reality to his own land. This was a sanctuary for the days when Russia was a mighty tsardom. The walls were off-white and each icon was framed by ornate gold that seemed almost humble compared to the iconostasis's massive gold structure. One could almost accuse it of being gaudy if it weren't so captivating. It was excusable in its extravagance because it felt like a museum to Christianity, a conservatory of this ancient faith hidden away amongst the bustling streets of downtown Chicago. But this was not just a church; it was a Little Russia being preserved here in the diaspora, as they called anything outside the borders of the homeland.

The bishop locked the doors into the cathedral behind them and then turned to Kyle. "You have made a grave mistake in coming here. Not everyone within the synod is as comfortable with our arrangement. Some have yet to understand the complexities of the situation."

"They have certainly benefitted from our efforts," Kyle spat back at the Metropolitan.

"Indeed, but that does not mean they must like it or you being here. This is not your place. Our ways are not your ways." The bishop continued, "You are a guest."

"And so you are you," Kyle asserted. "Remember that this is our country you are in. I serve America first, Russia second, and only as an ally of our mutual cause."

"Remember that I am an American citizen and a Russian." The Metropolitan was tired and ready to get to the point. "What brings you here?"

"I need to see The Doctor." He pointed at his wounded arm with his good one. "The son of a bitch shot me."

"Language in the house of God." The Metropolitan rebuked him before continuing, "I will get you to The Doctor. Does this mean you lost them?"

"We have Stephen Jenks," Kyle said with pride.

"How did you accomplish that?" Against his better judgment, the Metropolitan was impressed.

"A miracle, I suppose." Kyle genuinely looked baffled. "I was on his trail but had lost him. I was staying out in my car and a cop approached me. He really gave me a hard time about everything and I thought I was going to get arrested. I told a little white lie that I was working as a bounty hunter and was looking for Stephen Jenks. Would you know it? Just a couple of weeks later, some dope head dies at this shelter Jenks is hiding out in and who happens to show up? The fucking police."

"Language!" the bishop said exhaustedly.

"Sorry, the fucking pig shows up." Kyle continued, "He recognized Jenks from the photo I showed him and held him at the police station for me. I called the crew and they came up to get him. I decided to stick around a bit; where there is smoke there is Nadya, I thought. When the number was activated, I expected to find her, but instead, it was this priest Jenks had gotten caught up with at the homeless shelter. He was wiry."

"Was he Russian?" The bishop seemed surprised.

"No." Kyle laughed. "Some Roman Catholic priest he hooked up with while hiding out on the streets."

"How the mighty have fallen, it seems." The Metropolitan smirked. "Good! But you should have gone to your own headquarters. You being here only compromises us."

"You think I hadn't thought of that?" Kyle got uncomfortably close to the bishop. "But things are escalating a lot faster than we thought they would. I happen to think that is a good thing. The others of the Krest—"

"The Krest is a holy institution within our church," said the bishop, interrupting him. "Though you have adopted many of our institutional ways and symbols, you are not of The Faith. You have your own way. We have our way. I pray for the day you all join the Church, but until then, remember where you stand."

"The Brotherhood has not shared your anti-ecumenical sentiments, your gracefulness." Kyle patted the bishop on the back. "You want a restoration of Russia and your leadership; we want the same for ourselves. Your tsar was removed against the will of God and so was our president. Thankfully, our president was smart enough not to get himself shot, so our goal is a bit easier to accomplish."

Lazarus glared back. "I will forgive you this cruel blasphemy. But keep in mind that there is much more we must do before both our countries may be restored to their previous glories. If we are to achieve this, then you must do things with certain decorum and not this barbaric, what is a good word for it, hillbilly-ish mockery with which you present yourself."

Kyle laughed, not even remotely insulted by the highly accurate accusation. He was an arrogant man; even those higher up in the leadership of the Brotherhood would have been upset with him showing up at the synod like this. Kyle knew more than was good for him and he was ambitious. He fantasized about one day also ascending to the presidency. He felt that, after Trump, the doorway to anyone becoming the leader of the free world was possible. Sure, he was lacking in the millions necessary to win the highest office in the land; still, he felt he had the charisma to make it happen. One day, if he could make this current operation work, they could see their president back in the oval office. Many others within the Brotherhood had already run for state office. Still, he was prevented from doing so by the leadership, concerned that his pending court case over his January 6th involvement might be too big a distraction. If he couldn't fight the battle by way of helping to decertify the election through ascending to public office, he was more than willing to fight the ground battle. After all, when the American Revolution ended, they chose a general of that war to lead them. Maybe it would happen again, he told himself. All he needed was a war, and the Krest was ready to supply one.

The Metropolitan had walked toward the iconostasis and was about to open the royal doors when he could hear Kyle walking up behind him. "My friend, you can go no further."

This stopped Kyle in his tracks. This was not his first time entering a Russian Orthodox church since the Krest and the Brotherhood had linked arms in their mutual aid for the cause of restoring both of their great nations to their previous glory. He thought the services were long and lofty and he couldn't keep up. He would have been lying if he didn't admit he was curious about what lay on the other side of those royal doors. To him, the priests and bishops acted like they had the Holy Grail or the Ark of the Covenant back there. He wanted to see it. As much as the services confused him, he was intrigued. It all seemed so different from the lights and music he had experienced at the non-denominational church he attended back home. He may not have understood it all, but the militant way they preserved their faith mirrored how he felt about his own country. He couldn't help but feel that the brotherhood within the Russian Church was similar to what he had hoped to find within the Brotherhood here at home.

"Maybe someday I will ascend to that altar with you, Vladyka." Kyle bowed as he stepped away from the icon screen.

"May your prayers and mine unite in this." With this, the bishop extended his hand to Kyle.

Kyle stepped forward and clasped hands with the bishop. “For the Fatherland.”

“For the Fatherland,” Kyle responded.

Chapter Nine

In his entire life, Caspian had never slept by a fire and was not accustomed to all the unique feelings his body was now producing. He awakened with a tremendous crick in his neck and his tongue was so dry that it made the air taste funny as he breathed. Without his phone, he was not sure what time it was. The blanket Nadya had placed over him was now wrapped around his feet in a wad on the floor. He was a heavy sleeper and didn't remember removing it, but he was also a very warm sleeper, so it made sense to him that he would have found it uncomfortable. He untangled the blanket from around his ankles and then stood up to stretch out his body. The sun was up outside, but the way the shadows hung across the ground meant it was very early morning. He made his way over to the front door and began unlocking the deadbolts so he could have a look outside. The place was entirely surrounded by forest. His family was not the type to go camping when he was a kid and this scene was utterly foreign to him. He had always heard such nasty things about Kentucky growing up, and though he certainly couldn't yet say anything for the people, having yet to meet anyone, the landscape was breathtaking.

He took a step off the porch, walked around the back end of the house, and saw the greenhouse, which was easily half the size. The entire compound was quite an industrial feat and he was certain that he could never leave and be quite content for the rest of his life. About a hundred feet behind the greenhouse was a small pond. He didn't know much about acreage but guessed it must have been at least half an acre long and wide. A tree growing up from one end of the pond hung out over the water, giving shade to the little fish that swam along the edge. Something jumped out of the water that he assumed must be a frog. To the right of the tree was a single-seater wooden row boat and just to the right of that was a small shed, which he thought would be a perfect place to hide fishing poles and such things.

Behind him came a crunching sound of leaves; he turned to see Nadya approaching and holding a cup of coffee for each of them. They stood there for a moment, just soaking in the serenity of the environment that they had found themselves in. It was hard to believe it had been less than twenty-four hours since his life had turned upside down. As he looked out over the water, trying to find peace, flashes of the man with the gun going limp rushed through his thoughts like an unwelcome guest.

"It's beautiful out here," he finally said.

"It is." Nadya took a few steps toward the water. "When we built this, it was just supposed to be a worst-case scenario escape plan. But I fell in love. I don't think I could have ever imagined how much I would love it out here."

"Have you ever thought of retiring and letting the world go on without you?"

"All of the time. How about you?"

Caspian thought about that for a few moments. "All of the time."

Neither of them was eager to rush inside and rejoin the burning world around them. Inside were computers, emails, and encrypted hard drives with clues to what they were supposed to do next. Somewhere in the world was Jenks and they both needed to find him. They weren't the only ones looking for him but they were the only two people in the world who wanted good for him. Everyone else who was searching for him would want him dead, arrested, or something worse. The beauty of this moment would soon need to be shattered, but they each took in one last look before Nadya nodded back toward the cabin with her chin and began to lead the way. Caspian followed but was also becoming a bit nervous as he wasn't sure what help he would be. He didn't know much about

Jenks other than what limited things he knew about him when he was John Doe, and even that was shrouded in mystery. He wanted to be useful but didn't know what he could offer that Nadya didn't already know or suspect.

When they made it back into the cabin, she pulled up another chair to the computer area and Caspian joined her. The setup was seemingly pretty modest. Caspian was not sure he knew exactly what he was expecting, but it was hard to believe that this was all that was necessary to keep the world safe from cyber-attacks launched by one of the largest powers in the world.

"Do we have a plan?" he finally asked.

"Kind of." Nadya took another sip of coffee. "Last night, I spent some time poking around, trying to see if there were any tracks leading back to what he could have gotten himself into."

"And?"

"Well, I did find a trail of communication between him and someone called the Hieromonk." She shrugged. "I found an email address for him, so I made contact. But it's pretty common for us to use lots of disposable communication portals and email addresses. So it could easily be a dead end."

"Interesting name," Father Caspian said, mostly to himself.

"I figure it is something from some video game." Nadya shrugged again. "Lots of these guys use shit like that."

"No, I don't think so," Caspian said in a contemplative way. "I mean I suppose it could be from a video game, but a hieromonk is a type of cleric in the Eastern Orthodox Church."

"I've never heard that before." Nadya leaned in toward Caspian, giving him her full attention. "How is it different from a 'monk' monk?"

"Well, a monk is someone who has devoted their life to the cause of a particular religious order, like the Franciscans." Caspian repositioned himself in the chair so he could look at Nadya without straining his already hurt neck. "The same is true in the Eastern Churches, and the priesthood is similar as well to ours, except their priests can be married as long as they did so before ordination. Most clergy in an Eastern Church are married priests."

"Sounds like a better gig to me." Nadya blinked. "I guess you chose poorly."

"Nobody's perfect." Caspian laughed. "Monastics are all of the celibate ranks within the Orthodox Church, but some monasteries have priests attached who are also monks, which is what a hieromonk is. It makes you wonder if…."

"If what?" Nadya was genuinely curious at this point.

"I'm not sure yet, but it does seem strange." Caspian was fumbling with his mug as he thought. "I mean if he was getting entangled with the Russians in some way, I guess it wouldn't be the weirdest thing ever if someone on the inside were helping him. The Russians are notorious for using the Church as a means for their operations. They don't quite have the same idea of separation of church and state as we do in the West."

"What does it look like then, for them?" Nadya asked.

"The separation of church and state?" Caspian laughed. "There really isn't such a thing. The Church is older than the Russian government. The Russian Church has outlived the tsars and Bolsheviks and I imagine they will outlive the Federation. Without the Russian Church you have no Russia and sometimes it's hard to tell who is subordinate to whom. I imagine they are just one and the same."

"You aren't as dumb as you look." Nadya nudged her shoulder against Caspian's to let him know she was teasing. "Are you hungry?"

Caspian nodded an affirmative and they walked over to the kitchen together. The kitchen had an electric stove, but all the cookware was cast iron. He had never cooked using cast iron before. Nadya excused herself for a moment and went outside; she returned with a couple of eggs from the chicken coup. There was some lard inside the cabinet, so she began to heat the cast iron skillet and oiled it with the lard as Caspian cracked the eggs. He was shocked by how much thicker the shells were than the ones on the eggs he purchased at the store, and the yokes were brighter too. He dropped all six of them into a small mixing bowl and then began to whisk them until they were all smooth and bubbly. He handed the bowl over to Nadya, found some cured meat in the pantry and asked her if it was all right to use. After receiving permission, he started to cut the meat and look for plates while she served the eggs. Even without salt or pepper, these were the best eggs Caspian had ever eaten. They ate together in silence until their peace was broken by a dinging noise from one of the computers.

They quickly rushed back to their original perch in front of the computer screen. Surprisingly, the urge to get on social media was no longer overtaking him. This was now far more exciting than anything he could find scrolling mindlessly through the drivel of the exhausting attempts to be cool or relevant or have just the right selfie.

"He responded!" Nadya was ecstatic. She continued reading for a few moments and looked less thrilled than before.

"Do you want the good news or the bad news?" she asked Caspian.

"Bad news."

"He is just as paranoid as you would expect anyone communicating with Jenks would be."

"And the good news?"

"He's willing to meet with us," she said.

"Well, that doesn't sound very paranoid to me," Caspian responded. "That sounds kind of the opposite of paranoid."

"He says we have to know the responsory. I think it must be like a code he and Jenks have put together. But I have absolutely no idea what it would be." Nadya looked less defeated than someone else might in such a situation.

"May I see the whole email?" Caspian asked.

She pointed toward the screen and scooted her seat back so he could read it. The message was a bit longer than he was expecting:

I am sorry to hear about Jenks. I had warned him that meddling in such things could lead to this. But we must each do our part to keep this thing we fear from becoming inevitable. If you are a true friend, then you will know the responsory of our cause. If you do not, I am afraid I will be unable to help you. I will not be able to respond anymore here; it is too dangerous, but you may meet me at the skete - Hieromonk Jerome.

After a Google search, the two quickly found a Hieromonk Jerome who had been deposed for some reason and was currently living at a skete in rural West Virginia. It was about a four-hour drive. They agreed they would just start heading in that direction and figure out the issue of this coded message on the way. Though neither of them said it, they were becoming increasingly afraid that something more sinister may have happened to Stephen Jenks and they also knew that time was of the essence if they wanted to find him alive. If these folks were willing to harm Father Caspian, who as best they knew was a mere bystander, what would they be willing to do to Jenks? A nagging feeling was starting to work its way up Caspian's spine; if this story was starting to evolve into one with a hieromonk, a skete, and God knows what else, then maybe these people thought he was more involved than he actually was. The "I'm in danger" meme flashed before his eyes.

For about an hour, Caspian and Nadya closed the cabin down. She showed him how to properly clean the cast iron and he finished making sure everything was placed where it should be in the kitchen. He swept the floor and wiped down the countertops. He then had to sweep again because he should have wiped down the countertops before breaking out the broom. Meanwhile, Nadya took care of making sure everything was locked up outside, that the batteries on the automatic door for the chicken coop were still good, and then she returned inside to shut down the computers and checked to make sure the fire in the stove had gone cold and then shut the flue. Finally, she shut down the power so the solar batteries wouldn't accidentally overcharge if the charge controller malfunctioned.

She handed Father Caspian his very own backpack full of supplies: food, water, matches, ammo, and a gun. He was not particularly thrilled about the gun part. If he was candid, he had seen enough guns to last a lifetime, but he also knew they were in grave danger. These unique circumstances called for being reasonable; it was not just about his life but also Nadya's. The idea that he was carrying to help keep others safe gave him a bit of solace about the whole gun business. They started to march their way back through the woods but in a different direction this time than they had arrived from. After about a two-hour walk, they made their way into a small town.

Toward the center of a town was a small storage unit where Nadya and Jenks stored a small vehicle for such an emergency. There was no driveway on their property; they didn't even have a mailbox because the home was not officially registered. As far as anyone else knew, it was just a vacant lot. Hiding the vehicle inside the storage unit gave them access to an escape without having to expose their hideout. After all the complications of the day before, both Nadya and Caspian were relieved to see that the car was where it was supposed to be and that the engine started without any trouble. I am not sure Father Caspian's heart could have taken any more movie tropes in one twenty-four-hour cycle. Nadya reached over to her left and into the storage compartment in the car's door and handed Caspian a map.

"I hope you know how to use one of these." Caspian gave her an affirming nod, so she continued. "Now, what the fuck is a skete? Because I think I know what it means to the majority of the world and I'm just curious as to why a priest or monk or whatever would be inviting us to that."

"Oh!" Caspian laughed. "Like, 'Aww skeet-skeet, motherfucker.'"

Nadya stopped the car. "Don't do that again. Ever."

"No, it's not like that at all. If I remember correctly, a skete is like a little collection of cottages at a monastery. I stayed at one once during a retreat at a Uniate monastery. So my best guess is that we are heading to a monastery and that one of those cabins will be his."

"That is better than the alternative." Nadya laughed.

"Agreed." Caspian's mind then wandered off before he said, "I wish I had my phone so I could find out exactly what this guy got himself in trouble for. Maybe it would give us clues to the responsory we have to know."

Nadya leaned over Caspian while still steering and popped open the glove box. It was spotless inside. There was yet another handgun, two magazines, and then a small flat screen shining back at Caspian. It was a notepad!

"You can use that for fifteen minutes; then factory reset it and toss it," she said sternly.

Father Caspian made fast work about it and began reading several articles by Eastern Orthodox bloggers. Jerome had gotten into trouble quite a few times over the years, speaking on many social issues. He had advocated for transgender rights within the Church, arguing that there was evidence of transgender people in the Bible and amongst the saints. But that wasn't what ultimately got him on the outs with the Russian Orthodox Church; he had advocated a change to the liturgy and was a huge proponent of female clergy. He had written a book arguing that women first evangelized to the disciples and that, as a result, they should have first been considered for the priesthood instead of men.

"I've read this guy's work!" Father Caspian was excited to have put these pieces together.

"Does that help us?" Nadya asked.

"I am not sure." He shook his head. "I read it back in seminary, so it's been a while. We didn't read much stuff from Eastern Orthodox clergy, especially non-Uniate ones, but his stuff circulated online quite a bit. He made a lot of videos on YouTube. He was very popular, and then, one day, they were all gone. But I did read his book on the Virgin Mary and the priesthood."

"What happened to him?"

"It seems he was censured and sent to this monastery." Caspian was running out of time before he had to reset the device. "But it seems there was more to the story; I just can't piece it all together."

"Time's up," Nadya monotoned.

"Give me just a second!" Caspian was on to something.

"Caspian, you've got to get rid of it," she shouted.

Caspian continued to scroll through a Reddit post before Nadya yanked the device from his hands. She began to push some buttons and then tossed it from the window; it shattered as it hit the asphalt below them.

"Fuck!" Caspian shouted back. "I only needed thirty more seconds."

"So did they." Nadya pointed in no particular direction to indicate that whoever was looking for them was out there. "I'm sorry, we are just going to have to work with what you've already got in your head."

"Best I can tell he got in trouble for Eucharistic heresy." After sulking for a few moments, Caspian offered, "He proposed that women should be priests."

"Sounds like a reasonable guy to me."

"Well, not to his bishops he didn't." Caspian pulled a small black book from his jacket pocket. "There have been numerous arguments over time in favor of women priests but none as pervasive as the arguments presented by Hieromonk Jerome. He tied his entire theological argument down to the Theotokos, the mother of God. He posited that if she was the first to carry the Body and Blood of Christ and elevate him to the shepherds as the living Eucharist, then she was the first priest. Not Jesus, Peter, Mary Magdalene, but the Virgin Mary herself."

"What does this mean?" Nadya was suddenly unsure of what all this had to do with Jenks.

"It means that Jerome argued that it was Mary who taught Jesus; she trained him. It is why she knew he could perform the miracle of water into wine. More than that, he argued that Jesus was intersex." Caspian could almost feel the heresy crawling on his arms as he said it all out loud. "If Jesus only had one earthly parent, and received his entire genetic code from that one parent, then his genetics would have been exclusively from Mary."

"So Jesus was non-binary?" Nadya inquired.

"Fully God and fully human." Caspian paused to collect his thoughts. "The bridge to fill the gap."

With that, Caspian pulled out the lock-picking kit and began to try again. He had not made any improvements since last night, but it was the only thing he had to entertain himself with.

"Any luck?" Nadya asked.

"It's kind of difficult," Caspian conceded.

"You will get the hang of it." Nadya laughed. "I'll make a vigilante out of you yet."

When they finally arrived at the outer gates of the monastery, they were locked.

"You wanna give it a try?" Nadya asked.

"I'm not sure I'm ready." Caspian looked nervous.

"I'm kidding." Nadya laughed. "Follow me."

She decided it was safer to go on foot. The path split into three directions. They followed on toward the one that said "Skete" and came up over a hill that looked down into a holler full of about thirty little cottages embedded into the hills surrounding it. They were tiny little places and some were more ornate than others. One of the things Caspian had hoped to figure out was which of these cabins belonged to Hieromonk Jerome, but

Nadya destroyed the notepad before that mystery was solved. As they moved around in the shadows looking at buildings, he hoped to see any clues that might give it away.

"That's it," he whispered.

"Are you absolutely sure?" Nadya asked.

"Yes."

"How?" She wanted more reassurance before possibly alerting the wrong people that they were on the property and potentially involving the police for trespassing.

"That icon there of the Theotokos. That is the icon of Our Lady of the Sign. It depicts the moment of implantation of Jesus into the womb of Mary. That is the moment that Mary became the first priest, the first person to hold the body and blood of Christ. If I were a devotee of that theology that would be the icon I would have outside my cottage."

"Fine, good enough answer. Fuck it, let's go," Nadya replied.

They walked up to the cottage, one of the more ornate ones. It was a tiny building made of rough hewn lumber and painted a burgundy color. It was adorned with gold-painted fixtures. Even in the darkness, the whole place seemed bright. Above the porch was an onion-domed spire with a cross atop it. The little structure almost looked like a tiny chapel. The icon was more prominent in person, virtually occupying the entire exterior wall.

The little door was offset to the right. Nadya sighed and knocked on it.

"Fuck," she said, looking directly at Caspian. "What's the response thingy?"

"I've got it," Caspian responded confidently, though it was waning. "I think."

The door opened and a tall, slender man stood, taking up nearly the entire frame. His long robe reached down to the ground, but his toes could be seen poking out underneath, indicating his feet were either bare or sandaled. His grey beard split down the middle and nearly reached the bottom of his belly. He was wearing a gold-colored pectoral cross, barely visible behind his beard. He was wearing an epanokalimavko that covered his head and ears, so you couldn't tell if he had any hair adorning him other than his glorious beard. He was holding a polished wood stick that seemed to have been a branch someone had carved for him. The staff was nearly as tall as he was, and after opening the door, he moved both hands onto the staff and leaned into it. If he was surprised by the company that now appeared before him, he did not show it. He learned toward Caspian, looked over at Nadya and then back to Caspian.

"Christ is risen," he said in a thick Russian accent.

"As the women told us," Caspian responded.

With that, the hieromonk removed himself from the doorframe and extended his staff to welcome them inside.

Chapter Ten

Unlike the cabin that Jenks and Nadya had built, the inside of the hieromonk's cottage was much smaller than it even appeared from the outside. Part of what made it seem so small was the height of Jerome himself. He must have been at least 6'7" and possibly taller, but it was difficult to tell due to the added height of his epanokalimavko, which made his total height easily over seven feet tall. He offered to make them some tea and pancakes. Watching the hieromonk attempt to maneuver the minute kitchen area was quite a sight to see. Caspian was almost certain that the man would set his beard on fire, but, by some magic, he did not. The beard was as much a part of him as an arm and seemed almost to move on its own to get out of the way. The tea kettle began to whistle and then Jerome removed it from the stove, finished the pancakes, topped them with some whipped cream, and then served his guests seated in two rather sizeable maroon wing-backed chairs.

"It is a shame about Jenks," the hieromonk finally uttered without looking up from his tea, "but also a very foolish thing. I told him to be careful."

The response seemed rather abrupt, but Caspian assumed the brutality of his statement must have been cultural, and Nadya did not seem to take any offense to it. They all sat there in silence and took turns sipping their tea. Caspian placed down his cup before picking up the pancakes. They looked delicious and he hadn't realized how hungry he was until now. He cut into them with a fork and lifted the morsel to his mouth. At first, the taste did not immediately register, and then his mind instinctively caused him to spit the pancakes back onto the plate as if he was discarding poison.

"Father, I fear your whipped cream has turned," Caspian said, wiping his mouth with a napkin.

"Not whip cream—" the hieromonk chuckled "—sour cream and caviar."

After discovering that what he was meant to be enjoying was not intended to be sweet but instead savory, Caspian took another bite to be respectful. It was not particularly better the second time but was far less alarming. After consuming the singular bite to avoid disrespecting their host, he picked up the tea again. Of course, the flavor of the sour cream lingered on the back of his tongue and now ruined the entire tea experience as well. He felt stuck not knowing what to do with his hands now that he didn't want the tea or the pancakes. Then, thankfully, Nadya broke the silence.

"I am not sure what to call you," she finally said to the hieromonk.

"Jerome," he said back to her.

"Jerome," she responded, "do you know anything at all that could help us find out what happened to Jenks?"

"To business then?" Jerome said as he leaned back into his chair and set his tea on a nightstand between the corner of the room and his chair, which was even larger than the ones for guests.

"If that is all right," Caspian interjected.

"Yes, yes, always on to business." Jerome moved around in the chair. "It has been a while since I have had guests. People make pilgrimages to the monastery to visit holy men, not deposed relics like me. Yes, let's get to business."

Everything that Jerome said sounded grumpy to Father Caspian, but it was clear by his body language that he was not, in fact, grumpy. After almost every word, he would smile, and the grumpier the phrase sounded the more the twinkle in his eyes would grow. Caspian couldn't keep his eyes off of the hieromonk. He couldn't help but think about how he looked like something out of another time altogether. Sitting in this little room with all the beeswax candles and icons glistening gold in the light of the fire, Caspian couldn't tell if he had somehow stepped into another dimension. This could have easily been a room in Russia during the time of the tsars or even further back to ancient Rome as Constantine attempted to create consensus amongst all the churches. Wherever they were, it certainly didn't feel like a time when people had miniature computers that they carried about in their pockets. It didn't even feel like he was in America anymore; this was Russia, West Virginia.

"Business," Father Jerome said once again before settling himself enough into the chair that he felt ready for business. "I was helping your Jenks with a few things, but I do not know everything he was involved with."

"Anything you know will help, Jerome," Nadya said with a sense of urgency.

"Yes, my dear, yes." He continued, "I am afraid that there is a lot you will not understand, but I will do my best, forgive an old man my sins. Let me think where to begin. Yes, Jenks is a fool, but a very wise fool. You see, in Russia, we do not think of fools the same as you do in the West. The Lord uses fools all of the time. Jenks is a fool but probably a good fool doing many good things foolishly. He was on to something in his own foolish way. Some want to see things happen very differently, you see, than you or me. When I left Russia during the dark times, I felt that once the curtain fell, we would never see times like those again. But some want to see things go back to how they used to be."

"With the Soviet Union?" Caspian asked.

"No, no, Father." Jerome vigorously shook his head. "There are very few who want to go back to those times. Not many want to go back to those times. Most who say that they do did not live during them or know someone who stopped living during them. No, further back, my dear Father. Some wish to see the tsar return."

"But I thought the people chose to be a democracy after the Soviets?" Nadya interjected.

"Yes, of course," Jerome agreed. "But that does not mean everyone enjoyed this idea very much. There have been plenty who think it would be best to have the tsar again. And this is a great burden that many believe still today. This sentiment has grown stronger, and democracy in Russia has been less abided by, and over time, yes, there have been many who want the tsar once again. None more than the Krest."

Jerome paused for dramatic effect, picked his teacup back up, and navigated it around his beard. He immensely enjoyed the company and was much less interested in all this business. Both Nadya and Caspian felt like they had pressed him so much already that they couldn't just beg him again to continue explaining things, so they all sat there in their chairs and Jerome just enjoyed the presence of other people in his home with him. His life was much more of solitude than was even customary for most monks. He had been quite a polarizing figure. There was a time when he was on a shortlist to become a bishop within the Russian Orthodox Church of the Diaspora, but he began to advocate for things that others within the Church thought were contrary to Orthodoxy. For Jerome, rebellion had not been a short-lived friendship like it had been for Caspian but had been a longtime companion. As the leadership within the Church pushed back at him, he pushed right back harder, and eventually, he found himself as far on the outside as one could be without being fully removed. The other monks did not visit him, so he remained in this silence here in his little cottage on the hill.

"The Krest?" Caspian finally asked.

"Yes," Jerome said, rolling his eyes. "The Krest is a society of Orthodox laity in the Motherland that was once known as the Carriers of the Cross. They were a motorcycle gang, henchmen of the Russian mob, but eventually, they became a kind of brotherhood of people from many stations in life. When the Church needs dirty things to happen, for people to break bones, or worse, it is the Krest that the Church will call upon. Over time, they have made their way here as well. First, they came to extinguish the Rose, or at least that is what I have come to believe, but some of them remained."

"Who is the Rose?" Nadya and Caspian said in unison.

"Father Seraphim was also part of the Church in Exile with me during the dark period. He was a writer and musician who changed many things. He spoke his mind about the Soviets during the dark period, and the things he had to say were translated into Russian and circulated as contraband to the great consternation of powerful men. One day, Seraphim became ill and he was rushed to the hospital. He died shortly of a stomach ailment. I did not believe this and so I began to do some investigations myself. Of course, I was told I should not, but what could they do? As I did my digging, I heard from many that the Krest had been seen here in America, and not too shortly after, the Rose was gone and with him a great wealth of knowledge."

Jerome disappeared into his mind for a moment and Caspian couldn't tell if it was a look of sadness or if he was tired. But they all remained there in silence for a while. There was a tremendous amount of love and chaos in this small room. There seemed to be no rhyme or reason for the placement of the icons on the wall. One image stood out amongst all the brilliant colors: a singular black-and-white photo of a smiling monk with an equally large beard that seemed to be matted into accidental locks. Lying upon this image were some freshly cut pink roses and a vigil lamp hanging from the ceiling that rested directly in front of the face of the man in the picture.

"The Krest"—suddenly Jerome was wide awake again and continued without prompting this time—"they began to work within many of the Russian Churches of the

Diaspora and they set up chapters all over the Americas. They certainly were not as violent here because they did not have the law on their side, but they still had the same hope to one day see the tsar brought back to the throne of Russia. You can tell them because they each have tattoos around their necks of the cross joined with the gules."

"Gules?" Caspian interrupted.

"Yes, Father, the double-headed eagle of Imperial Russia."

"That is the symbol the man I shot had on his neck," Caspian said without thinking it all the way through.

"You shot someone?" Nadya was shocked that this had not come up until now.

"Well, yes."

"And you are just mentioning this now!" Nadya was livid.

"Well, you weren't particularly easy to talk to in the beginning," Caspian protested.

"Children"—the hieromonk disrupted them from continuing their spat—"you must understand that this goes so much deeper than you can imagine. But there is only so much I can tell you, you see, as much as I have enjoyed your company. I am not whom you seek. I only know what she has told me. If you will forgive me, I am a middleman for her."

"Who are you talking about?" Nadya was the first to jump on this, but she did so while sending Caspian a 'we will talk about this shooting people business later' kind of look.

"Matushka, my bride." Jerome smiled. "Allow me to get her for you."

With that, Jerome got up and Caspian was certain Jerome would hit his head on the ceiling, but somehow he did not. He floated across the floor and through the kitchen and then disappeared through a door in the back of the kitchen area. They could hear him speaking in Russian to someone in the other room. Nadya leaned into Caspian for a quick council.

"What is matushka?" she asked.

"Remember how I told you that priests could be married?"

"Yes."

"Well, there are different names for a priest's wife depending on whether they are Greek or whatever, but in the Russian Church the name for a priest's wife is matushka. But he is a monk. He can't be married." Caspian eagerly awaited the arrival of this mystery woman.

Just then, Jerome appeared back in the room with them, alone. He sat back down on his chair and snuggled himself back into it. He was quite jovial at this point and greeted his guests again. "I was not deposed for my theology, my dear ones. Yes, I was constantly in trouble for the things I would say, but it wasn't until I acted upon them that I got myself into trouble. A priest and his matushka are one, as Christ and the Church are one, as intertwined as the cosmos. I chose to be married in secret because together, as husband and wife, that is the fullness of the priesthood, you see."

With that, Hieromonk Jerome pulled out a small iPad from the sleeves of his robe and on the screen was an equally cheerful rosy-cheeked woman. She looked them up and down before greeting them. "It is so nice to meet you, Father Caspian and Matushka Nadya. I hear you are ready to understand the great battle to prevent the tsar from ascending again to the throne."

"No, no!" Both Nadya and Caspian interrupted her and then Nadya continued, "I am no one's matushka, just an ally here, ready to help however we can."

Matushka Dorcas continued with them for a while with many conversations about anything and everything other than what they needed to talk about. Caspian was beginning to see what she and the hieromonk saw in each other. They were a perfect pairing, without question. She told them the story about how they met and fell in love but were too afraid to say it out loud. About how a priest they both knew, who was part of their cause, was willing to help them marry. They received every detail about the wedding, who was present and who couldn't be for different reasons. At some point, Jerome propped up the iPad with some books and excused himself to make some more tea, and it was at this point that they realized they were going to be there for quite some time longer. After what must have been nearly two hours of conversation about a great many things, none of them concerning Jenks, the man with the gun, or the Krest, finally Dorcas calmly looked at the two of them and asked, "How can I help you, my little ones?"

"I'm not sure we really know what Jenks has gotten himself into, ma'am," Nadya said, "and we are very concerned that he might be in much danger."

"He certainly is," the matushka said. "Foolish boy. You warned him, didn't you, dear?"

"I did!" Jerome said with a vigorous nod. "I certainly did."

Then the matushka looked back at the two spectators and asked, "What do you know about the tsar and tsarina?"

"Not much," Caspian said and Nadya agreed.

"Sit down then, little ones." The matushka was ready to give them a lesson. "For over three hundred years, the Romanovs ruled Russia. There was a special relationship between the Church and the tsardom from the beginning of the dynasty. The Russian Orthodox Church predates any government of Russia. It was the Church that gave Russia its alphabet and culture. That is why the gule came to represent the idea that the tsar and the Church are co-equal rulers of the world. Much of the dynasty has now been defined not by its long history of rulers but by the last ones: Nicholas and Alexandra.

"They were deeply in love, which makes everything so very complicated. The tsar was a kind man as it pertained to his wife and children, but he could be a brutal ruler. There was nothing he loved more in this world than those children. But he also had a fatal flaw: he had absolutely no clue what he was doing as tsar. Even worse, he had been raised as an autocrat his entire life and did not understand his people. When the cries began to rise up for change, they were squashed repeatedly by the mighty hand of the tsardom. The first fatal blow came during the coronation of the new tsar. People came from all over the Russian World to be there to see their new ruler. The people appeared with hope in their hearts that change was coming.

"The peasants believed that this new tsar, unlike his father and grandfather, would soon be willing to listen to their cries for help and the need for change. To show his love for the people, he put together gifts and food to be given out to them. Sadly, chaos broke out and thousands of people were killed in a stampede as desperate and hungry people tried to reach the food before it ran out. The tsar desperately wanted to see the destruction and be there with the people, but he was told no by those within the court. This began a chain reaction that would stain his rule and lead to little sparks of revolution until, one day, the real thing began.

"The people had long hoped that a day would come when democracy and the tsardom could live in harmony. Attempts were made, but only surface level. This opened the door to dissent and the Bolsheviks walked right through it. They demanded change with zeal and a populist message that could no longer be denied. Tsar Nicholas could see the writing on the wall. He was losing Russia, and if he wasn't careful, he and his family would meet the same fate as many other tsars before him.

"Nicky eventually abdicated his throne in hopes it would spare his family more trouble. But it did not. After being shuffled around, his family was taken. . . ." The matushka drifted off for a moment as if she could see that basement room, the bullet holes riddled along the walls, the screams of the children. "Oh, the children, a tragic thing. Yes, the tsar needed to be removed and make way for freedom for all people, but not like this. What happened to those children was a warning of what was to come at the hands of our new leaders. The Soviets gave us another kind of tyranny. We traded one type of oppression for another. Now a time is coming where many hope to reinstate the tsar and see Russia once again as the autocracy it once was with both the tsar and the Patriarch ruling together, each as the crowned heads of the gule."

Caspian took a deep breath before asking, "And what would they do about Putin?"

"My dear child"—the matushka looked deeply at the both of them—"he is the very one they hope to be seen as tsar, and not just of Russia but the whole world."

Nadya looked at Caspian, who had not yet taken his eyes off the screen.

"Little ones," the matushka continued, "our time is growing short. I do have something for you that I believe may be of help. During our last conversation, Brother Stephen said that the answer he was seeking lay with the bones of the tsar. I wish I had more to give you, but I will bless you on your journey."

"Bow for the blessing," Jerome said sternly.

Jerome took the first knee in front of the screen; then Nadya and Caspian followed suit. Matushka Dorcas stood up from her perch and it was clear she was quite a short woman; her height did not seem to change as she stood. She lifted her hands as a sign of blessing. She then said, "O Lord Jesus Christ, our God, do Thou accept our fervent supplication and bless the good intent and work of Thy servants, that they may begin favorably and may complete it unto Thy glory without any obstacle. Amen." And the screen went black.

After offering them yet another glass of tea, which they kindly refused, Hieromonk Jerome gathered the remaining pancakes and placed them in a paper towel, along with some fruit and a large slice of ham. He gave them to his guests, along with his blessing, before walking them to the door. He hugged them both before they finally made their way out into the darkness and the silent walk back to where their vehicle was parked. When they got into the car, Nadya lit a cigarette and rolled down the window. She had done everything she could to avoid smoking in front of Caspian, but nothing could be done now. This was all too much for her to handle. As each ring of smoke shattered against that space between the cracked window and the roof of the car, she smiled at the absurdity of it all.

"What do we do know?" She sighed at Caspian.

"Well, we find the bones of the tsar, logically," he said.

Chapter Eleven

Nadya was a brilliant person. However true that might be, it was always difficult for her to believe that about herself because when she was a child, her family made her feel very stupid for not speaking until she was almost five years old. To hear her tell the story now, if she ever told you the story, she didn't speak because she found the conversations everyone was having around her very dull and didn't want to participate in them. This was probably pretty close to the truth because the day she finally did break her silence was when her parents were touring a university with her older half-brother from her father's first marriage. Typically, parents wouldn't bring a child to tour a university with their older child, but they were very protective of Nadya and her "special condition," so they never left her alone with others. As part of the tour, her brother Dimitri, along with her mother and her father, audited a class. They did not know that they would be auditing a class and all of the other more interesting classes had already been selected, so, instead, they were placed in a philosophy class. Dimitri found the entire thing extraordinarily boring and spent his time doodling on a piece of paper, in spite of his mother's frequent requests that he pay attention.

The professor had taken a small metal folding chair and placed it in the center of the room. It was a rather slow and awkward moment as the professor was quite old and not as quick as he used to be the first time he had done this little thought experiment. He also looked quite professor-y with a tweed jacket over his tweed vest, a very bright bowtie, and a handlebar mustache. He pointed at the chair as if people were supposed to be amazed by the placement of it.

No one was amazed.

"I would like a volunteer to sit in my chair," the professor finally said, dismayed at the lack of intrigue from his students. At first, no one volunteered. Nadya's mother even nudged her brother, but he was wholly disinterested. Eventually, one of the students reluctantly came forward, hoping to get this over quickly.

"Thank you, thank you!" As he motioned more vigorously towards the seat, the professor said, "Now, explain to everyone what you are doing."

"Sitting?" the student offered as a question but also the answer.

"Indeed! Quite astute of you," the professor said. "Brightest of the bunch so far. Now, what is holding you up? As we all know, gravity attempts to pull you down to the ground. That is how gravity works, I believe; even in times like these I think we can all agree on at least this much as a known fact. Would you say?"

He looked at the crowd of students and his auditors, awaiting some response. It was clear that, in the professor's mind, he was expecting his students to be much more responsive as if this was a game show and not a classroom. Once upon a time, this was the kind of response he got from his students, but not anymore. He wasn't sure if it was due to a lack of performance that comes with age or if the times had just changed around him.

"Now, again, if I may," the professor continued, directing his inquiries back at the young man in the chair. "Would you mind explaining what is holding you up, preventing you from falling to the ground?"

"The chair?" The student again posed this more as a question than an answer.

Before the professor could respond, Nadya decided that this would be the time she finally had something to say, so she said, "That is incorrect."

A lot happened at once.

The first of those things was a near instant look of consternation that fell across the face of Nadya's father. This was quickly observed by her mother, who responded in kind. To her mother's shock, after years of begging her daughter to speak, she was suddenly attempting to hush her. This was all happening against the backdrop of a giggling snort fit that had befallen her brother in chorus with the laughter and sounds of shock from the other students. Then the near-deafening sounds of rustling came as each student collectively turned to see where this tiny disagreeable voice was coming from.

"No, no!" the professor shouted across the classroom and towards Nadia's parents. "Let's see where the little one is taking us."

To the absolute shock of Nadya's parents, she was now being directed by the professor to continue, and continue she did.

"Little thinker," the professor continued, "what is incorrect about the assertion that the chair is holding him up?"

"It's true in a sense," Nadya explained, "if we think of things as they are. But in reality, there is no chair."

"Studious!" The professor was near gleeful, and then he directed his question back towards the students. "What is holding him up then?"

"Atoms," another student from the back offered.

"Incorrect again," Nadya responded indignantly and the professor almost looked young again with the gleefulness that emoted from his being.

"Then what is?" The professor directed his line of questioning back toward his newest pupil.

"Light," Nadya said plainly.

"Light?" the professor asked without emotion.

"Nichola Tesla theorized that all things are light. When broken down beyond just the atoms, all matter has its origin in light."

The professor stood there, still emotionless, for what seemed like an eternity as if he was giving dual lessons on Einstein's theory of relativity. Then, in monstrous applause coming singularly from him, he said, "Brilliant! Brilliant child."

The bell rang and the class came to an abrupt end. The professor attempted to speak with Nadya's parents after class, but her father was too angry to hear the accolades the professor was pouring onto her. No, her father was only thinking of all the ways she had now embarrassed him in front of everyone with her bluntness. He wished for her to go back to her state of silence, though he did not hold this opinion only about Nadya; he felt this way about all women, including his daughter.

Her parents scolded her the entire drive home, but despite the situation, Dimitri made it into the university. I want to say that this was the beginning of a beautiful journey for Nadya, but it was not. Instead, she was placed in special education classes and sent to many doctors who were supposed to help correct the fact that she went back to not speaking and wouldn't make eye contact. These doctors were supposed to help her be a normal child: the type of child who wouldn't correct a grown-up when they were wrong.

Nadya did not comply.

In high school, she found her voice again. She started working on computers. The students called her Gothic and the teachers called her a whore behind closed doors. After the Columbine massacre, she was one of six other students called to the office, and her troubles continued until she finally decided to drop out of school at sixteen. Her parents were not very thrilled about this at all. She wanted to explain it all to them. To tell them about the bullies, that her teachers had been unkind, and that she was learning more from the computer than she was in the classroom. There was so much she wanted to tell them, but they had already shown her that they didn't care at all about what she had to say from her very first words.

The only person in the world who did listen to her was Stephen Jenks, another kid who didn't quite fit in, just like her. They met in a chatroom for coders and eventually ran away from home to be closer to each other in real life. But this is not a love story. They were not in romantic love; they were family. The type of family you choose when the family you are given rejects the very essence of who you are. The kind that understands your brain.

The last time they spoke, her father told her that she would never amount to anything. She would die cold and alone on the streets, penniless and uneducated, that she was making the worst decision of her life running off with Stephen Jenks. Together, she and Jenks made many good decisions, specifically for all the reasons their parents said they were broken. They invested pennies into lines of code and turned them into millions.

Nadya was very, very smart.

This is why Nadya was so upset with how stupid she was when she got into the car with Caspian at the skete. She was not clinically OCD. She used to say that was the only gift she wasn't gifted with. But she did develop patterns for her life to keep herself safe. She usually did very smart things like checking license plates before she got into ride shares, she didn't drink out of bottles unless she opened them herself, and she always checked the backseat of her car to make sure no one was inside.

Until tonight.

As she stepped into her vehicle this evening, she did not follow the routine that would usually keep her safe from the boogymen that lived in her head and that now she knew for sure also lived in the real world. She wasn't sure what broke her from doing her routine this time, but I suppose it doesn't matter. At that very moment, as she and Caspian began their conversation after she lit the cigarette and blew smoke toward the cracked window, another person was in the car with them. This person lifted his body ever so slightly, and first, he placed something over Nadya's nose and mouth. The last thought she had before she slipped off into sleep was how disappointed she was in herself for not checking the back seat.

The man in the back seat was fully prepared to struggle with Caspian, but to his utter surprise, the sheer terror of someone popping up from the backseat shocked Caspian so wholly that he passed out. The man in the back seat did not immediately know what to do with this unexpected good luck, but he decided to go ahead as planned, placing the same piece of cloth over Caspian's nose to be extra sure. He then had to exit the vehicle to pull Nadya out of the front seat before dragging her into the back seat and returning to the front seat himself to start the ignition. He drove away from the front gate of the skete and then down the road until he reached one of the chapels on the property. He had not fully formulated his plan. He needed to unlock the building, something he should have done first so he wouldn't leave his victims unattended. Having no choice, he nervously left them both in the car, rushed to the back of the chapel, unlocked the door leading into the sanctuary, and then went back to the car, hoping they were both still passed out. They were.

He decided to collect Nadya because she had been the first one he had knocked out with the concoction on the cloth. He had never dragged a body before and was having a rather difficult time with it. Once he got her inside, he tied her hands and feet with some rope and then left again to retrieve Caspian. He had an even more difficult time getting Caspian into the building, first because he was already exhausted from having to drag the previous body but also because Caspian was much larger than Nadya. After finally getting him inside, he also tied his hands and feet. Now he was faced with the somewhat tricky part of such a messy business and he had to wait for them to wake up.

They were not asleep for terribly long before they began to squirm. Then Nadya started screaming, overtaken by panic to find that she was tied up. This resulted in the man who had been in the backseat of the car realizing he had not done anything to cover the mouths of his victims and it also caused Caspian to jolt up. He too began to scream when he realized that Nadya was screaming, equally shocked to find himself in such a precarious situation.

"Please, please be quiet," the man begged softly.

"Fuck you!" Nadya responded.

"I beg of you; please stop. I am very sorry about this; I truly am." The man pleaded, "But please, please be quiet! I beg of you."

"I'm going to rip your throat out!" Nadya yelled back at him.

"That would be very unpleasant," the man said, holding his small hands against his throat. "I would beg of you not to do this. I mean you no harm."

"The fuck you don't! You don't do this to people who don't want harm," Nadya spat back at him.

"Let me begin differently," the man said. "My name is Father Andrew. I must know what you have done with the hieromonk."

"Nothing," Caspian said sternly.

"Nothing?" Father Andrew was confused.

"Nothing!" Nadya shouted back at him.

"Please, I beg you; do not scream lest we alert the others," Father Andrew pleaded, "which, I am afraid, would not do well for any of us. Now, what did you do with the hieromonk?"

"Nothing, unless you count having tea with someone as something to be drugged and dragged against our will over." Nadya was so full of fire she could almost burn through the ropes.

"Oh dear, I do beg your forgiveness again." Father Andrew walked over to Caspian to begin untying him. "I am with the Cause of the Theotokos, along with Hieromonk Jerome. However, I have done so in silence. It is my silence that has caused him much pain as he sits alone all of his days in his cottage without any friend, even though he does have a friend in me. I have been charged to keep an eye on him, should anyone mean any harm. Please forgive me, a sinner."

As he pleaded this last time for forgiveness, he had already finished untying Caspian and was just finishing untying Nadya. As soon as her hands were free, she struck the monk just as he ended his mea culpa. He fell back towards the altar. He began to rub his jaw and a single tear began to form.

"I do apologize, dear lady." Andrew seemed very sincere in his contrition. "I was merely attempting to protect the hieromonk. Many would wish him harm to get to her, even some within our monastery, and I diligently keep watch every night to ensure his safety. Tonight, this was the first time anyone has breached our facility in search of him."

"What about Jenks?" Nadya asked.

"Brother Stephen!" Andrew responded with a smile. "No, he did not come in secret. Though he did come to visit us here frequently. Is he all right?"

"No," Caspian said. "He is missing."

"Foolish man," Andrew responded.

"So we've heard." Nadya was unamused.

"If Brother Stephen has gone missing, we are all in much more danger than any of us could have imagined. What may I do to be of assistance in your quest?"

This was yet another moment when Caspian felt he had stepped into a different time and place altogether. Even the old churches he had served in did not have the same sense of ancientness as these buildings. The chapel they were in was so covered with icons that it dwarfed the scene from the hieromonk's cottage. Every inch of the space was one intertwined painting. Whatever was not an image of a saint was a stunning network of royal red and blue floral flourishes connecting each piece to the next. The altar that Father Andrew was leaning against had been carved from a single piece of wood with intricate detail. The scent of frankincense and bread hung heavy in the air. This monk had a familiar look, but Caspian could not immediately place it. He too seemed like he had just been plucked out of another time altogether.

"I have some questions," Caspian finally said to the sulking monk who was rubbing his jaw.

"I want to get out of here." Nadya was angry, hungry, and uninterested in making an ally of their kidnapper, but Caspian urged her to allow him to ask a few questions, so she relented.

"Please, I beg you to allow me to be of some help for this grave sin I have committed." Father Andrew was perhaps one of the most contrite people Father Caspian had ever met.

"All right." Caspian stood up to pace as he was nervous and tired so he wished to stretch his legs. "First, Christ is risen."

"As the women told us," Andrew said, beaming.

"Okay, good," Caspian continued. "Now, when we spoke with Matushka Dorcus, she told us that Jenks … uh… Brother Stephen had told her that the answer lay with the bones of the tsar. Do you know what this means?"

The smile on Father Andrew's face grew even wider as if he could finally be helpful after all of the damage he had caused. He exhaled and then said with great jubilation, "I do not."

"Fuck it, Caspian." Nadya was frustrated. "Let's just go. This guy is a fool."

"Thank you," Andrew said.

"Jesus Christ." Nadya rolled her eyes.

"I mean to say," Father Andrew interrupted, "I do not know what Brother Stephen meant by this cryptic response, but I may be of some assistance with the location of the bones of the tsar if you will allow me."

"Make it fast." Nadya was ready to be on the move, but, as of yet, they had no real place to move to, and since it seemed that this bumbling man before her was the possessor of at least some knowledge, she began to cool her anger a bit.

Father Caspian took a few moments to explain what had happened in the cottage with the hieromonk and the matushka and their lesson concerning the tsar and tsarina. The little monk kept plucking at his beard as if he was also hearing all this information for the first time. His eyes were wild with anticipation at each word that came out of Caspian's mouth as if he were the greatest storyteller of all time and the monk was utterly captivated. When Caspian finished his recap of the earlier conversation, the monk clasped his hands together gleefully as if to let

Caspian know he had done an excellent job recounting the tale.

"That is so very wrong," Andrew said with a smile.

"Excuse me?" Caspian shook his head, confused.

"Forgive me, I beg you, I do not think wrong is the correct word." The monk bowed. "Incomplete would be the better word, I do believe."

Nadya rolled her eyes again.

"The tsar and his bride, Alexandra, cared deeply for all of their children but none nearly as much as they did their youngest, Alexei. It was in him that they had all their hopes for the continuation of the Romanov dynasty. But poor Alexei was exceedingly frail as he was stricken with a sickness known as the Royal Disease."

"Hemophilia?" Nadya asked, now finally engaged in the conversation.

"Yes, very good." Father Andrew was overjoyed with Nadya's brilliance but then caught himself and continued, "From a young age, he was unwell and they had to keep him as safe as possible. They did not succeed, nor did the doctors keep him well. The Royal Family chose to keep this secret from the whole of society. As revolution brewed in the streets of Petrograd and the hearts of the peasants outside of the city, they had no idea about the great cloud that hung over their tsar. He kept these things from the world, fearing it would make them appear weak. You see, they were deep in the throes of the First World War, and to make matters worse, the tsarina was a German, and many began to believe that she was working to destroy Russia from within!"

"Was she?" This was all new to Nadya.

"No, she was not. I am afraid that the Royal Family was very unconcerned with just about anything else in the world other than the health of their dear Alexei. The tsar, Nicky, had already been a poor leader up to this point, but after the frailty of his son, I am afraid he had abdicated the throne in his heart and mind long before he relented to the demands of the people to do so. He was losing the war and the hearts of his people, and soon he was harming them to try to keep order. Thousands were killed in the streets through multiple campaigns to quell the uprising. The images were too much for the people to bear, even children killed in the streets. It was terrible, inexcusable."

Father Andrew wiped away yet another tear, this time not for himself but for those images he saw in his mind. "The people prevailed and the military turned on the tsar and he abdicated the throne and removed his sickly son from the line of succession. With this, the Romanov dynasty came to its completion and the people took control of their own destiny for a short season. Now, without the help of Rasputin...."

"That is it!" Caspian rudely interrupted the monk mid-thought, but he had finally realized whom Father Andrew had reminded him of—it was Rasputin.

"Excuse me?" Father Andrew asked.

"That is who you reminded me of, Rasputin."

"Thank you!" Andrew beamed again. "Now, may I continue?"

"Yes," Nadya said to Andrew while glaring at Caspian for saying something that no one, except for clearly Father Andrew, would take as a compliment.

"After the tsar and his family were brutally murdered they were buried in the woods around the compound, where their lives were taken. But the Bolsheviks spread many rumors. One, I am sure you have heard many times that Anastasia had lived. Other such rumors persisted for years within Russia, including that Alexei had survived. See, as I have explained, none of the people knew how weak poor little Alexei was, so they had hoped that he could be alive somewhere. Those within the new government did not quell these rumors because though they thought many might have supported the execution of the tsar and even the tsarina, due to xenophobia of her being German, no one would have wanted harm to come to those poor innocent children."

"And so this is where the bones of the tsar are? Lost in some woods in the vastness of Russia?" Caspian now feared he should have listened to Nadya.

"Yes!" Andrew exclaimed. "Until…."

"Until?"

"Yes, until finally the curtain fell and they were able to be exhumed. Many priests went to smuggle the bones of the tsar and the family out before their time. They had fought for the Royal Family to receive an appropriate burial according to our customs. One such priest was an American by the name of Bishop Nicholas; he took the name for himself in honor of the tsar."

"I thought priests could only take the names of saints?" Caspian was now also confused.

"Yes, you are very right, quite smart indeed." Andrew tapped Caspian on the knee reassuringly. "The tsar and the tsarina were made saints, martyrs of the faith, after the ascension of Putin to the presidency and the restoration of the Glory of the Church in Russia. And it was this man, the American, Bishop Nicholas, who was blessed with some of the bones of the tsar to return to the National Cathedral of the Russian Orthodox Church of the Diaspora in the capital. Washington, DC!"

Father Andrew paused as if he was expecting some level of adulation or possibly even some clapping from his captive audience. But none came. It was difficult for him not to show on his face how disappointed he was at the fact that no one seemed particularly impressed with him, and to hide his shame he stood up and began busying himself around the altar. Finally, Nadya made an expression to let Caspian know it was time to get on the move now that they had a location and they both stood together to excuse themselves. Tilting his head down so they could not see the tears forming as an actual stream this time, Father Andrew led them to the door, apologizing yet again for the odd way in which they had met, and handed Nadya the keys to her car. She snatched them and walked off. Caspian turned back to the old little monk.

"Why would you be pleased to be compared to Rasputin?" Caspian didn't even realize how insulting the question was due to how tired he felt.

"Grigori Rasputin was a very complicated man, but there is much more to his story, as with each of us, than many of the rumors you have heard. The same men who assassinated the character of Brother Grigori ultimately assassinated the tsar."

"Caspian!" Nadya was over it and made a hurry-up motion to Caspian.

"I am sorry. I must go." Caspian embraced the monk. "You have been such a help."

With that, the waterworks finally burst at these kind words he had so hoped to hear, and as Caspian made his dash back to the car to continue with Nadya, Father Andrew waved them away. "Of course! I am but a humble servant; please forgive me, a sinner."

Chapter Twelve

Kyle was waiting on an exam table already dressed in a robe. He hated doctors and, more importantly, had an extreme distrust of them. However, he had found himself in a situation well beyond his survivalist training. His fever was high, his arm hurt even in stasis, and he felt he was becoming ill. The brightness of the room made him uncomfortable and the smell didn't sit well with him. He kept looking around the room, hoping for something entertaining. Little models of human inside parts were displayed around the room next to the cotton balls and other tools. On the wall was an otoscope. He had always wanted to touch one when he was a kid, fascinated by the little device the doctors would shove in his ears and then use to look at his eyes. He had not been to the doctor since he was a child, so this was his first opportunity, and he took it. He had just placed his hand on the otoscope when the door cracked open. He attempted to remove his hand before anyone came inside but, in doing so, dislodged it, and it fell to the ground, dangling there by its wire. The Doctor walked in, giving Kyle a disapproving look before he replaced the device in its rightful place.

"You shouldn't touch things that aren't yours," The Doctor scolded.

"I was just curious," Kyle said. "Always wondered about those things, what it was like to look through them."

"Then you should have become a doctor instead of a mercenary," The Doctor quipped back at him. "Now, what brings you in today?"

Kyle pointed at his bad arm with his good one and The Doctor walked over to inspect it. The wound was in terrible shape. It was greening around the edges of the impact point.

"Luckily, it somehow missed anything important," The Doctor said, "but it needs to be cleaned and stitched and I will give you a prescription for some antibiotics. Are you up to date on your vaccines?"

"Fuck that," Kyle responded.

"I figured as much." The Doctor had turned to his notebook and was writing.

"What are you writing?" Kyle asked suspiciously.

The Doctor looked up at him over his thick-rimmed glasses. "Patient is an idiot but is likely to live."

"Very funny," Kyle said.

The Doctor was a kind and handsome-looking man. He almost had the appearance you would expect of a doctor on some nighttime emergency room show. He was slightly older, maybe in his late fifties, but had taken care of himself. Kyle was squirming the entire time, and The Doctor sensed he was in quite a bit of pain.

"How would you describe your pain? The Doctor asked.

"It fucking hurts," Kyle said with a smile, "so really fucking bad."

"Worse than a cold?" The Doctor said without looking up from his notepad.

"Are you some kind of feminist?" Kyle asked.

"I am a doctor."

"That isn't an answer, doc." Kyle looked a bit nervous. "I thought you worked for us."

"I work for societies like yours, but I am neutral. I do not take a side in any of this; I am just here to serve," The Doctor said without emotion.

"So you aren't about the cause?" Kyle was confused.

"Am I about your little war? No." The Doctor put his pad down on the counter, pulled the otoscope from its place and inspected Kyle's eyes. "I have been around long enough to watch many members of societies such as yours start all manner of wars and conflicts. I am here to mend, not to opine on what each of you decides to draw us into."

"How am I supposed to trust you then?"

"You don't really have a choice." The Doctor was now checking his other eye. "You can't go anywhere else; they would have to report the gunshot wound. So, like it or not, I am your only option at this point."

"You just do it all, no matter who? What all do you do?" He was curious by this point.

"Whatever is necessary; patch up bullet wounds like yours, treat any manner of ailments, write prescriptions, abortions." The Doctor said all this without inflection of stance. "Whatever is necessary to keep the order."

Kyle pulled away from The Doctor. "Abortions?"

"Yes."

"That is disgusting." Kyle looked ready to kill The Doctor on the spot. "When we are done, that will be illegal."

"Yes." The Doctor nodded. "I am sure. Then I will be all the more necessary."

The Doctor had gone to the counter and found a depressor to place on Kyle's tongue. He told him to open his mouth and Kyle obliged. The Doctor poked around in his mouth for a few moments then made a sudden movement with his other arm and jabbed Kyle with something. They both looked down simultaneously and Kyle was shocked to see a needle in his arm. Before he could pull away, the Doctor had emptied the entire contents into Kyle's shoulder.

"What the fuck did you just do to me?" Kyle screamed.

"Lower your voice." The Doctor responded, "It is just a vaccine."

"Did you just…" Kyle's eyes grew wide. "Was that the…."

"Tetanus," The Doctor said again without any feeling.

"Jesus Christ." Kyle sighed with relief. "I thought you just…."

"Gave you a COVID vaccine?" The Doctor smirked. "I considered it. But at this time, this one is the most important for you to stay alive. As much as I am sure the world would benefit from you receiving lockjaw, I do have an oath to uphold."

"You can't just go giving people vaccines without permission like that!" Kyle almost shouted and then caught himself and said it in a mildly hushed tone.

"You didn't seem like a big fan of choice," The Doctor said, looking back down at his notepad, "I didn't think you would mind."

"So you are a feminist." Kyle pointed at him.

"I am a doctor," The Doctor said.

"I could report you." Kyle was furious.

"You could." The Doctor made his way to the door and opened it to exit. "But, of course, this isn't even my office. Be sure to take your antibiotics. You wasted a lot of people's time so you could live. Try not to make that a mistake."

With that, The Doctor exited the borrowed exam room and Kyle began to dress slowly. It was an arduous process. He fell over a few times trying to get his pants on, but he finally succeeded. He left The Doctor's office, now confused about where he had been sent. If this wasn't where The Doctor actively practiced, that would explain why they had sent him to a pediatric facility. Kyle made his way back to his busted-up vehicle. When he got inside, he opened the glove box with his key, pulled out his phone and placed it in a hands-free case on his dashboard. He had several missed calls from Boris. He wasn't looking forward to this chat but decided to return the ring as he pulled out of The Doctor's office parking lot.

"What were you thinking going to the synod office like that?" Boris began shouting as soon as he showed up on the screen.

"I needed some help," Kyle shouted right back. "I tracked them back up to Kentucky and then lost them. By that point, I was closer to Chicago than back to Florida. I did what I had to do."

"There is protocol; there are procedures—" Boris began to lecture.

"Blah, blah, blah." Kyle shot back, "Last I checked, this is a free fucking country, you communist bastard."

"I am no communist!" Boris said indignantly. "My family was killed by the communists, you sick fucking fuck; if you ever say something like that to me again I will succeed where the Roman failed."

"What do you want? Natasha?" Kyle was pulling into a McDonald's for a late lunch.

"We have an issue with the detainee," Boris continued, "he is not being compliant. Where are we in your efforts to find and apprehend Nadya and this Roman?"

"I've had some other priorities, like staying alive." Kyle leaned over, ordered a number three, and then started back in on Boris. "I am back on it."

"No, you are not." Boris was uninterested in any more of Kyle's shenanigans. "You are to return to Florida immediately. We will handle them from here. You are on babysitting duties."

"That's bullshit and you know it." Kyle hated being so low on the priorities list.

"Return, now." Boris sighed. "Or don't. I do not care."

"You know that Doctor whacko is an abortionist." Kyle took his first bite of the burger.

"We must align with many strange bedfellows as we attempt to meet our ultimate goals." Boris was now hungry. "These things are unfortunate but all in good time, brother. All in good time. Nothing comes quickly. Remember that even in the Fatherland there are abortions. Soon, they will end here and there. We will see the glorious end and a new day will be born for us both and for the whole world."

"Your mouth to God's ears, comrade," Kyle said.

"Do not do that." Boris hated Kyle but considered him a necessary evil, just like The Doctor. "I am now on my way to finish what you should have. I am not sure how much time Stephen Jenks will be of help to us."

Kyle was tired of having to talk over his meal, so he saluted Boris and hung up the phone. He pulled up the directions to Milton, Florida, on his phone and saw that it was almost fourteen hours from outside of Chicago. *Fuck that,* he thought before opening an app to purchase a plane ticket quickly. He drove from the parking lot and went up from the south side of Chicago toward the airport. Then he saw a sign for the future Obama Presidential Center and flipped it off, only to momentarily hit a curb since he only had one good hand, which substantially hurt his arm. In spite of all the pain, he felt very pleased with himself for having offered the gesture toward one of many that he soon hoped to see behind bars when their mission was complete.

"Lock him up!" he shouted to no one at all as he rushed down the freeway.

And everyone applauded.

CHAPTER THIRTEEN

Nadya decided they needed to drive straight through the night to Washington, DC. The drive was just under seven hours and she was very disappointed that they were making it shrouded in darkness. Not that she had any issue with driving at night, she preferred it, but she was sad to be missing all of the scenery as she had never driven through this region before. The destination was taking them through the Appalachian Mountains and just shy of Pennsylvania before heading on to the capital. It wasn't too far into the drive before Caspian had passed out in the passenger seat. He had never had anyone in his life to tell him that he snored terribly during his slumbers. Occasionally, Nadya would reach over and rustle his shoulder until he would move about slightly in his seat and she would get a reprieve from the sound for a few minutes before they would start up again. She was finally starting to get a little tired, so she pulled into a gas station to fill up and grabbed a coffee for Caspian as it was now time to switch out so he could take the second leg of their overnight journey.

She was sure that the bright lights of the gas station would wake him, but they did not. When she returned to the vehicle, she went ahead and began pumping the gas and then cleaned the windows in hopes that would do the trick. Finally, she made enough commotion that Caspian stirred himself awake and began his stretching routine. Not being able to fully get as good a stretch inside the vehicle, he stepped out to continue what was his usual morning routine. It was still very dark outside and they were just a few miles over the halfway point. After being good and exercised, Nadya tossed the keys to him.

"Your turn," she said.

"What?" Caspian looked nervous.

"Those are the rules of the road trip, Caspian." She was now wondering if he had ever gone on a road trip. "I took the first half. It's your turn. I got you a coffee and now I am tired."

"I am afraid I can't be of help. Thank you for the opportunity." He extended the keys back to her, but she did not take them. "But no, thank you."

"No, thank you. This isn't a negotiation." She pushed the keys and his hand back toward him. "I am fucking exhausted. We have to get on the road; let's go."

"I really can't be of help here." And with that, Caspian sat back down in the passenger seat.

"I am going to need some kind of explanation." Nadya crossed her arms.

"And I am not really interested in giving one. You politely asked and I am politely refusing."

"Whatever." Nadya grabbed the keys from Caspian's hand and tossed the lock-picking kit at him. "Just play with your fucking toys like a toddler."

Caspian leaned over to pick the lock-picking kit up. The wood had a slight scratch from it bouncing off his arm and hitting the floorboard. He was very disappointed by the damage; he loved his little gift. His sadness was fleeting as he realized that the lock-picking kit was also quite the mighty weapon and his arm was now throbbing at the impact point. Still furious and tired, Nadya turned the engine on, drove the vehicle to the back of the gas station, and then turned the car back off. She pulled her jacket over her arms and then laid the driver's seat back so she could sleep for a bit before continuing the rest of the journey on her own.

This gas station was not the beautiful and well-kept kind with a big brand name plastered out front and a little gift shop inside. This was a small building in the center of two pumps. The only button that worked on the gas pump was the premium one and you had to pay inside, which had been convenient for Nadya, considering she was only using cash. Inside, they did not have a little serving area with an assortment of hotdog flavors. There was not a bar of coffee selections but a singular coffee pot that looked like it had been the cheapest available at Walmart. This gas station was certainly not the best hotel, but it was the only one they had available on such short notice. Adventures like this were becoming increasingly impossible, considering that very few motels or hotels took cash anymore, and even if they did, they required a credit card for incidentals. This would not be the only time they would end up sleeping in the car, even if it happened to be the first. The final nail in the coffin of Nadya not getting a very restful sleep was that the entire back end of the gas station was covered in stray cats that came out of the overgrown vacant lot behind the dumpsters. These little critters were accustomed to travelers having some sympathy for them and tossing food their way. So they waited outside of Nadya's car, meowing until she would break. Between the crying of the cats and the logs sewn inside Caspian's nasal cavities, she was pretty doomed but eventually passed out.

She felt like she had only just closed her eyes when she was jolted awake by Caspian screaming. At first, she couldn't make the words out, but then they got louder and he began to wave his arms around a bit.

"No, no, no!" he kept saying.

Because she woke up with such a start and was sure that they had finally been discovered, she had pulled out her gun and pointed it toward the passenger side window. She did not have her finger engaged on the trigger and it was pointed away from Caspian, but the whole commotion woke him from his nightmare and into another one. He jolted up and then looked over at her extended arm with the gun. He began to scream “No” again, but awake this time; he looked out the window, afraid that the weapon was pointed at someone on the other side. Then he looked back at her, just screaming the whole time.

“Fuck, Caspian!” Nadya yelled back. “You scared the fuck out of me.”

“What did I do!” he yelled back.

“You were screaming ‘no’ like some asylum patient. Jesus Christ!” She grabbed her chest to be dramatic but could feel her heart beating out of it.

Though she felt like she had only just shut her eyes, they had slept for almost four hours and the sun was beginning to peak around the horizon. Caspian may have been blissfully unaware of his snoring; he was well acquainted with his screaming. He had been told about this numerous times by college roommates and other clergy at parishes he had been assigned to over the years. He apologized for startling Nadya and she holstered her weapon. They didn’t talk about that or much else as she made the rest of the way toward the Russian Orthodox Church in DC.

In the silence of their drive, a thought made its way into Nadya’s consciousness that they weren’t sure if the people they would find at this parish were friend or foe.

They were only operating on the assumption that the bones of the tsar would be there and that they might contain some kind of answer. What kind of answer it might be was anyone's guess. Caspian may have been accustomed to operating on faith, but Nadya was not a fan of the unknown.

When they finally arrived, Nadya was surprised at the peculiar building, which looked more like a medieval watchtower than a church. It was a slender structure made of red bricks reaching the heavens. Some would have quickly dismissed the place as a church; there wasn't much about it that indicated that it was such, other than a small wooden plaque out front with the name of the parish written in gold leaf and a half oval icon of Jesus above the door. They both exited the vehicle without a word. This was a sign of them not having a real plan.

As they walked around the back of the building, they saw that it extended out the back with a brick-walled open-air space behind it. There was ivy growing up the bricks of the hidden area behind the church, though you could see that the ivy had been picked away from the church's main structure. As they walked up and down the wall, Caspian silently had the idea that he could scale it, but before he had chance to suggest it, the silence of the early morning was broken by some hummed notes from the other side of the wall. Then a wooden side door to the wall was opened and a stout man in a riassa exited with a hoe and a bucket and made his way towards a storage shed wedged between this mysterious wall and the back of the main church. He did not acknowledge the visitors, which they both thought was unusual at first. Still, Caspian offered that maybe they were accustomed to tourists considering the location was so close to the capital. They slowly approached the man.

"Good morning," Caspian offered as a greeting.

The cleric stopped momentarily, looking up at the sky. "Indeed."

The little man continued on with his business, unaffected by their presence. Because of the length of his robe, he appeared to be floating along the ground. The thought had even crossed Caspian's mind that the man might be floating, as none of them had seen any indication yet that he was the owner of any feet. The humming of hymns also continued, and then occasionally he would stop humming and burst out a few words in Russian in a sing-song-type fashion that seemed adjacent to chanting. They just stood there watching for a few moments as he would float over to the storage shed, disappear inside, and then float back to the door of the mysterious wall and then back inside. This continued for about four such trips before Caspian decided to try again.

"May we possibly see inside?" he asked.

This stopped the man in his tracks again. "Oh yes, it is possible, I am sure."

But instead of offering for them to go inside, he just continued with his back and forth between the inside of the mysterious wall and the storage shed, bringing this and that back and forth with him.

"How would it possible?" Caspian asked a different way hoping to secure an invitation. This again seemed to stump the little man.

"All things are possible with God." And with that, he continued forward.

"For fuck's sake!" Nadya mumbled as she was about over all of this and then she directed her words at the cleric. "Can we go inside?"

The man abruptly stopped again, laid down two pails he was carrying, and then turned to Nadya. "Oh absolutely! I would love to show you."

With that, he walked over to them, extended both hands at once, took them each by one hand and shook them heartily. "I am Father Seraphim, deacon of the Cathedral of Saint Katharine. I am so pleased you have made a pilgrimage to see us. Would you like to see the garden? I so love the garden."

They walked through the mysterious wall by way of the wooden door and were greeted with a cacophony of smells. There were roses and basil and tomato vines growing up in little trellises. The place was alive with plants and winged creatures. Something zoomed past Nadya's head so fast she couldn't see it, but Caspian instantly recognized it as a hummingbird. There were plenty of bees buzzing around as well that were going back and forth between the plants and their little wooden beehive over on the back end of the garden. There was also the distinct sound of rushing water from a little koi pond with a small waterfall. The place was very peaceful; for a moment, Nadya missed the cabin in the woods. This was as if you took all of her little sanctuary's best parts and condensed them into this tiny space. The entire thing seemed so tremendously alive.

"I apologize; I am an odd little fellow," Father Seraphim finally offered. "I have been widowed many years and this is my little way to remember my love. I do believe I often get so caught up in it all, hearing her song in the bees and the birds, that I don't pay attention to much else. Please forgive my manners or lack thereof. Christ is risen!"

"As the women told us," Nadya responded.

Father Seraphim smiled and took them both by the hands again. "Shall we go inside?"

"I would like that," Nadya said, smiling back.

"We must go around to the front as I am afraid you will be unable to walk in through the back as we would be entering the area of the altar," Seraphim said apologetically. "Please follow me this way."

They followed the floating deacon as he returned to the front of the building, unlocked the front door, and welcomed them inside. The interior of the building surprised Caspian. In his mind, he had imagined the many stories of the building to have stairways that led up to offices or classrooms. Instead, the building was open-plan and icons led all the way up to the top of the onion dome with one massive icon of Christ with hands extended looking down at them. He wasn't certain, but he estimated the building must have been at least six stories high and all he could think about was that someone had to go all the way to the top of this building by some ungodly means to paint that icon at the very top. As he looked up, his stomach churned at the thought of all the scaffolding and climbing up and down it with cans and brushes to paint. He imagined himself at the top of it and then looking down, giving himself empathic vertigo. Nadya was also straining her neck to look up, but her thoughts were on the hanging of each icon, of which there must have been hundreds, and someone had to nail each of them up. They heard a clicking noise, bringing themselves down from the stars and back down to earth. They made eye contact with Father Seraphim, who was pointing a revolver at them both.

"Who sent you?" he demanded.

Nadya made a slight movement, which startled Father Seraphim. This caused him to point his gun even closer, demanding that she give over her weapon. "Reach for your gun slowly and then toss it over here to me."

She slowly unholstered her weapon, leaned over to the rust-colored marbled floor, and slid it over to Seraphim. His foot snuck out from under his riassa. Suddenly, he seemed much less whimsical now that Caspian could see his foot. And the gun.

"Now, you." He pointed his gun at Caspian, who looked confused for a moment. "You Romans, always looking for any chance for another round. I guess Constantinople wasn't enough bloodshed of God's true Church for you?"

For a moment, Caspian had forgotten that he did have a gun in his backpack, but the hatred in Seraphim's eyes helped remind him. He tossed the entire pack onto the floor quickly and then kicked it across the floor toward Seraphim. But his fear made him a bit feisty.

"Still holding a grudge over that, eh?" He stared Seraphim down. "I mean what's a couple of hundred years between siblings?"

"Your Church is not a sibling; you are nothing more than an imposter, a shell of what God intended for his Holy Catholic Church." Seraphim pointed with his gun for them to take a few steps backward toward the wall. "It is for this reason that God saw fit for the throne of the emperor and the Ecumenical Patriarch to leave Constantinople and, instead, the Holy Spirit fell upon Imperial Russia to be the Third and Final Rome, the true Empire of the whole world and the only religion that is pure and undefiled."

Nadya was entirely lost in their exchange. Instead, her eyes were darting around the room, looking for any opportunity to make a move to release them from the predicament they had found themselves in. Because the room was circular, there were no corners to run and hide in. The place was also completely devoid of pews. It was just a round open space. She had a morbid thought of how much the gunshot would ring through the rafters once the cleric finally decided to take his shot. This seemed like a truly impossible situation. Then the deacon made a move backward. There was an old rug in the center of the building he had been standing on. He tossed it to the side, revealing a door in the floor. He leaned down slightly and lifted the door by a round handle, which lay flat against the marble. He did this with the other hand still extended, pointing the gun back and forth between them. After opening it, he stood erect and walked back a few more steps before making a motion that they were supposed to circle the building so they could face the opening on the opposite side.

"The True Church survived your Crusades and weathered the storms of many perils. It was the truth that allowed us to hide in the catacombs during the reign of Lenin and prepare for the time when the Lord would see fit to reinstitute the tsar to his mighty throne to rule hand in hand with the patriarch for the Russification of the whole world. The final rise of the Third Holy Roman

Empire, the House of Romanov reincarnated in our new Imperial ruler, Vladimir Putin the Great." He took a deep breath. "And I'll be damned if after all of this I will not see that ascension. I certainly won't fall to some reprobate Roman concubine of the Whore of Babylon. Now get in."

Caspian decided to go first, seeing literally no other way out of this situation. The ladder that led down into the basement was not very long. He could reach the ceiling with his hand when he got there. Nadya began her way down and Caspian extended his hand to help, but she swatted it away. Then they both looked up, no longer seeing the extended arms of Christ but only the scrowling face of Father Seraphim before he slammed the door shut, placed a combination lock on the door and replaced the rug. They listened as he walked away; they heard a sound they assumed was him opening a door before slamming it shut, leaving them in total silence and a profound darkness.

"Well, fuck," Caspian said.

CHAPTER FOURTEEN

The little dungeon they had now found themselves in was the type of dark that causes your eyes to see little firework flashes across your line of vision in an attempt to make sense of this much darkness. Suddenly, there was a faint blast of light in the room as Nadya pulled a lighter from her pocket and Caspian flinched for a second, having already become accustomed to the darkness. With this newfound light, he quickly began to look around the room for something more sustainable than a lighter. There were a few folding tables against the walls with things strewn about them. Unlike the upstairs portion, which was entirely round, the basement was square. He found a long cardboard box on one of the folding tables with slender beeswax candles inside. They lit a few of them and placed them around the room. There was no way out other than the locked door above them. Coming to terms with this reality, Nadya began to take an inventory of the items in the room to see if there was anything to help with their hopeful escape. Unfortunately, the parish had not stored anything helpful like a crowbar or explosives in the cellar.

As the candles flickered, there were flashes of gold light that caught Caspian's eye and he became momentarily distracted by some of the icons that lined the downstairs room. A number of them were in disrepair; he assumed they'd fallen from the walls of the main church only to meet their demise on the ground. He wondered if this would be the icons' final resting place or if they would be repaired and restored to their original spaces in the sanctuary. Nadya had many questions about Caspian's exchange with their captor and so as she continued to investigate the room, she also began to assault him with a series of questions.

"You and Seraphim seemed to hit it off," she offered as an intro to her inquisition. "What is that about?"

"There are some ancient animosities between the Roman Catholic Church and the Orthodox Church dating back nearly a thousand years. Some of those differences that exist between us are bigger than others." He joined in the search as he continued, "Depending on how you look at history, the aggressions over the years can widen the gap between our two churches."

"Considering I am about to possibly die for whatever your boss did to their boss, I would like to know a bit more than it's a 'widening gap' if you don't mind." Nadya picked up a broom and then discarded it.

"It all began with the Filioque." Caspian intended to continue but was interrupted.

"Fil-o-what?"

"Filioque," he said flatly and exaggerating his enunciation of the word. "It is Latin for 'and the son.' According to the Eastern Churches, it is a phrase from the Creed that was improperly added."

"So this whole thing is over an argument about words?" Nadya said indignantly.

"Well, it certainly started that way, but like most things involving humans, it didn't end that way. For a thousand years, we were one Church. There were cultural differences, but we were in union on the basics, which was what mattered. But over time, each Church, Rome in the West and Antioch, Constantinople, Jerusalem, etc. in the East, started little spats over things like using leavened or unleavened bread during Communion, the definitions of original sin, purgatory, Hell, and whether we experience God cerebrally or as a mystery. Then there is this little issue of the Trinity, or at least that's what it looks like on the surface. There is debate amongst the Orthodox and Roman Catholic Church on whether or not the Holy Spirit proceeds from the Father or the Father and the Son. That is where the Filioque came into play."

"So you all changed it without asking permission; they got pissed, and what? You killed them?" Nadya was now taking a seat but not yet admitting defeat. She was recalculating the situation.

"You sound like you are Orthodox when you say it like that." Caspian laughed. "On the surface, those were the issues, but it really boiled down to power. We believe that the Pope is the supreme head of the Church and has unilateral power. For us, the Pope choosing to make a change to the creed would be within his authority."

"A pissing contest. Fucking brilliant. I'm doing to die over a thousand-year-old dick measuring between a bunch of fuckers who don't even use their dicks." Nadya had picked up a candle and used it as a type of phallus. "Awesome."

"I think history would agree that the Pope and the Patriarch knew there were arguments for all these issues on both sides. But, again, that's not really what it was about. The issue escalated over time and they essentially started doing the Middle Ages version of them sending each other several old-school mean tweets across their territories until they each excommunicated the other."

"They can do that?" Nadya was actually engaged and Caspian was a little surprised.

"Well, yes, they could. I guess you'd need to understand that, at that time, the Church was functioning a little differently than it does now. The ecclesiology is developing differently in the East and West as well."

"You've lost me again with the terms. Speak English." Nadya said that last part mockingly in a Southern accent.

"That is also another issue, language." Caspian was getting excited about teaching. Admittedly, he had repeatedly felt pretty useless on this adventure and was happy to be offering something that might be useful. "But ecclesiology is the governance of the Church: who is in charge, rank, and all that shit. In the West, the belief has developed over time that the bishops govern the Church but do not hold equal power. The sole authority of the Church rests on the Seat of Saint Peter as he was the first of the Apostles and the first bishop of the universal Church. We believe whoever sits on the Seat of Saint Peter holds the Keys to the Kingdom. We believe that the Pope is the central authority of the Church and that he controls, well, everything that happens throughout all of Christendom. This belief ultimately led the way for the Roman Church believing it had the authority to mandate certain things, such as adding the Filioque to the Creed without having to check with anyone else. We are the original Rome and the holder of all authority.

"In the East, the rest of the Church viewed the Pope as having what's known as the primacy of honor because it was the first apostolic appointment, but this didn't come with special powers. Instead, the Churches of the East viewed all bishops as equal and from the same line of apostolic succession linking themselves back to the Seat of Saint Peter. If decisions are to be made, they must be done by way of a council and not the unilateral decision-making of one bishop. This doesn't mean that this system doesn't have its own downfalls. It can be difficult to reach a consensus on issues when you don't have a centralized figure who can decide disputes, but this was the way of the East. They believe that Constantinople is the Second Rome and so they've got equal power and authority and no one is going to tell them what to do. I suppose one can empathize a bit with their understanding of the differences in the governance of the Church. In that case, you can now see why the Patriarch of Constantinople got a bit miffed over the Pope exalting his power in such a manner. So here we are at both of them excommunicating each other. There is just one minor issue: Pope Leo decided to go and die, so his excommunication didn't work out so well. But these two fellas went and launched the great divide between the East and the West and the rest of the world took a deep breath and then didn't give one flying fuck about it. In spite of this schism, things mostly continued forward without any real chance until things got quite explosive."

Nadya had been thinking about this whole escaping thing from a big picture vantage point until Caspian said explosive. She had been looking for something to smash the wood with, like an axe or hammer. She was not breaking the issue down to the micro point, so now she began investigating the hinges on the door. They were exterior, meaning they were facing on the upside of the door. Again, if she had a hammer or something like that, she could smash even the floor and maybe crack where the hinges were attached, but there was nothing on their side that could help make that a reality. Though she didn't think that this little basement area had been created for the point of holding prisoners, she was impressed with how well it was secured. If you wanted to make something that was nearly fucking impossible to get out of, they did a masterful job. Nadya reached down into her boot and pulled out the secondary gun she had hidden for emergencies, like a deacon stealing your main gun while attempting to take out a thousand-year-old grudge against you.

"This is going to be loud." Nadya shot the gun toward where she assumed the lock was.

She missed and accidentally hit the cement instead of the hinges. The area had been fortified with rebar; steel reinforcements were often put under cement to hold it in place and make it much more secure. This caused a minor ricochet and Caspian started yelling, "Stop!" But because the room was very small and the gunfire very loud, Nadya was having a hard time hearing him. Not that it would have stopped her anyway. She reset her position and pulled the trigger again. She pushed up on the door and it wiggled a bit. She stepped back and fired a third time. This time, the door gave way after a few shoves. It flopped up on top and made a thud that neither of them could hear. Nadya went up the ladder first and then Caspian followed.

When he made it topside, he was at first very relieved. That was until he tripped over something that he thought was the door but realized was far too squishy to be wood. When he looked down, he found the deceased body of Father Seraphim lying there. Hearing the first shot, Father Seraphim, who was just on the other side of the main door still making a telephone call, had come rushing back inside. Of course, Caspian and Nadya didn't hear him come inside because they couldn't hear anything well as their ears were ringing from the sound of the gunfire. As Nadya repositioned herself below him, Seraphim had run over to the door on the floor, and when Nadya fired the second time, the bullet made contact with the hinge. It then continued through the wood going straight up into his groin area, piercing several vital organs before he fell backward, bleeding quite profusely. He was dead by the time she fired the third shot that released them. And that was precisely the state he was in when they found him lying there.

As is the case when someone fires a weapon, they were now afraid that they had alerted neighbors or other concerned citizens with the gunshots. They now needed to make quick work of whatever they were going to do next. However, they also had the issue of Nadya now being rather fascinated by her history lesson and equally unconcerned with the untimely death of the man who had thrown them into the pit of this church. Then, without ever addressing the issue of the dead deacon, she turned to Caspian and said, “What happened next?”

While waiting for Caspian to respond in any meaningful way to her request for more knowledge, she started making her way toward the iconostasis. She may have been new to all this church stuff, but she had been a quick learner and determined that it seemed that these folks liked to store valuable trinkets behind the icons and around the altar.

“Follow,” she demanded, “and talk. Get to the crusades bit. That seemed to have him pretty miffed.”

As Nadya opened the royal doors and began looking around, Caspian complied as best he could between the ringing in his ears, the shock of seeing Father Seraphim dead, and the existential dread that they could at any moment be discovered.

“The Crusades were originally intended to liberate the Holy Land from Islamic rule. A little-known fact about these Crusades was that whenever the Roman Church would make its way into places like Antioch and Jerusalem, they would find Christian churches there. Admittedly, they should have allowed those churches to continue uninterrupted, but that was not the case. They set up competing bishops within the rightful jurisdiction of the Orthodox bishop. It was the Fourth Crusade where things got complicated." Caspian was speaking very fast at this point and also frantically looking around the room for any indication of where the relics of the tsar might be. "The purpose of this particular Crusade was generally the same as the previous Crusades, 'Muslims = bad. Christians = Good.' This time, the Crusades were supposed to go to Egypt and liberate everyone there."

"Liberate?" Nadya rolled her eyes. "And by liberate you mean swords to the abdomen paid for by indulgences?"

"Well, sure, but…."

"Can we skip the 'but' part where you try to justify this shit?" Nadya was uninterested in a revisionist white knight version of history. She was equally frustrated with their inability to find anything that looked like what they were looking for amongst all of the chalices, incense burners, and candles. "Where the fuck is this thing?"

"We should look under the altar." Caspian began delicately removing the chalice and other sacred items. "Often there are relics in the altar. It's actually required."

Nadya swung her entire forearm across the top of the altar knocking everything to the ground. Caspian looked mortified, but she shouted, "Just think of it like Jesus flipping the tables and move on."

Caspian began inspecting the altar without any luck. "Normally, there would be a small cutout of wood and the relic would be placed underneath that."

Just then, his eyes caught a small pink piece of cloth on the ground where Nadya had knocked everything down and Caspian quickly picked it up and placed it back on the altar.

"The antimension!" he exclaimed as he flipped it over.

"The what?"

Before Caspian could answer, they heard a group of people filing into the church building. Caspian stood up and poked his head above the royal doors just enough to see who was inside. There were six men holding guns. They were all wearing non-religious clothing but one of the men was wearing a leather vest with the Krest insignia. Caspian quickly ducked his head back down and could hear the men discussing splitting up and looking everywhere.

"Boris," one man shouted, "you are a subdeacon; you go look inside the sanctuary and make sure they aren't in there desecrating it."

Without having to say a word, both Caspian and Nadya began crawling their way toward the back door. Thankfully, it did not lock inside and they made their way out into the garden. It seemed substantially less beautiful this time. They ran across the courtyard to the beehives, jumping atop them, and made their escape over the wall. Nadya ran around the corner toward the car. Caspian was right behind her and they made it inside the vehicle without anyone noticing. But then Caspian could see the man he assumed was Boris making his way around the front of the church. Nadya was already backing the car up when Boris started shooting and hit the trashcan next to where they had previously been parked. They continued backward and then immediately forward to get onto the main road. Nadya was speeding in the wrong direction on a one-way street.

"One way!" Caspian screamed.

"No backseat driving from someone who doesn't drive! Teach, don't drive!" Nadya shouted back. Just then, she realized another car was following after them. Caspian wasn't really in a teaching mood anymore, but Nadya demanded it again, if for no other reason than to keep her mind off of how suddenly terrified she was.

"Okay, so that was the Crusade's mission: get to Egypt. Instead, they went some 900 miles east to Constantinople and decided to sack the city instead. The assault on Constantinople was brutal and lasted for nearly three days." Caspian grabbed the dashboard to hold himself in place as Nadya took a sharp turn. "We stole relics, gold, silver, and books. But to be fair, it's not like the East was particularly kind during this time either. Some of this was considered payback for them having killed a considerable amount of Latins during the Massacre of the Latins, which was genocide of Roman Catholics within Constantinople. So no one's hands are free of blood here."

"Stop making excuses!" Nadya yelled as she took another sharp right.

"I am not! Fuck!" He couldn't find a place to hold on to. "The sacking of Constantinople was not the plan and the Pope was pretty pissed about it. If the great Great Schism in 1054—"

"That's the excommunication thing?" Nadya was now certain that Boris was pursuing them and she was doing her best to lose him.

"Yes, the excommunication thing!" Caspian continued yelling his lesson over the screeching of the tires. "That was when the East and the West first broke up, but it wasn't the end of it. That came hundreds of years later."

Boris shot off the rearview mirror on the passenger side. They were coming up to an intersection and there was a cop directing traffic. If this hadn't been happening, Nadya had intended to tell Caspian to return fire from the gun in the glove box. Fortunately, it appeared that Boris had also caught on to the fact that law enforcement was in the area and had stopped firing. The cop was putting his hand up for them to stop, but Nadya had every intention of going forward. At this point, she would rather get caught by the cops than Boris, but Caspian had the exact opposite feeling because he wasn't so sure some of the police weren't working with the Krest or members of the Brotherhood. Now they were careening towards their doom and the cop was waving his arms. Caspian started just letting out information rapid fire as he was sure this was the end.

"The Ottoman Empire was making its way across Byzantium and the Byzantines were absolutely losing. Constantinople needed the Roman Church on its side to win the battle. They eventually relented and accepted the Filioque and papal authority in order to secure the support of the Crusaders."

"The creed thing-y?" Nadya could almost see the whites of the cop's eyes.

"But it didn't matter; it was too late." Caspian was almost screaming at this point. "Catholics and the Eastern Orthodox Christians met inside the Cathedral of the Holy Wisdom along with the emperor. They lost. Legend says that people within the congregation watched as the Holy Spirit left the sanctuary and then Constantinople fell."

They blasted past the cop just as he pulled his gun out. He was quickly distracted from Nadya because he could see the gun now in Boris' hand and he believed they must have been running from a robber. The cop began to run toward the car and Boris stopped for a second.

"I'll be damned, "Nadya said. "So that's why it's called Istanbul and not Constantinople."

"That's nobody's business but the Turks'," Caspian replied.

Just then, they were cut off from Boris and the cop by the presidential motorcade driving down the road. Soon, half a dozen cars were surrounding Boris. One of the cops pointed at Nadya and she quickly turned away from the crowd. They both took a breath and watched in the rearview mirror as the presidential limousine drove by with its little American flags waving in the wind.

"God bless America," Nadya said as she raced off down a side alley.

CHAPTER FIFTEEN

Nadya was confident that if the police weren't already pursuing them, they would soon be. Not only had they blasted through a red light and defied a direct order to stop, but they had done so during a presidential transport. This was a major fuck-up. It was only a matter of time until their license plate would be pulled from the traffic light camera and their car would be flagged. Fortunately, she and Jenks were well prepared for such an occurrence and this vehicle's registration matched fake identifications that they both had, should they ever be pulled over. This also meant that once the police traced the vehicle's tags, it would lead them to a fake address and fake identities, buying them both some time. However, that didn't prevent the car from being marked or that it would make it all the more likely that they could be found if they stayed with the car. After traveling about six blocks, Nadya pulled the vehicle over and demanded that Caspian immediately exit.

In the trunk of the vehicle, she had a complete change of clothing for both her and Caspian. Until now, he had still been wearing his clerical attire, which was especially conspicuous if the red-light camera had captured a front-facing image of the pair. Caspian changed into a blue-and-white-striped button-up shirt with a tie, a pair of surprisingly well-fitting jeans, and brown boots that fit a little less well, but he could manage. She also gave him a smartwatch that had been disabled and was simply for show. She had also been wearing all black for the entirety of their adventure together but had now changed into a burgundy top, a pair of gray jeans, and knee-high black boots. The couple had morphed from being a detective pair into tourists in a matter of minutes. Nadya had them walk about three blocks from where they had abandoned the vehicle and they found a small fleet of rentable scooters.

The backpacks with the change of clothing also contained some essentials, including five burner credit cards for emergencies. Nadya hated to waste one on something as trivial as these scooters but they desperately needed to get out of plain sight and into some public building until they could regroup as to their next options. Caspian had forgotten the thing of actual value within the car that was now abandoned: the antimension.

"Fuck," Caspian said as he dismounted the shooter. "I left the antimension in the car."

"What? How?" Nadya said, looking back toward the vehicle.

"It was in the back pocket of my clericals." Caspian started back toward the vehicle as quickly as he could.

As he headed toward the vehicle, Nadya pushed the unlock button on the key fob. He fumbled around the back seat for a moment as his discarded pants were inside out from his quick change maneuver. He finally located the pocket and pulled the cloth from it and then he heard a sound that made his skin crawl.

"Stop and place your hands in the air," the officer said.

Caspian slowly backed away from the car with his hands raised, the pink piece of cloth dangling from the grip of his right hand.

"Drop the handkerchief," the cop demanded.

"I can't do that, sir." Caspian improvised, "This is a sacred religious item; it can't touch the ground."

"You've got three seconds to drop that thing before I drop you," the officer shouted back. Caspian was suddenly left with very few options to escape this predicament and so he decided just to shoot his shot.

"Listen, I know it's going to sound crazy, but we are on the run from a group of Russian spies. I am working with a CIA operative to help uncover their plans. This item I have in my hand might have the answers we need to stop them and restore order to the Republic." As the words exited his mouth, all he could think was that when

Stephen Jenks had said something similar to him, he didn't believe him. He disregarded him as living in some delusion. Had he chosen to set aside his own engrained prejudices would all of this have gone much differently? And more importantly, would this officer have more faith in him than he was willing to place in Jenks?

"Drop the hanky!" the officer shouted back.

Guess not, Caspian thought. He then made one of those decisions that could easily have been fatal. He quickly turned to face the officer. They made eye contact for only a fraction of a second before a loud noise pierced through his ears and Caspian shut his eyes tightly, accepting his fate. He reached towards his torso to feel for a bullet wound, but there was none. Instead, as he opened his eyes, he realized that the officer had been plowed over by Boris, who was now facing him through the window of his vehicle. Not willing to push his luck any further, Caspian ran as quickly as he could toward where Nadya was waiting with the scooters. Boris was hot on Caspian's heels as he pushed his body to go faster.

Before Boris finally gained on Caspian, Nadya let off a single shot from her gun that destroyed the driver's side tire. Boris's car hit a curb and jumped into the air, flipping upside down before crashing to the ground, barely missing Caspian.

"Let's go!" Nadya yelled as Caspian jumped on his scooter.

They zoomed through the capital on their borrowed transport, quickly blending in with the tourists around the mall. In spite of it all, Caspian was enjoying the experience tremendously as he had never visited Washington, DC, before and was eagerly taking in the sights as they maneuvered through the area. He was surprised by how much smaller everything looked in real life. He almost felt like he was at a miniature golf version of these national monuments, not the real thing. He was also surprised by how close everything was to each other. In his mind, the White House was far from the Capitol Building. But everything one could want to see was all within a mile radius of each other.

Nadya's biggest concern was that if Boris and the others were intelligent, they would have accused her and Caspian of being up to some nefarious business. Not only would this make them a quick target for the police or the Secret Service, but it also meant they needed to steer clear of any monuments or locations that would be likely targets for terrorism, such as the White House, Capitol Building, Lincoln Monument, etc. These buildings were much more difficult to get close to following January 6th, so it was easy enough to avoid them. Still, she didn't want any proximity to them, so she began to steer them toward the Smithsonian museums.

When they finally arrived at the red sandstone building, Caspian was in absolute awe. He was struck by how at home he suddenly felt as they approached the landmark. The Romanesque and Gothic elements made him think of the universities and cathedrals he was accustomed to. He had almost a sudden urge to genuflect when he walked into the foyer but resisted the temptation. To their left was a small round table barstool height with literature and maps in plastic pamphlet displays. They walked over to this table and it was nice to have a rest for a moment.

"All right, what the fuck is that thing?" Nadya said, pointing to Caspian's pocket where the antimension was hidden.

He pulled the cloth from his pocket and it seemed rather unimpressive at first sight. It was folded in on itself, giving it the appearance of being nothing more than an oversized pink bandana. He delicately began to unfold it into the first grouping of thirds and then again until the entire rectangle sacramental was completely opened, revealing several icons printed on the cloth. The first was an image of the Theotokos surrounded by angels and saints as she held the body of Christ in her arms. On each of the four corners were icons of the Gospel writers and to the right of them, along each edge, were writings in Church Slavonic.

"Remember how I told you that some customs developed differently in the Eastern Churches than in Rome?" Caspian asked as he ran his hand over the antimension along the creases.

"Yes." Nadya nodded.

"Well, this is one of those ways." Caspian was now rubbing his hand in the opposite direction over the smooth silk. "In the Roman Church, the altar is one of the most sacred items in a church. It is blessed by the bishop, anointed with oil, and then a relic of a saint is placed inside. But this is not how it is done in the Orthodox Church."

"But the churches we have visited had altars?" Nadya inquired.

"Yes, they did. And they are considered holy, but they are not what is required to serve the Divine Liturgy." Realizing he had lost Nadya again, he offered a better explanation. "Divine Liturgy is the phrase used in the East instead of the Mass for the worship service of the Church. Antimension is a Greek word that means 'instead of the table,' so the antimension is, in essence, the actual altar and it is a portable one at that. Each priest has one and the bishop signs it; it is this, not some printed certificate, that shows they are ordained and authorized by the bishop to act as a priest. Without this, they cannot perform the Divine Liturgy."

"I guess we just fucked some priest's day up, huh?" Nadya laughed, but Caspian did not look as amused.

"Inside this is a relic of a saint; just like with our altars, they must be a first-class relic, meaning it is the bones of a saint, and I am guessing that within this antimension are the relics of Tsar Nicholas II of Russia."

"I think we have company," Nadya said, looking across Caspian's shoulder. "Don't look. Just listen."

Across the foyer were two men in plain-clothed suits who appeared to have earpieces in their ears. They were both looking intently in the direction of Nadya and Caspian. At first, Nadya had chosen this particular location because of the table, but when they approached it, Nadya enjoyed that it gave her the ability to keep her back in the corner of the building, which then empowered her to survey the entire building, its exits, and anyone who was coming and going. However, it now presented a new problem as she just noticed a third figure that appeared to be with the two. The original two had split up and together they formed a trifecta of doom that was closing in on them. If they were to run, it would only draw attention at best and, at worst, result in them getting shot. Though she wasn't interested in either of those options, seeing none other presenting itself she looked at Caspian and whispered, "Walk in different directions; meet me in the back."

With that, they both scattered; Caspian had grabbed the antimension and shoved it into his pocket without properly folding it in threes. He felt terrible about this, but he also wasn't very interested in dying today either. Nadya had shoved him toward the door when she ran, trying to make it out of the back exit. They were now out of sight of each other.

Caspian was enjoying the slowest chase in history. The man was fast walking toward him as he was fast walking away from the man. It seemed that neither of them wished to cause a scene. The sidewalk was coming to an abrupt end and his only option was to take a right turn, which he did. For a few moments, the man following him disappeared, but just as quickly he reappeared. There was a group of about six tourists ahead of them on the same style of motorized scooters that he and Nadya had just used. The group was beginning to move again. Caspian took the opportunity to stick his foot out just slightly enough to knock over the person leading the group. This caused the rest of them to fall over like bowling pins on top of one another. One of the tourists smacked directly into the man who was chasing Caspian. At this point, Caspian picked up his speed. He was about to round another block and could hear footsteps behind him. The man was gaining on him rather quickly and so his attempts to thwart the man had not been successful. He rounded the corner and found Nadya standing with one of the other men. He had his hand on her arm as if he was detaining her. It was at that moment that the first man caught up with Caspian.

"Father Caspian," the man with Nadya said, "my name is Michael and we mean you no harm."

"Who are you?" Caspian directed his question to Michael since he seemed to be in charge.

"We are Knights of the Third Order." As Michael said this, a car pulled up next to them, and the third man was inside. "We are in genuine danger here. The antimension you have with you does contain a relic of Tsar Nicholas II within it. I am afraid it also has a tracking device, which is how we were able to find you. Now, if we found you, it stands to reason that the rightful owners of that antimension are also looking for it."

"I don't feel great about any of this," Caspian said.

"Neither should you, Father," Michael continued. "Unfortunately, there are many things none of us feel great about that are happening at this time. You are welcome to come with us or you can wait to explain this to the Russians when they arrive. Whichever you choose, I will need the antimension."

"Absolutely not." But as Caspian said this, the man behind him plucked the antimension from his pocket and handed it to Michael.

For a moment, Nadya and Caspian looked at each other, hoping one or the other might have a better escape plan. Seeing as neither did, they watched as Michael began to inspect the antimension until he found a bump in one of the edges. Then, holding it in place with one hand, he reached into his pocket and produced a small knife. He cut open the cloth revealing a small off-white stone from the fabric. It took a moment for Caspian to realize that this small memento that Michael had removed was, in fact, a fragment of the tsar. Holding the now damaged antimension in his hand with the knife Michael dropped the antimension on the other side of a fence and then replaced the blade into his pocket. With the same motion, he produced a small, circular polished brass box from his pocket. Caspian recognized it immediately as a pyx, a small container for carrying around the Eucharist and other sacred things. It was adorned with a red Chi-Rho symbol on top of it. He placed the bone fragment into the pyx and then back into his pocket.

"Now, my dear Father," Michael continued, "you are welcome to wait here with the antimension and hope that the Russians are in a forgiving mood today or you can come safely with us."

Seeing yet again no other reasonable offer presenting itself, Nadya and Caspian got into the back of the vehicle along with Michael, the other unknown man, and the driver. The backseat was somewhat like a limousine as the seats faced one another, allowing for better conversations. As terrifying as the situation had been, both Nadya and Caspian welcomed being captured by folks who didn't feel the need to be pointing guns at them.

"Father, I am sure you have many questions," Michael said.

Nadya abruptly interrupted. "I have a lot of questions myself."

"You are a harlot," Michael said without ever looking at her. "I will be addressing the Father and no one else at this time."

Now that they were stuck in the car with these three figures, neither of them felt like getting into a confrontation over the offensive words that Michael had just said. Just because they did not have guns pointed at them did not mean that there were no guns in the vehicle. Caspian did not feel any desire to be agreeable to the words that Michael had just said either. He found them profoundly rude, so instead of saying anything, he just gave a solemn head bow toward Michael as an indication to continue.

"Again, Father, I apologize for the way in which we approached you. We figured you both would be afraid and would run. You have every reason to be afraid." Michael pointed towards a cooler with some wine in it and the other man opened it and offered a glass each to Caspian and Nadya. "You have found yourself in the bowels of a war, the third and final war. There are many players and we are but humble knights in service to see that this cause reaches a righteous end to all of the conflicts that plague mankind."

"With all due respect, Mike"—Caspian was becoming more emboldened as time moved on—"could you just cut to the point where you explain who the fuck you are?"

"Yes, of course." Michael shook his head as if to knock the swear words out of his ears. "We are Knights of the Third Order, a lay organization with a devotion to the

Virgin Mary in general but more specifically to Our Lady of Fatima. I believe that your friend Stephen Jenks was very close to discovering us as well as he too was quite close to uncovering the relic of the tsar."

"Do you know where Jenks is now?" Nadya asked. Michael ignored her, instead keeping his gaze locked directly on Father Caspian.

"Do you know where Jenks is now?" Caspian repeated.

"I do, Father." Michael immediately responded to Caspian as Nadya rolled her eyes. "He has been captured by the Krest, in union with the Brotherhood. He is at their joint headquarters along the Panhandle of Florida. I am also afraid he is in quite serious danger."

"Why haven't I heard of the Third Order before?" Caspian asked.

"Oh, Father, I am sure you have, if not by name then certainly by way of reputation." Michael chuckled in unison with the other gentlemen in the car. "We are those whom you like to call Trads. We have been fighting for some time for many causes within the American Church of Rome, for a restoration of the Latin within our sacred tradition, the reclamation of the Tridentine Mass, for an end to the liberalism of our faith, and exposing our current Pope as a false prophet hell-bent on the destruction of the True Faith from within. As of recent times, our cause has also shifted in a great many ways to the sole purpose of the completion of the Second

Secret of Fatima and the Consecration of Russia to the Immaculate Heart of Mary."

"I thought the Pope had put an end to you nuts," Caspian said unapologetically, but he still offered a "sorry" in there somewhere for good measure.

"No offense taken, Father." Michael continued, "We have been called much worse. The Fatima Prophesy is important for the continuation of the Church and we expect all manner of persecution."

The car came to a stop outside of a large restaurant building.

"What is the Second Prophecy of Fatima?" Nadya asked. Again, Michael did not look at her.

"Refresh my memory," Caspian said. "What is the Second Prophecy of Fatima?"

"As I am sure you remember, Father, Our Lady appeared to young Lúcia, Jacinta, and Francisco on numerous occasions in Portugal. Our Lady chose to appear to these young shepherds as shepherds have always been close to Our Lady's heart. These young prophets warned us about many calamities that would come to the world. There were worst-case scenarios if our mistress was not heeded, but there was also a promise of the absolution that would come if her words were heeded. As you know, Father, those within Russia have parroted our faith for centuries but have always fallen short. The apparition of our Blessed Mother made it clear and certain that Orthodoxy is a bastardization of the true path that she wishes us to follow. They must abandon this shell of the faith and be united once again with Rome as the Holy and Apostolic Head of the Church."

"And the prophesy?" Nadya asked.

"And the prophesy?" Caspian echoed.

"Yes, the second vision." With this, Michael closed his eyes and began to recite it as if it were the creed; the three knights repeated the words in unison. "Our Lady said to them, 'You have seen hell where the souls of poor sinners go. To save them, God wishes to establish in the world devotion to my Immaculate Heart. If what I say to you is done, many souls will be saved and there will be peace. The war is going to end, but if people do not cease offending God, a worse one will break out during the Pontificate of Pope Pius XI. When you see a night illumined by an unknown light, know that this is the great sign given you by God that He is about to punish the world for its crimes by means of war, famine, and persecutions of the Church and of the Holy Father. To prevent this, I shall come to ask for the Consecration of Russia to my Immaculate Heart and the Communion of reparation on the First Saturdays. If my requests are heeded, Russia will be converted and there will be peace; if not, she will spread her errors throughout the world, causing wars and persecutions of the Church. The good will be martyred; the Holy Father will have much to suffer; various nations will be annihilated. In the end, my Immaculate Heart will triumph. The Holy Father will consecrate Russia to me and she shall be converted and a period of peace will be granted to the world.'"

"Okay." Father Caspian looked baffled. "The Pope is just supposed to say some prayer, and then—poof—the Russian Orthodox Church falls and the Roman Catholic Church takes over in Russia and we avoid a Third World War?"

"If only it were so easy, Father." Michael pulled the small pyx back out of his pocket and held it in his palm. "Our Lady appeared to the three divine children and gave them three prophetic visions on July 13th of 1917 and nearly a year to the day later, July 17th of 1918, the tsar and his family were murdered by the Bolsheviks. Their bones remained hidden for decades. Once they were finally exhumed, they were held strictly by the Russian Orthodox Church under lock and key. We are unable to violate their sacred space, nor they ours. We must have the bones of the tsar, this holy relic, to complete the consecration, these bones which you have now provided to us."

"That wasn't exactly the plan," Caspian said.

"I am afraid, Father"—Michael closed his fingers back around the pyx—"that this is all much bigger than you or me or your harlot friend. There are forces at play here that want to bring about the destruction of the whole world at best, and at worst they wish to bring about a new reign of the tsar and global Russification. We will see, in our lifetime, a destruction of the Catholic and Protestant faiths, a march toward the total theocracy of the tsar and the Patriarch towards world domination."

"What about—" Caspian began to inquire more but was cut off by Michael.

"There is a great more you should know, Father"—Michael opened the door to the vehicle—"but I am not the one who can explain it all best. Here we are safe. A type of neutral zone, if you will."

Michael and the other knights exited the vehicle and motioned for Caspian to join them. Nadya waited a moment to compose herself before she too stepped out. Everything had been so dark inside that she had forgotten it was day. The light was blinding in that way you feel if you go to the movie theatre for a matinee and then exit only to be assaulted by the sun.

As the triune knights walked toward the building, Caspian did not follow.

"Father?" Looking back at the reluctant cleric, Michael asked, "Is everything all right?"

"What if the Pope chooses not to play into your little war game?" Caspian asked. "What if he refuses to consecrate Russia to the Immaculate Heart?"

"Then he will have proven himself truly unworthy and our Lady will remove him to the place where there is weeping, and wailing, and the gnashing of teeth to prepare a way for the true Holy Father to rise once again." Michael opened the wooden doors of the restaurant and welcomed them inside.

The quaint Italian restaurant's appearance was somewhere between genuinely authentic and a trope of itself. When they walked through the wooden doors inside, the smell of fresh herbs, roasting tomatoes, and rising bread made them suddenly realize how hungry they were. Michael led them down a hallway past the booths. He turned down a second hallway at the end of the first and the room became suddenly colder. Unlike the warm colors of the wood or the red-and-white-striped coverings over the tables, this hallway was stone and glass. Behind the glass were bottles of wine. Some of them looked to be so old that they might have been from the Last Supper. At the very end of the hallway was an arched doorway. A small plaque sat upon that door with a large single key lock and engraved there upon the bronzed centerpiece of this door was a young gentleman with a top hat and a tuxedo. Written above this figure's frame in Gaelic-inspired letters were the words: The Statesmen Lounge.

Chapter Sixteen

As much as the sting of failure hurt, Kyle was happy to be home back at the compound in Florida. Home was an unusual concept for him as he had never felt at home within his own house growing up. He was a constant outcast at school and within his given family, not unlike Nadya had been. However, their lives went down very different paths. Hers led her to a place of wanting to fight for equality that she was never given whereas Kyle wanted to crush those whom he despised into submission. He considered finding the Brotherhood and the Krest, by virtue of them, a blessing from God. He would have been in prison or worse if it wasn't for them.

After graduating high school, he wrote a manifesto and posted it online. He had every intention of killing as many people as he possibly could at his old school. He had a list starting with a few teachers and then working his way down. If he could escape the school without being detained or shot, he would head to the local mall and, if he could, the airport. It was a perfect plan and no one could stop him.

Then David had reached out to him.

"I think you've got the right idea, kid. Can I buy you a coffee?" David said in an email to Kyle.

They met for that coffee and Kyle instantly felt at home. He was still going to be able to enact his revenge on all those whores who wouldn't sleep with him and fight for a world where he didn't have to compete with lesser races to make it into college or be afraid if the person in the bathroom with him was the correct gender. He would still get to shoot that gun someday but no longer as a lone gunman whose name would ultimately become forgotten in the long list of school shootings. No, he would be a general in the war to make America great again.

The headquarters of the Brotherhood was very unlike the prestigious feel of the Statesmen Lounge, nor was it filled with men in well-pressed suits like the Knights of the Third Order. The men at the compound were working-class folks. The members of the Brotherhood were primarily real estate agents, a few cops, one EMT, and the rest worked in varying levels of trade skills like plumbers and electricians. Most of them had served in the military. The compound was impressive, albeit primitive. Two of the founding members purchased it together from a government auction. It had been a former campground for middle schoolers that had gone defunct after the recession. The property was eventually sold at a tax deed held by the state and was in some major disrepair. However, it had many elements that made sense: a lake, a shooting range for guns and bows, an office building, a chapel, a rather large house, and ten cabins with bunks that could sleep twenty each. Every two cabins had a bathroom between them and there was another building with an industrial kitchen and dining hall. The entire campus was covered in large pine trees and the ground was laced with pine needles and sand. It abutted a national park, so they had no neighbors to complain about them constantly shooting off weapons while doing drills.

After January 6th, there were some significant changes in leadership. One of the founders had already been tried and convicted and feared more arrests were imminent. That was when the Krest started to take a more active role in the day-to-day operations at the compound. If Kyle was honest with himself, he welcomed much of the change. Even though he thought Boris could be disrespectful sometimes, he was an intelligent guy. The Krest seemed better organized and well-managed. Kyle also liked how much further along Russia was at addressing some of society's wrongs; he felt they could all learn a thing or two from what the Russians had accomplished.

One of the first changes the Krest made was converting the small chapel on the property into a Russian Orthodox mission. Father Mark, the chaplain of the Krest, was coming to the compound later that week to bless weapons and officially receive nine of the Brotherhood members as catechumens: Kyle was one of them.

Kyle was excited to be back, though this journey took him longer than expected because he was making it on foot. He abandoned his vehicle back in Chicago, selling it to a junk car buyer for a few hundred dollars. The car had grown far too conspicuous and had already resulted in him being pulled over once; he wasn't willing to risk that again. Watching the red clay of the old dirt road dust up under his feet almost gave him a sense of urgency to run down to the main area and see who was there. He also hoped to get a glance at Jenks.

As he rounded the corner of the main campus, he saw that almost everyone was congregating at the chapel. The parking area was full of motorcycles, all bearing the Krest insignia. At this sight, Kyle picked up his speed, making his way directly toward the chapel instead of the mess hall or the main house as he had planned. In the distance, he saw one of the members of the Krest that he knew, a man by the name of Orlov. Kyle shouted a greeting toward Orlov, so he waited for him outside of the chapel.

"What's going on?" Kyle asked in a breathy tone as he had run the rest of the way. "I thought Father Mark wasn't coming until next week."

"He is not here," Orlov said sternly. "We are having a panikhidas for Father Seraphim of the Cathedral of Saint Katherine. He was martyred for the cause."

"What happened?" Kyle was shocked. He had never met Father Seraphim, but he knew him by reputation.

"You." Orlov shook his head contemptuously. "You failed at your mission to capture the girl and the Roman. Now Seraphim is dead. Boris and the others arrived just moments too late to save him. His body now lies in wait at the cathedral."

"May his memory be eternal," Kyle said solemnly.

"Amin."

With that, Orlov walked into the chapel and Kyle followed behind him. They walked into the narthex, where Kyle remained to watch from afar, as is the custom. Catechumens and penitents are prohibited from entering the nave or the sanctuary. Kyle enjoyed the narthex because the room was warm and full of light. On either side of the entrance door to the nave stood two tables with sandboxes. Before entering the nave, believers would light a candle and place it in the sand. Sometimes, they would draw small symbols in the sand before placing the slender beeswax flame into the box. The narthex was full of icons and other decorations. He was also able to see into the nave from there.

The chapel was dimly lit and there was a small table in the center of the nave with a picture of Father Seraphim placed upon it. Flowers brought in by the faithful surrounded the picture frame. As someone approached the image of Father Seraphim, they would make a solemn bow toward the ground, touch it with their right hand, and then make the sign of the cross. They would repeat this motion three times, leave their gift upon the table, and then move about the nave making similar genuflections towards other icons throughout the room.

They did not have a full-time pastor or deacon stationed at their little mission, but one of the members of the Krest was a cantor. He was already vested and entered into the nave from behind the iconostasis. He was carrying a large icon of a bishop or priest that Kyle did not recognize. The cantor held the icon outward, facing toward the congregation, while standing directly behind the image of Father Seraphim. Orlov was still standing in the narthex with Kyle as he lifted a candle and said some prayers before placing it into the sand with the dozens of other candles already burning.

"What is he doing?" Kyle asked. The sincerity of his inquiry softened Orlov ever so slightly.

"The icon itself will be performing the panikhidas," Orlov said plainly.

"How does that work?"

"It is an old custom from Siberia and other rural areas. The belief is that in the absence of a holy priest or deacon, if one cannot be found or the clerics in your village have fallen into sin and corruption, the icons themselves may substitute for the priest."

"I don't understand," Kyle said.

"You understand that the icon is a window into Heaven, yes?" Orlov whispered as the service had begun.

"Yes."

"Then it is not a great mystery if you can understand this ancient truth." Orlov placed his arm around Kyle to bring him in closer so he could hear him over the chants that had begun. "The icon is an imperfect image of the perfection of the saint it represents. On the other side of the veil, that saint can receive our prayers and petitions to take them to God. In this same way, they can also pray for us, though we cannot hear it."

"Let us attend!" the cantor sang.

"Wisdom!" they all chanted back.

"Do you see and understand?" Orlov asked Kyle.

"I think I do."

For Kyle, the ancientness of the faith reminded him of how the world used to be: simple and full of mystery. He didn't understand all of the "smells and bells," as his grandfather used to say, about the Catholic Church but was ready to learn. He had always felt a little out of place, even in the Pentecostal church he had attended growing up. He always felt there had to have been more than this and he was pretty sure he had found it in the Russian Church. They had achieved what he had always hoped for in his own country: a complete symmetry between the Church and the state. They worked in perfect unison together toward a common goal of morality and culture that he couldn't believe was truly possible until now. He had even thought on more than one occasion that maybe Putin would be a good president of the United States. Perhaps in all this restructuring they would be doing Russia and America could create their own kind of confederation.

Orlov stayed in the narthex with Kyle for the remainder of the panikhidas, explaining the words and movements to him in hushed tones. Growing up in the Protestant Church, he was scolded for asking questions or challenging the pastor or Sunday school teachers. Never in his life had he experienced such a sense of community as he felt within this small chapel. Every movement and word had a purpose, which connected him with the whole Church throughout the world but also brought them back in union with Christ and the Apostles. *This is what home feels like,* he thought to himself as he leaned into Orlov's embrace.

After nearly an hour, the service concluded and he watched as the men moved around the chapel, continuing their venerations of icons and greeting the cantor with reverence. Kyle and Orlov exited the chapel together and were greeted by the hot, sticky humidity of a warm Southern night. Fireflies danced around the open area where the bikes were parked. One of the Krest opened a bottle of vodka and shouted something in Russian. Red Solo cups were passed around and they each took a shot.

"Seraphim!" they shouted and then served another round.

A few of the men had gathered around the fire pit and they began tossing branches and logs collected from around the property onto it. The entire area was piled high within a few minutes and they lit it. It was a monstrous blaze.

"Seraphim!" they shouted before pouring another round.

As the night continued to draw on, they began to rev the engines of their motorcycles until the roar was so loud you were sure that you could hear nothing else. Others shot their guns off into the air to compete with the noise of the exhaust.

"Seraphim!" they shouted; another case of vodka was brought out from the main house.

Around midnight, most of them had drunk their weight in vodka. Two men were fighting in a dirt area near the fire pit and others were betting on who would win. With each pounding blow, they would shout louder and louder. A few of the wives had arrived and joined in with the revelry.

"Seraphim!" they shouted and began to remove their clothing.

They chanted hymns and shot their guns and revved their engines until someone yelled out, "Plavat'!" All of the men began to run toward the water. Orlov joined them in the run and Kyle followed, albeit drunk and confused.

"What are we doing?" Kyle panted as he struggled to keep up with Orlov.

"To swim!" Orlov shouted back to him over his shoulder.

The men continued to drink and splash; the two who had been fighting on land had begun to fight in the water and the others continued to place their bets. The stakes were getting higher and everything felt more dangerous. Kyle had never felt so alive. One of the fighters now had the other man's face under the water and he was sputtering to catch a breath. Eventually, the fighter let him go and the man accepted his defeat before passing out. Everyone began to make their way back to the fire to settle their bets and find their clothing.

Orlov placed his arm back around Kyle's neck as they walked away from the beach towards the woods where the trail back to the fire was. About halfway up the trail, Orlov shoved Kyle against a tree and then placed his hand against his thigh.

"What the fuck are you doing?" Kyle shouted and so Orlov covered his mouth.

"Another Siberian tradition, catechumen." Orlov breathed heavily against Kyle's neck. "If we never sin, what do we have to confess? If we never sin, what is the point of redemption? If we never sin, what is the point of the cross?"

Kyle's heart was beating out of his chest. Part of him wanted to refuse for fear that this was some kind of test, but if it was a test, he had already failed as he was visibly hard.

"Would you like to sin with me so that we may find redemption?" Orlov asked.

"Yes." Kyle was afraid and excited. He welcomed the touch and moved Orlov's hand up his thigh until he was holding his cock in his hand. Without letting go, Orlov dropped to his knees and placed Kyle inside his mouth. With each thrust of his head, Kyle could hear his friend repeating, "Amin, amin, amin."

When they finally returned to the camp, the fire was nearly out and there were men strewn about sleeping on the ground in varying stages of undress. Orlov's wife was there and she brought him his clothing. Kyle placed his hands over himself and was a bit embarrassed.

"What took you so long?" Tatiana asked Orlov.

He smacked Kyle on his wet back with such force that he thought he might cough up a lung.

"Just preparing him for his first confession." Orlov smiled.

"Amin." Tatiana rejoiced.

"Amin," Kyle said in response, feeling himself becoming hard again under his hands.

CHAPTER SEVENTEEN

They had expected the three Knights of the Third Order to follow them inside and were surprised they did not. The room seemed to mirror the tables and booths within the main restaurant, except these booths had red velvet curtains that could be pulled back for privacy. There was no one else inside; Nadya even checked under each booth to make sure. Realizing this was not enough, she took a second look by pulling each of the curtains to ensure that no one had propped themselves up on a chair. Above all of the booths were different insignias. She recognized some of them. There was the image of the square and compass of the Masons' lodges, the three-lined circle that the Third Order knights had been wearing, then the barred cross and gules of the Krest; there was a Gadsden flag serpent, the skull and bones from Yale, and the open palm with a heart under interlocked chains for the Order of the Odd Fellows. There were plenty of other symbols she did not recognize.

In the center of the room was a round table with three place settings. The entire room felt rather ominous and Nadya was having a hard time understanding how this was all sitting inside a little restaurant like this. *Do people not notice?* she wondered. Caspian now had his look around at the different symbols along the wall.

"I don't recognize them all," Nadya whispered to him.

"This is the strangest thing I have ever seen," Caspian responded. "None of this makes any sense. That over there is the Masons' symbol."

"I do know that one."

"Right." Caspian almost seemed to be talking to himself. "But that over there is the Knights of Columbus. Those two groups are about as opposite as you could get. They are at complete odds with each other. That over there is Opus Dei. Basically, every Catholic lay organization is represented, along with Protestant and secular groups that would never have any association with one another."

"That is the mystery of the world." A voice came from behind them. The man must have entered through the door without them noticing, which was very disconcerting. He stepped further toward the center of the room and the round table. "I am The Doctor."

"What's your name?" Caspian inquired.

"I am afraid, for the sake of order, I am only known as The Doctor." He motioned for them to sit. "But I will do my best to explain. I am sure you are hungry."

Nadya sat first. "Very much so."

"And tired." Caspian was exhausted; even though he did get to nap in the car, it was not the truly restful kind of sleep.

"I am sure of that," The Doctor said kindly. "There are three things I can promise you: a genuine meal, information, and then an authentic night's sleep without fear of retribution from anyone."

"And how can you promise that?" Nadya was very suspicious of such an offer.

"Because I am a doctor," he said with a smile. "My oath to this organization provides me with certain privileges and assurance for your safety. At least for one evening, your safe passage is one of them."

"What is this place?" Nadya asked.

"That is an excellent question." The Doctor looked around at the insignias that had confused both Nadya and Caspian. Nadya was particularly excited to have someone willing to respond to her. She couldn't have put up with too much more of that nonsense. "You are in the Statesmen Lounge. It is a society that was formed, as most are, by a group of young men with the purpose of providing privilege and access. However, unlike many of the other groups you see represented here, they took a stance of neutrality. They intended to be without agenda, simply a meeting ground for the sharing of ideas. Over the years, they developed into a bit of a United Nations of sorts for many other societies. This eventually evolved into them providing certain services to the other groups, which is where I come in. My function is as The Doctor. I am summoned whenever there is a need that others would like to keep out of the media."

"Like what?" Nadya was pretty skeptical.

"Like when a high-ranking officer of a Catholic organization's daughter needs an abortion," The Doctor offered, "or if a senator has an STI. Or if an operative is shot, but not killed, by a priest who has found himself in over his head."

Caspian was suddenly relieved to learn that he had not killed someone, though he was also feeling another odd feeling. He was beginning to wonder if his relief at The Doctor's statement only brought the release of the burden for his intellect and not his heart because as the news broke about his lack of murdering Kyle, he also felt a slight tinge of sadness at his lack of success.

"So you are a bad guy?" Nadya wasn't pulling any punches.

"I am a doctor," The Doctor said.

"Yes, but you are helping the bad guys," Nadya protested.

The Doctor sighed. "Your criticism is not unfounded, which is why I have called you here."

Just then, a back door opened up and a waitress walked in. Suddenly, this all felt less mysterious as she walked over and greeted them just like she would have if they were sitting anywhere else within the restaurant. She handed them menus that looked just like regular ones, except that they had the Statesmen symbol on them, which seemed to be an abbreviated selection. However, abbreviated did not mean lesser; on the contrary, the options were exquisite. They ordered their food and the waitress took back each menu and then left.

"Everyone has a red line," The Doctor continued, "and I am afraid mine has finally been crossed."

"What would that line be?" Nadya was curious.

"Freedom," The Doctor offered.

"No offense, doc," Caspian jumped in, "but that is a pretty vague response. We see freedoms disappear all the time, not just in our country but worldwide. Some of those atrocities have been exacted by the organizations whose banners we are eating under today."

"You are correct, Reverend." The Doctor clasped his hands together and leaned into them. "There are certain things I have seen or participated in that very well may have blown past your red line many times over. What has brought us here today, to this point, to my desire to meet with you is not about your red lines or the things you think I have done over the course of my life and career that would have wounded your sensibilities. I am not claiming to be a moral or righteous man. I have done many immoral things and likely will do many more.

But there are certain things I cannot abide and we are careening quickly toward some of those same events that, I would hope, any person with even the spark of a conscience would stand up against, regardless of the cost."

The waitress returned with their drinks and salads. The three of them enjoyed the silence together for a moment. Nadya felt almost like she was consuming life itself as the greens entered her body. This was the first nutritious thing she had consumed in days. She had never appreciated a salad so much in her entire life and was almost sure she could eat nothing else for the rest of her days. Caspian was having a similar emotional moment with some bread set in the center of the table. The Doctor watched as they consumed their food for a few moments then leaned back into his clasped hands.

"My friends," he finally continued, "you have found yourselves in the midst of a holy war."

"Everything is a holy war," Caspian said glibly with a mouth full of bread and butter.

"To be sure." The Doctor handed Caspian a napkin. "There have been plenty of them throughout history. Might I add that it is one thing to pontificate about them safely from history books and it is another thing altogether to find yourself a leading character that undoubtedly will be judged by history once this is all said and done?"

"What makes this a holy war and not just a regular war?" Nadya asked.

"Patriarch Kirill of Russia has stated, in no uncertain terms, that this is, in fact, a holy war," the Doctor responded. "That, in and of itself, should tell you something."

Caspian jumped back in, having finally finished his bread. "But that doesn't just make it so. Even ideological wars aren't necessarily a holy war in the sense the Crusades were."

"No," The Doctor conceded, "but the players certainly do. Allow me to explain: The issue you have now found yourselves in is far bigger than you can imagine. You basically have three players maneuvering this conflict. Let me correct myself, war; I say war because Putin wishes us not to say war: this war is about more than meets the eye.

"Our friends waiting outside, the Third Order, hope to complete a war that began nearly a thousand years ago. They want to see the Orthodox Church come to her knees and be reunited with Rome with the Pope as their supreme authority. They know that this can only be achieved through Russia. They are the largest of the Orthodox jurisdictions; for them, it is catching the big fish. The Fatima prophecy justifies their purpose. The goal is the same as it has been for a millennium, to regain control of the whole of the Church and for her to be under the same roof again. They are being opportunistic because, suddenly, so many people are angry with Russia and no one is even questioning it. The Consecration is just colonialism by another name. Orthodoxy is part of the national identity of Russia and for that to be erased by the Catholic Church would be a disservice to society and the Russian people. They don't need more erasing; they need new leadership.

"The Knights consider the Krest and the Brotherhood an enemy here and position themselves as the good guys. But their ideological goals are not that far away from each other. The Third Order has just as much intent to see an end to human rights: marriage equality, regressive policies for trans people, and an absolutist view on overturning Roe v. Wade. All three groups have this in common. Even though they should all be able to agree on the basics, this battle is an ancient one. The same war that existed when Rome went after Cyril and Methodius: language."

"Who?" Nadya was starting to wish she had paid more attention in history class before dropping out.

"Father?" The Doctor said, yielding the floor to Caspian.

"Cyril and Methodius were two brothers and arguably the fathers of the Russian Orthodox Church. They came to evangelize the Kievian Rus' people. My team had already been in the region and had been rejected because they demanded adherence to the Latin language. In stark contrast, Cyril invented the Slavonic alphabet and translated the Bible and the services of the Church into the language of the people. Just a few years before the Great Schism, this action set the wheels in motion for the Russian Orthodox Church to become the powerhouse it is today."

"Cyril?" Nadya pondered. "Is that why we call it Cyrillic script?"

"Yes." Caspian looked back at The Doctor. "All right, so I get it. Same battle, different century, but what about the Krest and the Brotherhood? That seems like an odd pairing."

"Not particularly," The Doctor countered. "The Brotherhood was an invention of the Russian Federation misinformation campaign."

"Explain," Nadya said flatly.

"The goal was always to get Donald Trump in. The plan was to use the same rulebook they did in Ukraine: divide the country ideologically and you can divide the country in reality. They wanted a civil war in Ukraine and got one. That opened the door for them to eventually invade. Don't you find it fascinating that both our country and Ukraine elected television personalities?"

"Are you insinuating that Zelensky is a bad guy?" Nadya was shocked and a bit offended.

"No, I am not," The Doctor said cooly. "I am simply saying that Putin got more than he bargained for in Zelensky. He could never have anticipated the backbone on him. So he lucked out with Trump and failed with

Zelensky. But the plan was still the same: destabilize the nation through misinformation, petty infighting, and eventually an ideological ground war that opens the door for invasion. They got their civil war by proxy in Ukraine; now they wish to conquer it in reality … piece by piece."

"And you think they can do that here?" Caspian sounded unsure.

"Father, they already have." The Doctor gave them a moment to let those words penetrate. "We can only tango with words for so long before someone throws the first blow. In your mind, wars are directed by Stephen Spielberg. They look like the beaches of Normandy and star one of the Fiennes brothers. That is not what civil war looks like, my friends."

"What does it look like?" Nadya asked obligatorily.

"Three hundred mass shootings a day," The Doctor said coldly.

"That is hardly the same," Caspian protested.

"Is it not? How many continents have you been on during civil war, Father?" The Doctor asked sharply.

"None," Caspian relented.

"None," The Doctor scoffed. "I have been to nine. I have sawn off arms and buried the dead in these conflicts—these wars. I've also made love to women in fancy hotels in those same countries. Dined in fine restaurants and drank cappuccinos outside of cafes in the spring. Everything seemed fine in those moments; there would be peace until suddenly there wasn't. Another mass shooting, a blast at a shopping mall. A child is killed by a mortar bomb. So what do you think a civil war looks like? It looks like this."

"And the Krest is behind it all?" Nadya asked.

"The Krest has been available to the Kremlin, the Russian Mob, and the Patriarchate as the ugly arm of Russia for decades. They are like a resurrection of the Tsarist military generals, willing to do anything for the state. If you look at the things that the far right in our country are becoming angered about, they are things that Russia has already waged war on in their own country: gay pride parades, trans rights, feminism. For a moment, it appeared America was making headway on these issues, and then suddenly a dramatic shift backward. The man whom the Kremlin selected as our new leader was pushing these ideologies. That is what brought us right to the front door of January 6th. But no, this isn't the doing of the Krest in the sense of it being their idea. All this has come down from the top: The Kremlin and the Patriarchate. The Krest are merely soldiers in the army."

"But they failed," Caspian offered. "They didn't succeed; the election process moved forward. The inauguration happened."

"Do you know how many uprisings happened in Russia before the tsar finally fell?" The Doctor asked.

"No," Nadya responded nervously.

"A lot. Little uprisings, an attack on the royal family here, blowing up a general there. They even assassinated Tsar Nicholas II's grandfather. A lot happened before we got to the February Revolution that brought about the end of the Romanov Dynasty. Bloody Sunday in St. Petersburg was twelve years before the ultimate fall of the dynasty. The revolutionaries played the long game." The Doctor leaned back into his folded hands again. "This is what is so strange about Putin's operations: he is using Bolshevik tactics to achieve the return of the tsarist regime. It's like he is pushing the rewind button on history and we are watching it all play in reverse."

"So you are saying that January 6th was just one of many operations?" Caspian was now very concerned.

The waitress returned with their food, though, admittedly, both of their appetites were diminishing. It is hard to eat such luxuries while imagining a world crumbling apart outside the walls. But The Doctor told them they couldn't help anyone if they didn't have their health. *Doctor's orders,* Caspian thought before jumping in. The Doctor allowed them to enjoy their meals in silence. They ate quickly, as most do when they are starving. As soon as they finally allowed themselves to eat, they realized how truly hungry they had been. When all was complete, The Doctor made the now familiar pattern of folding his hands into a clasp and then leaning into them. He almost seemed as if he were emulating something he had seen in a movie.

"How was it?" he asked.

"Delicious." Nadya seemed genuinely grateful.

"Thank you," Caspian offered and then he gestured for The Doctor to continue.

"In all his attempts to modernize Russia, Nicholas II allowed through the Duma a type of freedom of the press that had never been seen before in their country. Almost immediately, they came after him in that same press." The Doctor put his finger up to correct himself. "More importantly, they came after the tsarina and her relationship with Rasputin. It was an embarrassment to the dynasty and the country. It was also a deliberate disinformation campaign. Rasputin was a devil in his own right, but much of what was being printed was absolute falsehood intended to diminish the power of the tsar further."

"But to what end?" Caspian was getting lost.

"The missing piece here is who." The Doctor leaned in harder on his hands. "Nicholas II was paying for the sins of his father. After the successful assassination of Nicholas' grandfather, Alexander II, his son immediately took his place on the throne. That is the problem with dynasties; there is always someone to replace them. So another attempt was planned on Alexander III. One of those conspirators was Aleksandr Ulyanov, a young revolutionary hoping to see a change for Russia, a world without the tsar and a truly democratically elected Duma with real power. They attempted to finish off Alexander the III, but the revolutionaries failed. Aleksandr Ulyanov was hanged along with his co-conspirators for treason. Something his little brother Vladimir Ulyanov would never forget."

"No offense, Doctor," Nadya interjected, "but you say this like any of these names should mean something to us."

"They certainly should." The Doctor paused. "You know him as Vladimir Lenin."

"Are you trying to tell me that Lenin is responsible for the false reports against Rasputin and the tsarina?" Caspian sounded skeptical.

"There is reason to believe that is quite possible. Lenin would use any possible way to bring about an end to the tsar." The Doctor paused again. "And it certainly explains why he was so keen to assassinate the tsar and his family when the time presented itself. The brutality of it all, the slaughtering of even the children, makes more sense when it is not only about the political differences but revenge for the execution of his brother. Making sure that you succeed where others fail, end the entire line of the Romanovs once and for all."

"That must have been what Father Andrew meant when he said, 'It was the same man who assassinated the character of Brother Grigori ultimately assassinated the tsar,'" Nadya said, leaning into Caspian.

"So if by the scales of history January 6th was our Bloody Sunday and not the February Revolution, there is time?" Caspian asked, hopeful.

"If you are looking at the world through the lens of an American, yes," The Doctor said, "if you are a Ukrainian lying cold on the ground, no. We are all being pulled into this conflict, this war, from different angles. It is this very thing that your friend Stephen Jenks was on to. And it has become my red line."

"And what is your red line, Doctor?" Nadya was suddenly very interested at the mention of her old friend.

"For all of our flaws as a country, as with any democracy, there are checks and balances in place. Such erosion would be catastrophic, but we have begun to see that erosion occur. Loss of faith in the Supreme Court, suspicion about the integrity of our elections, police brutality, and the list goes on. Most wars are for money and we have started most of the wars. This is not a war we were looking for; it was one being brought to us. This is no longer about fighting wars to fill their coffers with blood, money to sell more weapons, or getting their hands on more oil. The real devil in the details for me is that there are rules, procedures, and policies, but Putin doesn't give a damn about any of them. He has just blasted every red line out of the water and continues forward with his bloody campaign. His war. There isn't a too far for him, which is the too far for me. This is about fundamentally changing our system of government to dismantle us as a nation. He wishes to consume Ukraine and other border countries back into Russia and rebuild Russia and the United States into tsardoms, theocracies with the State and the Church ruling side by side: one body, two heads."

"The gules." As she rubbed the chill bumps from her arms, Nadya asked, "But what about the Brotherhood?"

"The Brotherhood is an apocalyptic cult that believes that the second coming cannot happen until there is a one-world government, a singular currency, the mark of the beast, and destruction of the planet. They don't want to stop climate change; they welcome it." The Doctor leaned into his hands for a final time. "Putin and the Patriarch are ready to give them the war to end all wars. They want to light the skies up so bright that God would have to come down to see what the fuck we had gotten ourselves into now. Putin and the Patriarch want their one-world regime, a total takeover of the planet, replacing it with the Imperialistic vision of the Third Rome. And the Third Order wants all that too; they just want to steal it from Russia."

"What can we do to stop it?" Nadya pleaded.

"Sleep," The Doctor responded, "because without it you are useless. The only thing I can promise you, with absolute certainty, is sleep."

With that, he abruptly stood up and handed them a piece of paper with an address. "Here is the location of your Stephen Jenks. I have arranged another car for you, for a place where you can lodge for the evening, and this is all I can do. Maybe you can find the answers and prevent us from reaching our February Revolution and stop the Apocalypse."

"Jesus, we aren't just going to be in the history books." Nadya laughed. "The way you are talking about it, we will be in the new Bible too."

The Doctor laughed, leading them out the door to where the Knights were waiting for them on the other side. They were taken to their car and the house, where they were safe for the evening. The Doctor escorted them to the front door. It was a small blue house in the middle of a residential neighborhood. It seemed positively normal minus a small crest of the Statesmen hanging above the door. When they got inside, each room was made perfectly. Caspian found a new set of clerical attire waiting on his bed, along with the liturgy of the hours. Nadya had a brand-new nightgown, a new set of clothing, ammunition, and two guns. Their doors were directly across from each other.

Caspian leaned his head back enough to see Nadya. "What now?"

She shrugged back at him.

"Sleep," The Doctor yelled as he went up the stairs towards the main bedroom and study. "Doctor's orders."

Caspian and Nadya passed out almost instantly. They were both too tired to even dream. As the hours passed while they slept, The Doctor rested in his study as he mindlessly responded to a few emails and began working on some paperwork he had neglected. No one knew who his safe house visitors were, except for the Knights of the Third Order guarding the house for the evening.

The landline rang and he walked over to answer it; it was never good news at this late hour. When he got a call this late, it meant someone was in trouble and it was time to activate The Doctor to fix whatever problem someone powerful had gotten themselves into. Maybe they overdosed their sex worker or ran a red light and had a wounded pedestrian needing mending and a payoff. Whatever the problem was, whatever the ailment, whatever the sin, The Doctor was there to fix it. That is what The Doctors had done for as long as there had been Statesmen. He answered the phone and heard a static-filled hum. He stood there, motionless for a few moments before he methodically walked over to his nightstand where he kept his revolver. He checked to ensure it was loaded before placing it against his right temple.

The gunshot woke up Nadya first.

CHAPTER EIGHTEEN

Nadya jolted out of bed with her gun pointed toward the door. She ran first to Caspian's room to make sure he was all right and found him lying in bed, petrified. She put her hand over his mouth and made a hush motion with her finger to her lips. He slowly nodded in agreement before she went upstairs to check on The Doctor. She found him lifeless on the floor with the phone on the ground. She turned around the room to see if anyone else was there. Finding no one, she walked over to the phone receiver and placed it against her ear. No one was on the other end, just the obnoxious dial tone of a phone left off the hook. She wiped the receiver with her shirt and then made her way out of the room and back down the stairs.

"Get dressed," she demanded of Caspian.

He quickly complied and gathered his things together. Though it all felt like it had taken far too long, everything happened in minutes. The Doctor had given Nadya keys to a vehicle they could use, but she was now uncertain if that could be trusted. Then she was struck with a different fear: where were the guards from the Third Order? Not knowing where they were made her incredibly nervous. If they were guarding the place, shouldn't they have run in when they heard the noise, and if not, didn't that mean they committed the crime? She opened the door to the front of the house and saw two things that made matters worse. The first was one of the guards lying, presumably dead, in the shrubbery next to the front door of the house. The other thing she saw was a neighbor a few doors down speaking with a police officer. It was only a matter of time until they would be questioning more neighbors until they found this house. She shut the door and went on to find out what was taking Caspian so long. She found him in the kitchen looking for food to take with them.

"Stop!" Nadya whisper-shouted at him.

"What?" He was startled.

"You are touching everything. Stop touching things!" Nadya began wiping things down.

"What is going on?" Caspian asked.

"I don't know." Nadya was still wiping things down. "The Doctor is dead; one of the Third Order guards is dead; I am assuming that the other two are dead. And if we don't get out of here soon, I fear we will be dead too."

As soon as Nadya said this, there was an abrupt and loud knock at the door. It was the type of knock that could only be from one type of person: a cop. Nadya knew that the longer she took to answer the door the more suspicious the officer would be, but she also couldn't answer it too fast because that would also seem suspicious. There was a real sweet spot she had to shoot for not to seem overly suspicious or do something that would cause them to ask to come inside or, worse, ask her to go outside. She made her way over to the door to open it. Just before doing so, she remembered that there was a dead body directly to the right of where the cop was standing.

"Sorry to bother you, ma'am," the officer said. "Some of your neighbors heard a noise and reported it. Did you hear anything?"

"Can't say I did," Nadya responded.

"The neighbor across the street said he heard a gunshot coming from this direction. Your neighbor next door said that it sounded very close; they also called." The officer poked his head around the door frame. "You sure you didn't hear anything?"

"Nope." Nadya shook her head. "Not a word… uh… sound."

"Right," the officer said with that tone that Nadya was hoping to avoid. "Is there anyone else in there with you?"

"Well…" Nadya was a bit stuck. She and Caspian hadn't put together a plan, and if she said no, the officer might hear or see Caspian, which would then tip him off that she was lying. However, if she said yes, Caspian might say or do something stupid.

"Yes." Caspian's voice surprised them. "I am right here, dear."

"Father?" The officer sounded confused.

"Oh! No." Caspian laughed. "Well, we didn't hear anything because we were a little preoccupied."

"Preoccupied?" The officer repeated it as a question.

"Just a little role-play," Caspian said, pointing at his outfit. "Have to keep things spicy after all these years together."

"I see," the officer said, continuing to look around. His head was tilting slightly toward the ground and Nadya was sure he was going to see the dead guard.

"Any idea where we could get a cop uniform?" Nadya asked sheepishly. "You know, for next time."

"I don't," the officer said, looking back at the couple. He was now quite uncomfortable and ready to leave, which was precisely what they wanted him to do. "All right, you two, have a safe night."

"Oh! We will." Caspian waved at the officer in a sitcom kind of way and then followed up with, "God bless you."

Unamused, the officer waved his hand into the air as he continued back to his cruiser. Caspian shut the door and Nadya turned around to him, looking kind of shocked.

"That was brilliant," she said, smirking. "Absolutely brilliant; I didn't know you had it in you."

"The power of Christ compels me?" Caspian shrugged.

Together they decided to head out in the car The Doctor had given them. They waited as long as they could and then headed to the garage. It was there that they found the other two guards. One of them was behind the rear wheels of the car, so they had to move him before they could drive away.

"There is no blood," Caspian observed.

Nadya leaned down and looked at one of the guards. While she was observing him, Caspian saw a small pill near his foot, and he, too, leaned over to inspect it.

"Don't touch that!" Nadya yelled quite loudly. "It's cyanide."

Caspian jumped up with a bit of a gasp.

"They must have had it on them in case they ever got caught," Nadya speculated. "But why would they take it? None of this makes any sense."

"It also doesn't make sense for a Catholic to kill themselves." Caspian was also confused.

"Well, you know how fundamentalists are; they think the rules apply to everyone but themselves." Nadya stood up and grabbed the guard's feet to move him out of the way.

Once they had moved the guards, they covered them with a large blue tarp in the garage so that no one would see them for the brief moment that the garage door would be open. Inside the car, they found a garage door opener, an envelope with some cash, and two fake ID cards with their photos.

"I'll give him this; The Doctor was thorough," Nadya said as she pulled out of the garage. She tossed the garage door opener out the window a few blocks away from the house. Caspian had the piece of paper with the address where Jenks was located. They had a fourteen-hour drive ahead of them, and without Caspian being able to drive, they would have to break the trip up again. It would be another day and Nadya was very nervous about how long it was taking for them to find Jenks.

Maybe it was the length of the drive ahead of them or just the exhaustion, but the two companions didn't talk about anything to do with any of the calamity that surrounded them as they traveled. They didn't discuss the death of The Doctor or the strangeness of the societies. They didn't mention patriarchs, presidents, or deities. Instead, they spent their time together talking about their childhoods and growing up in a world where they were still allowed to ride their bicycles around the neighborhood. There were many differences in their experiences, but there were plenty of commonalities to be found as well. Saturdays wasted at the roller rink and playing with yo-yos at the mall—slumber parties with truth or dare, twenty questions, and first kisses.

"All right, twenty questions, go," Caspian said.

Nadya laughed and then asked, "Favorite television show?"

"Serious show or guilty pleasures?" Caspian smiled back at her.

"Both!"

"Serious show, *Gilmore Girls*," Caspian said.

"Jesus, Caspian, I am scared to know your not serious show." Nadya looked at him, shocked.

"That show was great. It dealt with all kinds of important issues. You cannot tell me that the plight of Lorelai and Rory wasn't speaking directly to our generation." Caspian was an aficionado. "The characters were fun and complicated. It was a seasoned balance that not many other shows can capture."

"If you say so." She was still baffled but now needed to know more. "And your guilty pleasure? Even though I think *Gilmore Girls* should count."

"*Keeping Up with the Kardashians.*" He now braced for her response.

"I'll give you that one." She could tell she had stumped him.

"Really?" Caspian was shocked.

"Who is your favorite Kardashian?" She was now quizzing him.

"Scott Disick."

"Solid." Nadya followed up, "Did you always want to be a priest?"

"No."

"What happened?" she asked sincerely.

"Long story."

"We have a lot of time." She was correct.

"Next question." Caspian vetoed.

"All right, why don't you drive?" Nadya really wanted to know the answer to this one.

"Next question." Caspian vetoed again.

"Come on, man," she said jovially. "You are the most surface-level person I have ever met."

Caspian took a deep breath and then let it back out. "Do you really want to know?"

"Yes." Nadya was sincere in her tone.

"They are the same story," Caspian said. "I wasn't very devout growing up. My girlfriend and I both went to Catholic high school."

"You had a girlfriend?" Nadya seemed surprised. Not because Caspian was an unpleasant person to be around or to look at, but she had just mentally made him a eunuch. Mentally, he was a Ken doll to her.

"Her name was Amber," Caspian continued. "She was a year older than me and I thought I was so cool. We went to senior prom together. We were madly in love. The type that you would tell your kids about, the kind that lasts forever. Have you ever met someone who you could just see your whole future in their eyes? All of the houses and the cars and the kids and the careers?"

"No." Nadya sounded the kind of whimsically sad you are after watching *The Notebook*. "I have not. I think everyone wishes for that."

"Well, I had found it." Caspian looked out the window like it was all playing out in front of him. "She was everything. I just knew you know? Our senior prom night was perfect. My mom took a million photos and we drove off to meet up with our friends. The actual prom was very boring. The nuns at the school and Father Kevin were all there. It was kind of difficult to have a fun time surrounded by clerics. You could just feel the judgment. After a while, my best friend and our friend group decided to skip out and meet down at the water. We went skinny-dipping and drank awful beer. We made love in the sand under the stars in that shameless way that you really only can in your youth, completely unconcerned that our friends could hear us. It was getting close to midnight and I had to get her home before curfew. On our way back, I wasn't paying attention because she was so beautiful in her dress, and then... another drunk kid from another prom slammed into our car. We rolled a couple of times. I was completely fine, I had my seatbelt on, but she didn't because she didn't want it to wrinkle her dress. Two kids died that night. I was the only one that survived the crash."

"Oh my God, Caspian, I am so sorry." Nadya was shocked and genuinely didn't know what to say.

"She was still breathing when I found her a few feet away from the car. Then the ambulance and police arrived." Caspian shuddered for a moment like it was all happening again. "My mom came to get me and she took me to the hospital. We waited outside with her parents and family. Her dad kept looking at me like he wanted to kill me. Father Kevin arrived and he went to speak with the doctors. Eventually, he came back and we all went back together to be with Amber. I watched as Father Kevin lit the candles and he anointed her head with oil. He chanted all the prayers. I had always only seen him as the principal and the long arm of the law at our school. He always tried to be goofy with us and we never, ever thought he was cool. I had never seen this side of him. When it was all done, her father made the decision for them to remove her from life support. He cried into Father Kevin's arms. They spoke for a long time and then Amber's dad came over and told me he wasn't angry with me, that he knew it wasn't my fault. I am sure Father Kevin said something to him; I just don't know what."

Caspian looked around the glove box to see if there were any napkins in there for him to wipe his face with, but there was nothing, so he just used the sleeve of his new shirt. "I knew that Amber was it for me. When her eyes closed that last time, there went the house, the cars, the kids, and the careers. I didn't need anything else; there was no one else for me. I started spending a lot of time with Father Kevin. I got a scholarship to seminary and that was where I met Nick, who is my bishop now; we went to seminary together. Funnily enough, he also became a priest because of prom."

"He didn't…." Nadya couldn't believe that their stories were so similar.

"Oh no." Caspian laughed through his snot and tears. "He didn't also kill the love of his life. He just felt guilty for having sex."

He and Nadya laughed at that for a while and then they continued to play twenty questions as they made their way through Virginia and North Carolina. They stopped in at a Waffle House and had breakfast together. Strangely this part of the trip didn't feel at all like they were trapped in the middle of a horrific world that was falling prey to a holy war led by zealots eagerly seeking world domination. Without their phones and all of the late nights eating a steady diet of unhealthy foods it all kind of felt like being teenagers again. There was no news feed beckoning them back to the constant stream of drama, court cases, wars, and rumors of wars. Caspian hadn't even spent too much time thinking about the world of trouble he would be in back at home, that he was likely excommunicated. That he had let his friend down, or that, in reality, the bishop had let him down first.

Nadya was finishing up her eggs and smothered, covered, and topped hash browns when Caspian realized something.

"We are going to drive through Georgia, right?" He wished he had brought the map in with him.

"Yes, that's what the GPS in the car said," Nadya agreed.

"There is someone I know there who might be of help." Caspian was excited.

"Who?" Nadya wasn't so sure.

"There is a Uniate priest there; I have met him a few times at different conferences and events over the years."

"What is a Uniate?" Nadya had heard the word several times and hadn't bothered to ask about it until now.

The server brought over a fourth helping of coffee for Caspian. "All right, so when the East and West split, we both developed our differing traditions. But over time, the Catholic Church slowly set up its own Patriarchates, mimicking the original Patriarchates of the Orthodox Church. If they couldn't get them to get in line, the papacy decided they would just replace them. Eventually, some Orthodox Churches decided they wanted to regain individual unity back with Rome."

"So they are Catholic Orthodox?" Nadya was confused and also probably needed another cup of coffee.

"Sort of," Caspian continued. "The other Orthodox Churches don't recognize them; it's complicated. But they do follow their own traditions; their priests can be married—"

"Wait." Nadya put her hand up to pause him. "There are married Roman Catholic priests?"

"Yes." Caspian nodded. "Not just the Uniate either. There is an Anglican provision that also has married priests. It is just the ones, like me, who adhere to the Latin rite that are celibate. Well, along with all monks and nuns, regardless of which rite they are."

"I am truly lost." Nadya indicated to the server that she was ready for that other cup of coffee.

"Anyway, if I remember the story correctly, this priest was originally a Russian Orthodox priest, and at some point in 2012, he and his entire parish appealed to Rome to be received as Uniate." Caspian drank his coffee rather quickly. "It's a bit unusual, but it does happen from time to time. I don't remember all the politics of it all, but I have this feeling that he could be of some help."

"To the not Orthodox, Orthodox priest we go then." Nadya toasted Caspian with their dueling Waffle House mugs. "I am stealing one of these coffee cups."

"Everyone does." Caspian laughed.

Nadya slipped a coffee mug into her backpack and Caspian made a blessing toward her as if to absolve her for the theft. They went up to the register to pay before taking their respective bathroom breaks.

They stood out in front of the restaurant while they watched the sunrise as Nadya enjoyed a cigarette and Caspian finished his coffee. Neither of them was particularly eager to make their way back to the car, back onto the road, back to the war. But eventually, they would have to do it. They finished one more round of twenty questions before slowly walking toward the car. They almost bumped into each other as they walked toward the driver's seat.

"I'll take this leg," Caspian said, looking at Nadya.

"You sure?" she said, holding the keys.

"Yeah." He smiled.

She tossed him the keys and he held them in his hand as he made the sign of the cross with a smirk. They got into the car and Nadya started singing, "Jesus Take the Wheel." He laughed and shook his head. They hopped onto the interstate heading south.

Caspian pointed at the sign saying, "I guess they meant it when they said they would rise again."

"Except this time," Nadya cautioned, "the geographical lines aren't so clear; they are everywhere, north and south."

Chapter Nineteen

Father Caspian hit two curbs on their journey to the parish of Saint Basil outside of Atlanta. During the first traffic infraction, Nadya had been asleep and was jolted awake, absolutely certain that Caspian had killed them both. She was unable to sleep again after that. The second violation came as they pulled into the parish parking lot and Caspian nearly took out the mailbox. This would have been an especially egregious offense because the mailbox was a custom-made piece by one of the parishioners and was a mostly to-scale replica of the parish building. The mailbox and the church's actual structure were unique from anything they had yet visited. Unlike the Roman or Russian architecture of the previous establishments, Saint Basil's was profoundly Greek. The portico outside the parish entrance had large whitewashed Grecian columns and the bricks were painted an almost faded gold color. The building had the appearance of what someone would build if they were trying to make something look like it was from Greece but failed ever so slightly. The type of structure you would see at a putt-putt golf course or at one of those roadside attractions on your way to Disney World.

Around the back of the building was a small parish hall that shared a fenced-in playground with the rectory. The parish hall was blue and had white embellishments that gave it the appearance of being a Greek restaurant. The house was as unique as the parish itself. It seemed to have been constructed almost as an afterthought with the leftover materials from the parish. Not that the place was uninhabitable, rather just very old looking; not old as in ancient but old as in the '80s and forever stained with the uniquely bad architecture from that period. Everything about the house was wrong in some way. It should have been just slightly taller, the roof was unsettlingly flat, and the door was too large, which caused it to touch the border of the roof.

When they exited the vehicle, Nadya was a bit surprised to see some kids playing on the playground equipment. This was the first church they had attended that seemed lively. They approached the oddly sized door of the rectory and knocked.

A woman could be heard yelling, "Simeon, get the door!"

There was a momentary silence before the pattering of feet could be faintly detected before the door was swung ajar: there stood a short little boy of about eight years old who the two visitors deduced must be Simeon.

"I'm Noah!" the boy exclaimed. "Simeon is slower than me."

"Am not!" a voice that must have belonged to Simeon yelled from the other room.

"Are too!" Noah barked back just as his mother appeared. She quickly made her way to the door as she rubbed some flour off her hands and onto her apron before extending her hand to them.

"My apologies," she said with a smile, "I am Presbytera Claudia."

"I am Father Caspian and this is Nadya," he said, gesturing toward his companion.

"Nice to meet you, Presbytera Nadya," Claudia said with an even bigger smile.

"Oh, no, no," Caspian and Nadya said in unison.

"I am just Nadya." She laughed. "Just a friend of the good Father's."

"What a shame." Claudia shook her head. "Every good priest needs a good presbytera. I assume you are here to see my husband. Do you have an appointment? I didn't see anything on the calendar. But Father rarely puts things on the calendar, so I sometimes wonder why we even have one."

"No appointment," Caspian said, "but it is urgent if he has some time."

Presbytera Claudia ushered them inside, inviting them to sit at a coffee table in the kitchen. It was covered in crayons and was in extreme disarray with paper dangling precariously from the edges. Without asking, the presbytera brought both of them coffee with sugar and creamer. She excused herself for a moment to search for her husband. She was only gone a few moments before she came back in a hurry with an apologetic face.

"I am sorry, I don't think Father will be able to meet with you today…" But before she could finish the thought, the priest came busting into the room. He was wearing a long black cassock, which made his fiery red beard seem all that more fierce against the black backdrop. He was a robust man who looked like he could throw a tree a hundred yards. In Caspian's mind, the house was shaking as this troll-like man was rushing down the hallway at them. He was like a human cannonball.

"Do not make excuses for me, my sweet!" he yelled in a thick Russian accent as he approached the visitors. "I will handle them myself in my way."

Before Caspian could even comprehend what was happening, Father Maximos had him around the throat with his meaty fingers, pressing him against the pantry door. Without hesitation, Nadya pulled out her gun and placed it against the large head of the hulk-ish priest. He growled, looking in her direction while still holding Caspian, now turning purple, by the throat. Maximos barked, "The children!" to his wife and she vanished from the room quickly to gather them.

"You fucking fool!" He smashed Caspian's head against the pantry door as he said, "I have crossed oceans, lost my family, all to live in peace, and then you bring this fight into my home?"

"Let him go," Nadya demanded.

Maximos released Caspian's throat and he fell to the ground gasping for air. In the same motion of releasing Caspian he disarmed Nadya, dropping the magazine from the gun and catching it with his other hand before it reached the floor. Then, in his booming voice, he demanded they follow him to his study. The now disarmed and bewildered duo followed behind the fiery-red cleric as he made his way down the hallway full of family pictures, school awards, and hand-drawn stick figure images with enlarged child signatures.

When they made it into the study, it seemed more like the office of an attorney than that of a priest. Everything was perfectly spaced and he had one of those Newton's Cradle devices you see for sale at bookshops and office supply stores. His seminary degrees and other such credentials were neatly placed along the walls. There was a picture of him with the Ecumenical Patriarch and another with the president. Two chairs were facing his office desk and he violently pointed at these seating arrangements.

"Sit," Maximos demanded. "You have sixty seconds to explain why I should not pick up this phone right now and turn you over to the authorities this very moment."

"Authorities?" Caspian asked, confused.

"Everyone is looking for you: CIA, FBI, Homeland Security, Secret Service," Maximos explained. "I imagine if they are looking for you, then also the Krest and Brotherhood are on your trail as well. Not to mention your bishop wishes to have a word with you, I am certain of that. You are marked, my friends."

Nadya and Caspian sat there in silence for a few moments, coming to terms with the reality they now found themselves in. With all their attempts not to be traced, they had cut themselves off from the whole rest of the world and had been living blissfully unaware of how much trouble they were actually in. They had been walking around in the open, going to gas stations, and eating breakfast at the Waffle House, completely exposed with no idea that they could have been detected at any moment. They didn't even know to be hiding; though, in retrospect, they should have assumed this to be the case. Neither of them could find the right words to justify why Maximos shouldn't call the authorities and their sixty seconds were disappearing quickly. Maximos reached for the phone on his desk.

"Wait!" Nadya jumped up from her chair, holding her hand out in protest. "I just want to save my friend. He is like a brother to me and he is in danger."

Maximos relaxed his hand away from the phone and looked at Nadya. "This I understand. How may I help you?"

"We are missing pieces," Caspian offered. "We've walked into something that neither of us fully understands."

"I will do my best to help you understand." Maximos sighed. "But I do not enjoy having to relive any of this. I do not wish to be drawn back in. If I agree to help you in this way, do you promise to leave my home, leave me out of this, and that there will be no interruptions of my tale until I am complete? Agreed?"

"Agreed," they both said.

"I am the fourth generation of priests within my family. We have served Russia under the tsar, the Soviet Union, and now the Federation. My lineage has served but also suffered. During the Soviet period, my grandfather pushed back against the institution of the Living Church. An attempt was made on his life; he survived, but my grandmother did not. Like many others, he joined the Church of the Catacombs. He remained in Russia and continued to serve in secret, eventually becoming a bishop. He sent my father to Alaska for a season and it was there he met my mother. After the death of my grandfather, my father returned to the Motherland. Much had changed, but they were still under Soviet rule. When the Iron Curtain fell and the restoration began, my father was honored for his service. By the first election of Putin to the presidency, my father was a high-ranking official within the Church. Eventually, he was appointed the head of the Committee for Morality and Culture.

"My father had hoped that my brother and I would both become priests. I followed in the footsteps of the patriarchs of our family, but my brother had other ambitions. I loved my brother very much. He was the older brother in every sense one can be, even though he had only been born a few minutes before me. He went to college and became an architect, much to our father's anger. After completing seminary, I was given the opportunity to come to the United States. You see, the Russian Orthodox Church in America had been cut off from the mainland Church during the Soviet period. The Russian Orthodox Church of the Diaspora here in America and the Russian Orthodox Church within the Federation began reunification proceedings to bring them back into perfect unison, which culminated in 2007. Shortly after my ordination, my father believed it would be best to have those he trusted on the ground in the States to ensure this reunification would preserve the Russian ways. He sent me here to serve but also to be his eyes and ears.

"My dear brother remained in Russia and was living a happy life. He was renowned for his work and loved by his peers. However, my father refused to love him.

My brother did not see eye to eye with my father on many things: the role of the Church and politics, the things that mattered to our father; they were in complete opposition. Our constitution prohibited Putin from seeking a third term as president consecutively. He made his second-in-command run for president and then Putin was immediately appointed prime minister. It was no secret that he remained in complete power and this new president was merely a patsy. My father was highly loyal to Putin. In his mind, Putin was the tsar, if not in name then certainly in every other way. It grieved him to see Putin made to appear second fiddle. When it was announced that Putin would seek a third term after completing his time as prime minister, thus meeting his obligation to step away from the presidency for a time, my father was overjoyed.

"The Committee for Morality and Culture was striving toward many changes. They began to push for opposition to what they called gay propaganda. They wished for the Duma and Putin to fight for legislation that would criminalize certain activities: gay pride parades and the waving of the rainbow flag, these things they viewed as attempts to lure young people into also becoming gay. My brother began volunteering for the opposition in hopes of defeating Putin's third ascension to the presidency in 2012. My father felt this brought great shame to our family and our heritage. He and my brother met one final time before the election. It was a brutal match of words.

"Putin won the election, but there were widespread accusations of voter fraud. My brother joined in the protests, causing my father to publicly disown him. Shortly after the election, the Duma passed the Russian Gay Propaganda Law. My dear sweet brother and his partner joined in those protests as well. My father had been working with the Krest to ensure crowd control during these protests, and my brother, along with many others, was beaten in the streets. Eventually, my brother was arrested for his crimes and sentenced to six years in a work camp. He appealed to my father, who would not hear him. His partner was prevented from visiting him as they had no legal rights. After serving two years at the work camp, it was reported that my brother took his own life. He hung himself after secretly collecting laces from his boots.

"I went to Russia upon hearing the news, leaving my pregnant wife alone here in the States. Upon my arrival, I learned that my brother had been cremated, which is prohibited by our faith. His cremains were unceremoniously disposed of. My father refused to listen to me as I pleaded with him. He quoted Patriarch Krill to me, saying, 'Homosexuality is a very dangerous sign of the Apocalypse!' This apocalyptic thinking was not something known to Orthodoxy; it is a foreign thing altogether that one sees in Evangelical Churches but not what we believe. The Russian World was changing into an even darker place. The Russian government had been fomenting dissent within Ukraine. Eventually, it moved to illegally annex Crimea by 2014, the same year my brother died, and it was all unfolding during my visit.

"I pleaded with my father to listen to reason, to see that our Church was moving further away from the grace of God and being cruel to His children. He would not listen to me and said, 'Maybe you are a faggot like your brother. Maybe you are just like him. You are corrupted in your heart. You have left the True Church for the Church of the West. Sending you to America was a mistake. You have become defiled.'

"That night, after dinner, I made my arrangements to head back to America. Because of the battle now raging in Ukraine, this was exceedingly difficult. I had booked a plane out of Russia that would leave in a week's time. As I lay down in bed, my chest began to hurt. My throat felt constricted. I thought I was having a heart attack. I was able to call for help and I was taken to hospital. They stabilized me and it was discovered that I had been poisoned. Was it by my father? The Krest? Is there a difference? I do not know. I was able to meet with a Catholic priest at the hospital and he arranged for safe passage out of the country as there was a plot to arrest me after I was released. I did not make my flight, instead I was taken to Poland by automobile and then I flew out from there back to the States. Once I returned, I made the appeal to the Roman Church to be received as a Melkite priest. The process was lonely and difficult, but I was eventually brought to this parish, where I am a Russian serving Greeks in Greek under the authority of Rome. It is the same liturgy but a different language, a different culture, and yet the same altar.

"Now I live here peacefully with my family. I do not engage in these things, which may make you call me a coward, but my father already took my brother from me. I will not allow him, Putin or Kirill to take their father from my children. This is why when you appealed to me that you wish to save your brother, this I understand; if I could have saved my brother, I would. This would have been a worthy thing to die for, but with him gone, I will not die. If you wish to go die, I bless you in your endeavor and I pray it will be a righteous death."

With that, Maximos took a sip of coffee. Nadya was crying. This surprised Caspian because he had yet to see her show this kind of emotion. With all the pain, suffering, and death around them, she had remained stoic until now.

"Do you know where your brother is?" Maximos asked.

"I do," Nadya said, handing him a piece of paper with the address written on it.

"This is the headquarters of the Brotherhood," Maximos said without emotion.

"I thought you said you were staying out of it." Caspian looked suspicious. "How would you know that?"

"I said I was staying out of it, not that I was an idiot who wouldn't know where his enemy lies." Maximos took another sip of his coffee. "I would be quite foolish not to know. Of course I know. As I am certain they keep eyes on me, I keep eyes on them."

"We have to stop them," Nadya said defiantly.

"Dear child." Maximos walked around his desk and knelt before her. "You cannot stop them. Not any more than my brother could stop them. Not by yourself, anyway. The Republic is not for one person to save. It has always been the People's and it is for all of us to save if we are able."

"How do we do that?" Nadya felt tears welling up in her eyes again.

"The way that lies are always defeated." Maximos pulled a handkerchief from his sleeve and handed it to her. "With the truth. The weapon of Putin and Kirill has always been lies. They lied and said people like my brother were evil, a danger to society. So Pussy Riot stood up and exposed the truth; they were cut down for a time. I spoke truth; I was poisoned. But we must continue to fight for truth, each in our way. I am fighting by raising children who will do better than we have done. You are fighting to save your brother. There are those fighting in Russia by protesting; there are those fighting in Ukraine with farming tools. The time has come, my dear friends, to beat our plowshares into swords."

"Do you really think the war is coming here?" Caspian asked.

"Brother, it is already here. They are already here; recruits of the mind and of ideology." Maximos was preaching now. "Russia began by pumping misinformation into Ukraine. They fought each other, a war by proxy at first, and then when Putin felt the sovereignty of Ukraine was weak enough, he attacked. But patriotism was stronger than he expected."

Nadya shuddered.

"What?" Maximos asked.

"I just hate that word," Nadya said.

"Learn to love it, child. Don't despise it because these white nationalists, these terrorists, have coopted it. Patriotism and nationalism are not the same evil. If Russia is to win this battle, it will not come by way of these far-right fools hoping to align with her but because those on the left roll over and say, 'Take our country, it is a stupid country, a bad country, we have no use for it. This can't possibly be worse than it already is.' This nihilism has been the devised plan of the Kremlin all along. Putin is a mad genius hell-bent on the destruction of democracy and decency from the inside. He wishes for us to cut our own throats and then he will rush in like a ravenous dog to gnaw at our bones. With his misinformation campaigns, he has bolstered a false kind of patriotism on the right and so weakened any love for country on the left that both are willingly handing the nation over into the hands of Tsar Putin, one by way of a fake news war paint known as nationalism and the other by defeatism."

"Father, may I ask a question?" There were still a few details Caspian hadn't worked out.

"I believe you just did." Maximos chuckled. "But you may ask another."

"Why Rome instead of appealing to the Greeks or Antiochians?"

"Because, my dear father, Russia is attempting to poison the whole barrel," Maximos replied. "You see, the Ecumenical Patriarch, there is no one to replace him. There is some fear that he may be the last Patriarch of Constantinople unless some things change. Orthodoxy is tearing at the seams; this is what Putin and Kirill wish for because they will be the last men standing. They will become the Orthodox Church. I chose the safe route."

"So do you not truly believe in the papacy?" Caspian asked a third question.

"I believe in living. In seeing my children's children. In being there when they graduate college. In not missing life." Maximos took a breath and then pointed to the door. "With this, I must ask you to leave. Not because

I do not love you but because I must protect the next generation. It is your time to die, not theirs. Go, I bless you in your efforts; die with brilliance and grace."

Maximos walked them down the hallway and the presbytera had baked them some bread with some cold cuts and cheese. The two visitors apologized for the intrusion and returned to the car.

"Just for the record," Nadya said, looking at Caspian, "I am not planning on dying."

Caspian looked right back at her. "Yeah, me neither."

CHAPTER TWENTY

Kyle was standing in the kitchen fuming about something. In his mind, everything was beneath him and no one could see his true value. He had joined the Brotherhood because he felt that they shared similar ideologies, but he did not feel as if they were able to see his real potential. Things were stagnating and he had ideas that could move this process along. He was tired of being told, "Wait and see." He had waited. He had seen. The time for action was now. As far as he was concerned, the Second Civil War began years ago when this country chose to elect Barack Obama.

"It's called the White House for a reason," Kyle used to say to anyone who would listen. "It's not that I am racist; I am ethnocentric; everyone prefers to be with their own kind. That is just science."

He was sick of seeing American cities burning to the ground and protestors blocking streets. He would run them all over if he had the chance, but he knew he was more important to the cause on this side of the bars. Of course, why would he be behind bars and not these animals who block roadways? Because the liberal elites and fake news media sided with these monsters. They wanted to see America destroyed. They were running us straight into a communist dictatorship! To avoid this, he believed America needed to align with the Russians. And with Russia on their side, that also meant China would back them. He hoped that these nations could help us prevent our downward collapse into totalitarianism.

Boris had finally made his way back to the compound and Kyle hated it. He liked almost everyone except for Boris. The others took him seriously and thought he was important. Not Boris; he treated him like he was a child and incompetent. He felt it was for this reason that Boris had asked him to stay behind to keep an eye on the prisoner instead of joining everyone for their super-secret meeting in town. They were the generals and he was just a pawn, a foot soldier in the war to end all wars. He would show them all what he was capable of. He knew they wanted to dispose of Jenks, but none of them dared to do it. They were too weak of stomach to do what needed to be done. Not him. He could do it. He would do it. Then they would all see that he was more than just some silly babysitter and gopher. He was strong and powerful. They would see.

"Kyle!" Boris shouted from the other room.

"Yeah!" Kyle shouted back, popping his head around the refrigerator. "What?"

"We are leaving. We will be back in a couple of hours." Boris had walked closer to the kitchen, so there wasn't so much shouting. "Don't forget to check on the prisoner, logical things."

"I am not a baby." He shrugged. Boris started walking toward the door with about ten other men and as soon as they got outside with the door shut behind them, Kyle muttered, "Or a babysitter."

He walked out of the kitchen and into the living room area of the house. He sat down on the couch for a few moments and flipped through a few channels, but nothing interested him. He was walking back toward the kitchen to grab a beer when he heard a thud come from the room where they were keeping Jenks. He closed the refrigerator door without retrieving his beer and unholstered his gun as he started walking down the hallway. When he got to the door, he tried to open it, but it wouldn't budge because Jenks was in front of it, along with the chair to which he was tied. It took Kyle a couple of tries to push the door open. He kicked Jenks twice in the stomach before picking him and the chair up then dragging him by the chair toward the center of the room.

"You are a fucking idiot," Kyle said, spitting in Jenks direction. "You know, I said we needed to get rid of you a while ago. It isn't like you've been much help. Now that we've got you out of the way, you really aren't of any use to anyone. Just another liability, in my opinion."

Jenks had many things he wanted to say to Kyle, but he couldn't. They had his mouth taped shut. What frustrated him about his current situation was how much it was like a bad movie. He did think that, to their credit, using zip ties instead of rope was a brilliant move. Something he probably would have complimented them on himself if they didn't have his mouth constantly taped shut. It was not as if the zip ties were more comfortable than a rope or handcuffs; they were just more difficult to escape. *True masterwork,* he thought to himself often, unable to express anything else except for internal screams that echoed out into the void of his mind. Compliments on their unique style of imprisonment were not what he wished to express to Kyle at this moment.

"You got something to say?" Kyle said, looking down at Jenks.

Jenks nodded. He was smirking under the tape, imaging Kyle removing the tape so he could speak his piece. He hadn't eaten in days and he was imagining biting Kyle's ear. It was not that he particularly enjoyed the idea of eating human flesh. He would have savored the moment of shock on Kyle's face. First, he wouldn't believe it. The pain would take a few moments to set in. Then he would begin to feel a warm trickle down his neck and he would reach for it. He would place his hand along his veins and then pull it forward to inspect his hand. There would be a lot of blood on his hand and he would instinctively check his ear again. Some of it would still be there and he would slowly finger the rough ridges where the other part used to be. This is when he would scream. It would be a delayed scream that only shock can induce. *They can reattach it,* Kyle would think, like they did with that Bobbitt guy's dick. He would lunge at Jenks to open his mouth. This would be the moment that Jenks would relish. Just as Kyle would begin to lean down to pry his mouth open he would make a big dramatic gulping sound and motion with his neck before sticking his tongue out to prove that he did swallow his ear.

"Well, too fucking bad." Kyle laughed. "No one gives a shit about what you think."

Realizing that Kyle had no intention of removing the tape from his mouth, he had to come to terms with the fact that he would not be enjoying rare ear for dinner. What if he threw himself backward and smashed his head on the desk behind him? He would probably begin bleeding pretty badly if he aimed right and hit the edge. Sure, Kyle had said he wanted him to die, but did he mean it? *I mean I am still alive,* he thought. Maybe they would have to rush him to the hospital. They hadn't gotten anything out of him yet and they had tried everything. On the first day, they went all Operation Iraqi Freedom on him and did a little waterboarding. That didn't work.

On the second day, they removed one of his fingernails. That also didn't do the trick. Jenks had been a nail-biter from childhood and he had done some considerable damage to his digits himself. By the third day, a little electro-shock therapy. It was during this that he began to devise the ear-biting fantasy. He had imagined at first that it was Boris and then Orlov; now, at this moment, it was Kyle. Not because he thought Kyle was anything special, it could be anyone really. He didn't discriminate. On the fourth day, they just left him in his room for hours. It had blackout curtains and it was completely dark. He couldn't tell anymore what day it was. He had fallen asleep at some points but wasn't sure for how long. He did have his first wet dream since high school. But the dream didn't involve any ear biting.

"You know," Kyle said, "you've got some real hate in your eyes. That's the problem with all you leftists, just so full of hate."

Jenks didn't consider himself a leftist, whatever that was supposed to mean. He had been a registered libertarian since he could vote. He didn't always vote that way. It was a mixed bag. He and Nadya had debated about it a lot. But at this moment, as Kyle paced around the room with his gun, rambling back and forth about stolen elections and the liberation of the white Christian male, he was pretty sure he was going to register as a democrat when he got out of this, just to piss these fuckers off. *What is that?* he wondered. *Is that hope? Goddamn, that is hope. I actually think I am going to get out of this. Fucking hope and change, motherfucker.* Then the thought of the ear thing popped back into his mind. This was what was getting him through the whole thing. The only thing he couldn't wrap his brain around was the cartilage, it seemed like it would be chewy and maybe he couldn't get it down. He would swallow it anyway, but what if he choked? What a fucked-up way to go, making it all this way and then dying of asphyxiation just as he was on the brink of escape. Maybe this was a foolish plan. Then again, the hieromonk always said he was a fool, but it sounded like a compliment. Without knowing it, Jenks had become hyper-fixated on Kyle's ear. He wasn't sure how long Kyle had been ranting; he just kept looking at that delicious-looking appendage. Just seven little lbs of pressure and pop goes the ear.

"The fuck are you looking at?" Kyle shouted.

Jenks sort of blink stuttered his way out of his trance on Kyle's ear and then shrugged in his direction, unable to respond any other way. With that, Kyle placed his Glock against Jenks' forehead and made an explosion sound with his mouth. Kyle shook his head, turned toward the door and turned back to Jenks again. He slowly lifted his gun into the air with his arm completely erect.

Fuck, he's going to Wyatt Earp this shit, Jenks thought. *This can't be good.*

When he died, Jenks wondered if it would be a happy ending kind of death where you are ushered off into some fluffy clouds and then are greeted by your grandmother. Maybe it would feel like endlessly floating through a void. Maybe there was nothing. He would just be having all these thoughts and internal monologue and images of chewing on the cartilage of Kyle's ear and then, suddenly, nothing. He wouldn't even be aware of the nothingness of it all because there would simply be nothing. No more consciousness, no more thoughts: just gone. People would mourn him and he wouldn't know. They would attend his funeral and he would have no awareness. Then again, perhaps he would be reincarnated as a bear. One day, Kyle would be going on a walk through the woods of the Amerirussian Federation at the Tsar II Nicholas National Forrest; Kyle would lean over at a river to splash some water on his face. In that brief moment of blindness, bam! The reincarnated Jenks the Bear would jump out of the woods and chomp right down on Kyle's ear. *I bet a bear wouldn't have any trouble chewing through cartilage;* he was confident of that.

Kyle slowly lowered the gun down towards Jenks' face and then the gunshot echoed through the entire house. In most neighborhoods, this would have resulted in someone calling the police. Instead, they were surrounded by hundreds of acres of forest, and if a gunshot goes off in the woods and no Karen is there to ask the local neighborhood association Facebook group if that was gunshots or a firework, did a gunshot really go off? Jenks was momentarily aware of himself still having consciousness. Is it possible that consciousness remains just long enough until all oxygen is cut off from the brain? That would be an interesting thing. You are just there; your body is technically dead. You have no heartbeat or pulse, but for a while, your brain is still active. Your eyes can still see. You watch as the EMTs arrive and check your pulse. You are dead, someone would say. That is weird; *I am not dead,* you think to yourself, but you can't tell anyone you are thinking it because you are dead. You just aren't brain-dead yet. And then nothingness. Or Nana is waiting at the Pearly Gates with an apple pie.

Kyle reached for his chest and felt the warm blood trickle through his fingers. He looked down at the gushing liquid in surprise for a moment. He had so much potential. He was supposed to see this revolution through to the end and ascend to the throne someday. He was supposed to stand at the edge of the balcony of the West Wing and look down at the America he had helped to make great once again. Kyle had always wondered what his soul felt like. Was it what helped him feel sad or happy, pain or pleasure? Was this sudden dark tugging feeling floating in his chest his soul? He kept having this sensation like a falling dream stuck on a loop. He hit the ground and Nadya was standing there behind him.

She rushed over to Jenks and hugged him. Caspian flipped open his knife and began to cut the ties around Jenks' hands and she ripped away the tape from his mouth. He was so excited to be able to breathe and speak that he didn't even think once about biting anyone's ear. Jenks was crying uncontrollably with the shock of his rescue. He fell over into Nadya's arms.

"I love you," he said, weeping.

"I know," she said.

Jenks reached over for Father Caspian. "I never expected you to do all this."

"Going after the ninety-nine to look for the one is kind of our gig." Caspian shrugged.

"We've got to get out of here," Nadya said to Caspian.

Caspian and Nadya lifted Jenks up. He was a mess. He had visibly taken more than one beating and was having trouble standing. Though no one knew it at this moment, he was dehydrated, had three broken ribs, and his shoulder was dislocated. He had also urinated all over himself on more than one occasion, so he smelled rather rough. No one had allowed him to bathe unless you counted the waterboarding and he had that ripe onion smell of body odor. They made it into the hallway cautiously, afraid that someone would come barging into the house at any moment.

A gurgling noise rose from behind them, faintly sounding like, "Father."

Caspian turned around to see Kyle lying on the ground, reaching toward him.

"Father," he said again, still reaching.

"Don't," Nadya said.

"We can't leave him suffering," Caspian pleaded.

"The fuck we can't," Nadya protested.

Caspian walked over to Kyle, who was now a very pale color. He looked suddenly much older, now on the brink of death. Yet, simultaneously, Caspian couldn't help but notice how young this man was.

"Father?" Kyle said again, blood dripping from the sides of his mouth.

"Yes." Caspian's voice had changed. He sounded very much like his old principal, Father Kevin, had sounded that day in the hospital as his Amber was leaving. It was a tone reserved for the dying and bereaved. "I am here, my child."

"I'm not baptized," Kyle pleaded.

Caspian looked at Nadya. "Get me water, please."

She reached into her backpack and pulled out a water bottle. She popped the cap off before handing it to Caspian.

"Are you truly sorry for all the sins you have committed?" Caspian asked.

Kyle looked toward where Jenks was leaning against the wall and said, "Yes."

"Do you renounce Satan? And all his works? And all his empty promises?" Caspian continued.

"Yes." Kyle was fading quickly.

"Do you believe in God?"

"Yes." Kyle was losing focus.

"I baptize you in the name of the Father." Caspian hurriedly poured water over his head. "And of the Son." He poured water a second time. "And of the Holy Spirit."

The third time he poured the water Kyle grabbed Caspian's hand, which caused him to drop the bottle. Kyle could feel that falling dream sensation again. He couldn't lift his head any longer. He was now very aware that he couldn't move anything anymore. Not his hands or his feet or even to close his eyes.

"Is this my soul, Father?" Kyle asked. But before Caspian could answer, he was gone.

I suppose at that moment Kyle knew the answer to the question of who was right in all of this. Was there a Heaven? A Hell? Purgatory? Tollhouses? Nothingness? Was it the Muslims, the Buddhists, Protestants, Catholics, Orthodox, Scientologists, or atheists that figured it all out? Had Caspian truly, in this last moment, forgiven all his sins and washed them away in the waters of baptism? Had Kyle been truly penitent of all the right things? In those last moments, did he genuinely have thoughts of repentance for all his wrongs, the cruelty, the attempts to steal others' rights away? Had he been sorry? More importantly, would it be enough to wait until the last minute like this without any opportunity to make amends in this life? Would he be damned to roam the earth in chains like Jacob Marley? Those answers lay with Kyle on the ground.

"Was that necessary?" Nadya asked.

"Even in times of war," Caspian said, "we attend to the wounded on both sides. Otherwise, are we any different than them? He is God's to judge now."

"I hope He calls me as a witness." Jenks laughed briefly until he realized that made his broken ribs hurt all the more.

Nadya and Caspian carried him out to the car. They laid him in the back seat and he sipped on some warm Gatorade like it was the best meal he had ever had. To the surprise of everyone, there was no gunfire as they made their exit. There was no high-speed chase off of the compound. In Nadya's mind, they were going to make it to the car, and, just as they were about to escape, they would suddenly be met with floodlights and they would be surrounded. Large men with guns would approach the vehicle and they would be detained. Maybe that would have been the end of it all and they would have died in a blaze of glory or they would have bested their enemy and gotten away. It was supposed to be more complicated than this, but it just wasn't. They drove for quite a while until they were off the property and then they were on the highway. Then, like the dog that caught the car, they had no idea what to do next.

"What do we do next?" Caspian asked the obvious question.

"I thought you two had a plan," Jenks coughed out.

"Rescuing you was the plan." Nadya shrugged. "We didn't have a plan after that."

"I'm not sure we thought there was going to be an after that," Caspian interjected.

"There almost wasn't an after that for me," Jenks said, looking at Nadya. "You know that bullet went straight through him. You could have hit me."

"Oh, here we go." Nadya rolled her eyes. "You were just rescued, on your deathbed, and you have a fucking opinion about how you could have done it better. Let's recap that you are the one who got in over your head, got caught, brought in a novice, and needed rescued. And I didn't shoot you, did I?"

"No." Jenks conceded.

"But it was close; I am on Jenks' side about that." Caspian smiled at Jenks, but it quickly faded when Nadya brought him back to reality.

"Don't think that you are out of the dog house just because we successfully saved him." Nadya shot Caspian a glare.

"Shit." Jenks jumped in, "What did you do?"

"Just a disagreement," Caspian deflected.

"Bullshit." Nadya looked at Jenks in the rearview mirror. "He's been the sleeper cell this entire time. We brought the enemy along with us."

"What did you do?" Jenks said, looking at Caspian and then, looking back over at Nadya, "What did he do?"

"Oh fuck," Nadya gasped.

Up ahead of them was a roadblock. Nadya looked behind her in the rearview mirror and there was an unmarked car that was, without question, a cop. They hadn't turned their lights on, but they were straddling the yellow line. The woods on either side were dense with those same types of pine trees that had been on the compound. If it had just been her and Caspian, they might have had a chance to make a run for it into the woods, but Jenks was in no position to be running from the cops. This was quite literally the end of the road. They were trapped. Nadya had made it up to the roadblock; then the truck in the front hit their flood lights. *There they are,* Nadya thought to herself.

There were guns pointed at them from every direction and someone over a loudspeaker demanded that they get out of the car slowly. Nadya was having difficulty seeing because of the bright light, but then she noticed that one of the official-looking people was wearing an FBI field jacket. Suddenly, she felt a little less scared. At least this wasn't just the local police; that gave her some level of reassurance. She got out first and then Caspian followed, both with their hands raised.

The man with a bullhorn said, "Nadya Nichols, Caspian Anthanos, you are under arrest."

"We've got a wounded man back here," Nadya shouted.

The officers ran toward them in slow motion. Time stood still as both Caspian and Nadya looked at each other. Their hands moved from the air to behind their backs. The same style of zip ties they had just moments before released Jenks from now imprisoned them. Medics attended to Jenks as Nadya was taken over to a separate car than Caspian. An officer placed his hand on Caspian's head and lowered him into the back seat. For the first time in nearly a week, the two were separated.

As an officer walked Nadya past Caspian to a separate car, he said, "Do you know your rights? Would you like me to read them to you?"

"Yeah, I would love to hear my rights," she said. "I'm a woman, so it should be a pretty short list."

As Caspian heard her say this, he knew those words were not for the officer as much as they were for him.

CHAPTER TWENTY-ONE

The officer slammed the door to the back seat of the cruiser, which caused Caspian to jump a little. He had never been in the back seat of a cop car before. However, this was not his first time in a police cruiser. One year, a number of the clergy of his diocese had been invited to the citizens' police academy, a two-day event held by the local police department to try to build community engagement. Riding in a police car was not part of the schedule of the citizens' academy, but Caspian had struck up a conversation with one of the officers after the first day and he invited him to drive along. He enjoyed the entire experience a great deal. The day was filled with several events: a look at the evidence room, a tour of the detectives' unit, and the grand finale was a routine by the police dogs. They jumped through hoops and even took down one of the cops like they would a criminal, except the officer was wearing a padded outfit.

"This is how we catch criminals," the commanding officer said at the event.

"Suspects." A voice came from within the crowd.

"Excuse me?" the officer had replied. "Who said that?"

"Emily Papadelias, public defenders' office," Emily Papadelias from the public defenders' office said. "They aren't criminals, they are suspects. Just because you catch them doesn't make them a criminal."

"The suspect," the commanding officer said, slowly annunciating every syllable. "This is how we catch the suspect."

The commanding officer did not find any of Emily Papadelias from the public defenders' office's commentary very amusing, which had brought her tremendous amusement in return. The officer rolled his eyes and swapped suspect for criminal for the rest of the police dog routine, but the word seemed to taste very bitter to him as he said it. It was clear that the commanding officer didn't want to catch suspects; he enjoyed catching criminals. On the day of that event, Caspian had agreed with the commanding officer. Emily Papadelias from the public defenders' office had put a damper on the whole affair, and now the commanding officer was cross. He didn't even laugh when Sergeant O'Malley the Patrol Pug, the mascot of the police dogs unit, ended the show by also taking down an officer, I mean suspect.

Even though Caspian had found Emily Papadelias from the public defenders' office rather annoying on the day of the Citizens Police Academy, he suddenly wished he had her number now that he too was a criminal. He could have used someone in his corner who realized he was just a suspect.

There are many differences between driving in the front seat and the back seat of a police car. The first thing you will notice when you are in the back seat of a cop car is that there are no door handles. They have those in the front of the vehicle. The back seat doesn't have real windows; they have windows that have metal grates over them, so you can't escape. The final thing you might notice is that they don't have seat belts. All of these realizations were causing Caspian to feel quite claustrophobic about the whole being captured thing. Whether he was a suspect or a criminal, it didn't matter; he was in the back of a car without a seatbelt, windows for escaping, and door handles, and his hands were being involuntarily held behind his back.

It was not a great day.

Another observation that Caspian made as he sat alone in the car was that, since he didn't have any seatbelt or windows that could open or a door that could open, should they get into a car accident, he would have no way to escape. He would bounce around in the back of the cruiser as his bones would break and then just have to lie there at the officers' mercy to decide to let him go. None of this felt particularly like freedom or liberty. His mind then began to play out the scenario to its fullest extent. What if he moved from being a suspect to being a criminal? He would go to prison. Then he would also be stuck in another place with no exits and no knobs for him to turn to come and go as he pleased. Once he was released, he would be a felon. He imagined it would be pretty challenging to continue working as a priest after that. He would likely be defrocked anyway. He couldn't vote, own a gun, or find a job. The situation looked rather dire from the vantage point of the back of a cop car.

The door slammed shut. He jumped. The officer opened his door and sat down, immediately putting on his seatbelt. *Lucky bastard,* Caspian thought.

"Women," the arrested officer said. "Y'all are some lucky bastards, Padre."

"Excuse me?" Caspian asked as he was a bit jolted by the officer pulling him out of his thoughts and back into reality.

"I said women, am I right?" The officer chuckled. "Then I realized y'all are lucky bastards, you priests; you don't have to get married. So you wouldn't know."

Caspian realized that the officer must have been referencing Nadya. More specifically, he was referencing what Nadya said to her arrested officer when he asked about her Miranda rights. She responded to the officer, "Yeah, I would love to hear my rights. I'm a woman, so it should be a pretty short list." It seemed that the officer who was now driving Caspian away to the police station must have taken personal offense to what Nadya had said. This was, of course, silly because even though she said those words to the other officer, those words weren't for him; they were directed at Caspian. Maybe it was directed at both of them. Or really all of them. The whole collective of men who held the power.

Even while sitting in the back of that cop car, Caspian still had more rights than Nadya did. He still had more privilege than she did. They were both, at this moment, being momentarily stripped of their rights as they awaited to see what charges would be levied against them. This was a new feeling for Caspian, the sense of powerlessness, of feeling trapped, of not being able to escape, of wanting to run but fearing what another man might do to him if he did. He had never had these feelings before until now, trapped in the back of this car, wholly uncared for and without protection, at the whim of what other men would think of the decisions he had made.

"I did it to protect myself."

"I was just helping a friend."

"I felt our democracy was being destroyed and I had to act."

Would any of this be good enough justification for his actions? He wasn't so sure.

On the other hand, Nadya knew this feeling of powerlessness and fear all too well. She had felt it for as long as she could remember. From the first time her father disregarded her or her uncle hugged her in a way that did not feel familial. Caspian walked down the street with his eyes pointed directly forward, always marching through the world with absolute confidence. Not Nadya; she looked over her shoulders with her keychain clutched in her fist and each little key poking through her fingers. Caspian had never done that. Had never been taught to do that. But he had undoubtedly said things from the pulpit that contributed to the culture that created a world where Nadya had to. And not just her but countless others throughout all of human history.

The conversation that Nadya and Caspian had right before arriving at the compound kept rushing through his mind over and over. He couldn't respond now; he was stuck in the back of a cop car. Would this count as cruel and unusual punishment, he wondered. *I'm sure that's not what the founders meant when they wrote about it, but this was pretty cruel and unusual, having an unfinished conversation with someone and now you are both in the back of separate cop cars, unable to finish your debate.*

Caspian kept thinking about how their drive to Florida had been remarkably peaceful. Maybe it was the fear of sure and certain death that gave them a serenity just to enjoy the moment, or perhaps the twenty questions just settled them into such a sense of familiarity and nostalgia that there wasn't any room for fear of sure and certain death. Whatever the case might have been, they had made it from Georgia to Alabama and then to Florida without a hitch. It was a lovely time between two now very close friends.

After several hours of twenty questions, they were both running out of original content to ask. If they'd had access to their phones, they might have been able to Google lists, which would have helped them come up with fresh ideas, but that was not an option. They instead had to rely on their brains. The secondary dilemma was the fact that their relationship was clearly platonic. As a general rule, games like truth or dare and twenty questions are designed to help teenagers make out or get naked. Those are the unspoken rules of such a sport. However, Caspian and Nadya were not attempting to get each other naked and so there was an entire line of questions that could not be asked. Nadya was not inquiring about Caspian's shoe size any more than he was asking what color underwear she was wearing. The most risqué question that had been asked so far was when Nadya inquired about how many sexual partners Caspian had. She promised to keep it a secret, however.

"How many kids do you want one day?" Caspian asked while laughing off Nadya's previous answer about some innocuous point that he could not remember now.

"None," she said quickly.

"You never want to have kids?" Caspian was surprised.

"Who are you to judge?" Nadya laughed, pointing at his collar.

"But you are a girl," Caspian said plainly.

"The fuck does that have to do with it?"

"Well, most girls want to have kids." Caspian seemed very serious about his surprise.

"Not me. I got pregnant once and they couldn't get it out of me fast enough."

Often pundits will pontificate about the dangers of echo chambers. They will say how important it is to surround yourself with opposing viewpoints. There is certainly some value to this advice, but there is also something to be said about community as well. When we find community or a chosen family, people who share our ideals and principles, we avoid many societal pitfalls. When we are with our people, we can speak freely and without judgment. This happens because the communities we build are based upon the foundations of mutual care and concern for one another in the shared ideas we collectively hold. Nadya had begun to feel that sense of community with Caspian over the last few days and that caused her to let her defenses down and be a type of vulnerable with him that she had not been with anyone in a long time. When we use the word intimacy, we often think of it as a sexual term, but it really just means closeness. That is precisely what Nadya had begun to feel with Caspian and he with her: closeness. Because of this closeness, she forgot who he was and what his position stood for in the broader scope of society. The sudden chill that entered the vehicle when she said, "They couldn't get it out of me fast enough," was palpable. The icy feeling was so thick that she could feel goosebumps rising up her arms and legs. She patiently waited for Caspian to say or do anything that would indicate that he was, at a minimum, understanding.

"I see," Caspian said calmly.

It wasn't exactly outward violent protests outside of an abortion clinic, but his words stung like he had just shoved a billboard of an aborted fetus down her throat. The words themselves weren't patently cruel and the tone lacked a particular zeal to be called judgmental. It was something else entirely; it was disappointment. It was that tone teachers use when they know you didn't do your best or when your parents find out that you did something you weren't supposed to do. It isn't quite judgment; it's more "I thought better of you than this." Maybe that hurt more than judgment.

"What do you see?" "Nadya asked while holding back emotion.

"I see." Caspian was searching for other words. "I understand."

"What do you understand?" Nadya asked.

"I understand what you did." Caspian was desperately trying not to be cruel.

Caspian didn't want to judge Nadya. He wanted to love the sinner but hate the sin. He cared deeply for her, but that changed nothing about the profound disappointment he felt in his soul as she just so nonchalantly spoke about discarding the sacred life she had in her womb like it was common trash. Being a parent is a sacred duty and a child is a human life. How could she do this? This entire time he had gotten to know her everything she did was about protecting another human at all costs. How could she not see that this was the same thing? She was charged with protecting the precious life inside her; instead of doing that, she had been the very thing to cause that child danger. It didn't make sense to him at all. It seemed so out of character. He couldn't understand it. In that sense, he supposed he had lied when he'd said, "I understand," because the truth was he did not understand.

"Actually, I don't understand," Caspian said.

"How could you understand?" she snapped back at him. "But honestly, why should your understanding matter? Do you have to sympathize with everything in order for you to care about it? You have to have experienced the thing for someone to be considered equal to you? Empathy isn't a fucking thing they teach in seminary?"

"Listen," Caspian shot back at her, "I'm not judging you, okay? Everyone makes mistakes."

"The mistake would have been having a baby!" Nadya was yelling now.

"A baby is never a mistake," Caspian shouted back.

"You don't think Hitler was a fucking mistake?" Nadya was ready to smack him if he said no.

"Hitler was a grown-up who made adult choices to be evil."

"Do you know where grown-ups come from, genius? They start as babies." Nadya rolled her eyes.

"So you think your baby was the next Hitler? Is that what you are saying?" Caspian had a look of disgust on his face. "What if he would have cured cancer?"

"That is your brilliant comeback? That my zygote might have cured cancer?" Nadya was almost laughing at this point. "Even if that were true, some corporation would just buy the patent and prevent it from being released. Give me a fucking break. You are so goddamn naive."

"I'm just saying if you had a baby today, you might feel differently." Caspian put his hands up like he was retreating. "But what is done is done."

"That's such a bullshit copout, Caspian. That is like the 'but I will adopt your baby' couple. They think it sounds so fucking clever. It's not clever. I don't want to have stretch marks and my hips expand and lose function of my urethra just so some dingleberries from the suburbs can feel better about themselves. And I sure as fuck don't want to be forced to do it." Nadya was the one doing the preaching now. "You all think it's so clever, just have the baby anyway, maybe you'll like it. Maybe you can give it to someone else if you are heartless, does that really sound clever to you? I can go through all of those body changes and trauma and possibly die in childbirth so that your conscience can be clean—about what? My own personal choices about my own body. Fuck that. And fuck you. So I can go home and lie in bed bleeding until my boobs experience letdown."

"What's letdown?" Caspian blurted out, almost as surprised as Nadya that he asked it.

"You don't know what letdown is and you think you have any fucking right to have an opinion about my body or my choices?" Nadya slapped the steering wheel to let out some of the rage and then started to laugh uncontrollably. "I bet you think we pee out of our buttholes."

Caspian sat silently in the car for a few moments as Nadya laughed. He was confused. He wasn't sure if she was testing him, pranking him, or just wanted him to feel stupid because he was almost certain that they peed out of their buttholes.

"This is a trick question, isn't it?" he asked.

"Jesus fucking Christ!" As quickly as the fit of laughter overtook her an equal rush of somberness befell her. "Who did you vote for in 2016?"

"I don't see why that's anyone's business," Caspian said.

"Fucking hell, Caspian, who did you vote for?"

"The pro-life candidate," he said flatly.

"Say his name," Nadya said through her teeth.

"I didn't vote for him; I voted for his policies. For the Supreme Court Justices he would appoint. I voted for my party's platform." He paused. "I voted my conscience. I voted with the principles of my faith."

"You know what was missing from your little list there, Caspian?" A single tear bitterly fell down her cheek that she slapped away with contempt. "Freedom. You didn't vote for freedom."

"I just—" Caspian started to say, but Nadya cut him off.

"You just what? Didn't think it would matter? Why? Because you knew that whatever was going to happen wouldn't affect you, so who gives a fuck, right? Everything we've had to fight this entire time together has been to undo the hateful rhetoric of that man and Putin behind him."

"But I agree with you on that!" Caspian spoke over her. "I don't think the insurrection was all right; I do think that what happened was wrong. I did wear a mask, mostly. I got vaccinated. It's not like you think. You can't paint everyone with the same broad brush like that."

He began to try again at his lock-picking kit. It had become his way of disassociating from all the complicated feelings and thoughts, not just this conversation but all of the chaos. He was vigorously trying at one of the padlocks that were dangling from a loop. He wasn't having any more luck with this lock than he had with the deadbolt.

"Caspian, you'll never be able to pick the lock," Nadya said.

"Why is that?"

"Because you'll never be an outlaw, you'll never be one of us. You don't have the magic." Nadya was visibly shaken. "You can't break the lock because you are one of the pillars that uphold the powers of oppression."

There was so much more he wanted to say to her, but those were the last words she said to him as they turned onto the compound. The game of twenty questions had finally come to a bitter end and this could have been the last conversation they would have before they rushed into the headquarters of the Brotherhood and the Krest. Now, as he sat in the back of this cop car, those words just rang and rattled around in his brain.

Nadya was right. He should have been able to have empathy. Being here in this cop car, without any way to escape, he realized that his entire future was gone: his career, his education, his freedom in an instant, a man took all of that away from him. Now he was trapped. Except there was a way he could be free. He could get an attorney, make his case, and his freedom could be given back to him. His rights, his future, his education, and his career. He had a choice, to plead guilty or not guilty. To take his chances with the system he was given. His body was trapped in a car; he couldn't imagine if his prison was his own body. No way to appeal, no way to get a second chance at freedom. No opportunity to plead his case.

"I am the enemy," Caspian said out loud to himself.

"That a confession there, Padre?" The officer laughed.

"Yes," Caspian responded.

"Well, you can save it for the detectives. We are here."

The officer took his seatbelt off and exited the vehicle. He walked around to where Caspian was and pretended that the door handle was stuck. *This guy really thinks he's funny,* Caspian thought. The officer helped him out of the cruiser and they walked up into the main waiting area. Caspian didn't see Nadya, but he could feel her presence there somehow.

"Would you like me to take those zip ties off, Padre?" the officer asked.

"I would like you to take them off Nadya first," Caspian said.

"No can do, Padre; she is a dangerous woman," the officer said, nodding toward the room where Nadya was being held. "But aren't they all? Then again, you wouldn't understand. Lucky bastard, Padre. You are one lucky bastard."

Caspian was a suspect. Nadya was a criminal.

CHAPTER TWENTY-TWO

When Nadya and the arresting officer pulled into the police station, she was supposed to feel afraid, yet she couldn't help but laugh at how much the place looked like the station from *Twin Peaks*. It was a long single-story brick building with twin glass doors. It had never dawned on Nadya before how much schools and police stations looked alike until now. The officer opened the door for her and she walked into the reception area. It was even hokier on the inside than she could have imagined. The walls were lined with cork boards holding wanted posters and other information pamphlets. There were two hallways on either side of the reception area and above the entrance to the hallways was a sign in large gold lettering: "In God We Trust." *How appropriate,* she thought. Though she had seen some FBI field agents at the sight of their arrest, she was now a bit nervous not to see any of them here at the station. She didn't particularly like the idea of being in the hands of the local police. The officer led her down the hallway to the right and placed her in a room.

Nadya waited there for the better part of thirty minutes. Whenever she heard someone walking up or down the hallway, she wondered if that would be the moment someone would finally step in. The anticipation of it all was giving her extreme anxiety. After all, they had been through it: kidnapped by a monk, car chases, trapped in a dungeon, and shot at on more than one occasion; none of this had scared her as much as being zip-tied and waiting to see how this was all going to turn out. She began to imagine what it would be like if this were just a dream.

The door would open and a man in a trench coat would walk in. He would apologize for the wait while removing his coat and placing it on the back of his metal chair, revealing a black suit with a thin black tie. He would kindly remove Nadya's handcuffs; since this was a dream it would be seemingly more appropriate to have handcuffs than zip ties. Once removed, she would rub her wrists as one does when your handcuffs are removed. Then the agent would take his seat before pulling out a notepad. A knock at the door would startle them both and a receptionist would pop in with a coffee pot and two mugs. The agent would then offer her a cup, which she would refuse, and he would pour himself a glass.

"Lucy, excuse me for saying it, but that is a damn fine cup of coffee." Before letting the receptionist go on her way, turning his attention back to Nadya, the agent would say, "I am Special Agent Cooper. It seems you've gotten yourself into quite a mess."

Then a phone would ring in the room; Agent Cooper would stand up to answer it. A man would be heard yelling over the other line. He would then pace back and forth as they spoke for a bit. Finally, Agent Cooper would say, "I agree, Chief Cole," before hanging up the phone and returning to his seat.

"It seems to all be a mix-up, ma'am. Just a little bit of paperwork and you will be on your way." He would take one more sip of coffee. "That hits the spot. You really should have a cup before you leave."

A knock on the door jolted Nadya out of her fantasy. She looked up to see a man standing there in khakis with a white polo shirt. His badge and gun were visible on his belt and he was wearing a blue baseball cap with FBI in bright yellow letters. He was not nearly as cute as the television characters in her mind. He did not have a cup of coffee and did not offer to remove her zip ties. Instead, he sat down, rolling through some paperwork and files.

"Do you realize how much trouble you are in?" the man asked, looking up at her over his glasses.

"Who the fuck are you?" she asked, but she also answered her question in her head. *I didn't get Cooper; I got Rosenfield.*

"All right," the agent said, folding his hands and placing them on the table. "I am Special Agent Turner with the FBI."

"Do you have credentials?" Nadya demanded.

Agent Turner removed his badge from his belt and dropped it on the table. He wasn't particularly interested in this level of hostility, but he had anticipated it. "Good enough for you?"

"What am I being held for?" Nadya asked.

"Right now?" Agent Turner looked at his paperwork. "Nothing more than your safety. What could we hold you on? Murder. Breaking and entering. Murder again. Destruction of private property. Destruction of government property. Grand theft auto. Denying a direct order and blowing through a red light, disrupting a presidential motorcade. Aiding and abetting a fugitive. Failure to report a crime. Failure to report a murder. Failure to report an auto accident. Dereliction of duties. Leaking classified information. Stealing classified information. Violation of your federal contract. Conspiracy. Treason. And unpaid parking tickets."

"That's all?" Nadya smirked.

"Listen," Agent Turner said, "I want to help here. You got in over your head; your friend was hurt and scared;

I get it. I have a partner too and if he were in a mess, I would do what I could to help him. But at some point during all of this, you should have thought, *I am in over my head. Maybe it's time to bring in the authorities and let them handle it.* You chose not to do that, which is why we are in the pickle we have found ourselves in today."

Nadya's mind was still wandering. This was just too much to process; worst of all, now she wanted coffee. She also knew that the coffee would never taste as good as it did in her mind. She was also concerned for Caspian. She was sure he was far more afraid than she was in this situation. This was not her first time being interrogated by high-ranking government officials, but it was probably Caspian's first. Then there was the issue of Jenks. Was he also in trouble? Was he at the hospital? She looked over at Agent Turner and got the impression that he wasn't the kind of guy who would be willing to answer any of these questions if she took the time to ask them.

"No," she said.

"No?" Agent Turner said back.

"No, I didn't at any point think that any of you would be helpful in our attempts to save Jenks." Nadya said pointedly, "Quite frankly, this is the first time I've been scared during any of this. I don't trust you."

"Well, you are going to need to find some trust real quick"—Agent Turner was clicking the button on his pen repeatedly and Nadya wanted to stab him with it—"because how this meeting goes will determine many things concerning your future. Do you understand that?"

"I understand some of that," she acknowledged.

"What do you not understand?" Agent Turner was getting annoyed.

"I understand that we are zip-tied because we wanted to save someone from harm. Are the leaders of that militia group back there tied up?" Nadya pointed her head in the direction she felt the compound must be, but she wasn't sure why she felt that way considering her bearings were all off. "I can go ahead and answer that question for you, no. You never arrest those guys, at least not until it's too late. You wait until the mass shooting or the next assault on our democracy. They just blast off at the mouth with their hatred and vitriol and write their manifestos and you just let them. You wait by until someone is dead and then still do nothing."

"That is inaccurate," Agent Turner protested.

"When you catch them, you just let them go or give them slaps on the wrist!" Nadya was not quite shouting, but she was getting close. "Those guys that wanted to kidnap that governor, they were going to fucking kill her, but somehow that is protected. These guys meet and have training exercises to overthrow the government, the will of the people, and what do you do to stop it?"

"We are monitoring the situation," Agent Turner shot back.

"Monitoring until the next January 6th? Monitoring until the next kidnapping of a government official? Monitoring until the next slaughtering of innocent people buying groceries, going to the mall, or worshiping their god in the safety of their sanctuaries? The next school shooting?" Nadya was now shouting. "And when does it end? Are you just planning to monitor them until this escalates to the point of no return? Until they get their apocalypse?"

Agent Turner stood up for a moment and walked towards the corner of the room to collect his thoughts before turning back to Nadya. "So in your perfect world, we would just round them all up, arrest them, and send them off?"

"Yes," Nadya said without any hesitation.

"Miss Nichols"—Agent Turner returned to his seat—"there are hundreds of groups like the Brotherhood all over this country accounting for thousands of disgruntled individuals. Many of them are just blowing off steam. If we were to arrest them all, what do you really think would happen? Don't answer that. I will tell you what would happen. We would play right into their persecution narrative and whatever you fear would happen because of what they fear would happen."

"Bullshit." Nadya was indignant. "We are supposed to just sit by as they plot and plan. Then you do nothing, the president does nothing, Congress does nothing, and these leaders continue to stoke the flames of discord in our country until the bottom falls out. That is where we are heading. Jenks was on to something, I don't know what, but he found something that scared him enough he felt he needed to expose it or run from it."

"Your friend Jenks felt that he found evidence of Russian sleeper cells active in the United States." Agent Turner mindlessly flipped through papers. "He felt that these groups were working closely with some of the militias. We are working to corroborate these claims."

"So you can do more nothing?" Nadya asked.

"So that we can follow the rules of law and order, Miss Nichols." Agent Turner rubbed the bridge of his nose. "You may not like the process, but there is a process. We are a nation of laws and we can't just go around doing whatever we want."

"Unless you are a militia attempting to overthrow our government through a civil war?" Nadya was full of questions. "If I say we are militia can we go home?"

"That is your opinion. But we don't see it that way." Agent Turner stood up and said, "Please excuse me for a moment."

Nadya was not thrilled about being left alone for another indefinite amount of time, but there was nothing she could do about it. Agent Turner exited through the door and walked down the hallway until he reached another room. Upon opening the door, he found Jenks sitting there with his partner.

"I'm sorry to keep you waiting." Agent Turner said to Jenks, "You are correct; Nadya didn't find anything."

"I told you I kept everything hidden." Jenks took a sip of coffee. "No one knew except for me."

"Except," Agent Turner observed, "you were taking the information to someone."

"Listen, I was doing the best I could with what I had at my disposal at the time." Jenks was being cautious with his words. "If this weapon got into the wrong hands, I can't even imagine the effect it would have on society."

Agent Turner looked at his partner. "And you will help us understand this weapon if we let your friends go?"

Jenks nodded. Turner looked at his partner, who gave a shrug of affirmation.

"I think we can work with that." Turner exited the room, made his way down the hallway, and opened another door. He looked inside to find Father Caspian sitting there.

"I plead the Fifth," Caspian said defiantly.

"I'm sure you do." Agent Turner smiled. "Just hang tight."

With that, he shut the door and made it the rest of the way down the hallway to where Nadya was waiting. He sat back down at the table and clicked the pen again. He could see the eagerness on her face to disarm him.

"What happens now?" Nadya wished she was no longer tied up and began to squirm in her seat. "Not just to me, but to Jenks, to Caspian?"

"You will be afforded the same privileges of law and order that these groups you hate will be given." Agent Turner stood up and walked around to Nadya's chair and cut the ties. "We will investigate, we will determine if any crimes were committed, and then we will proceed from there."

Nadya rubbed her wrists. "And the Brotherhood? The Krest?"

"We will continue to monitor the situation," Agent Turner replied calmly.

"Are we free to go?" Nadya asked.

"For now, yes." Agent Turner passed a piece of paper over to her. "I will need you to fill this out. There will be some other procedural things we will need to do. But then you will turn over your clearances before returning home to somewhere we can find you once we are ready to make a determination in your case."

After what seemed like multiple hours, Nadya was released. She walked down the hallway and found Caspian waiting for her in the reception area. Before they exited the door, she noticed a small table with a coffee maker on it with little Styrofoam cups. A little red light on the maker indicated there was hot coffee in it. She walked to the coffee table and poured herself a cup without asking permission. She took a sip and thought, *Damn fine cup of coffee.*

"Everything okay?" Caspian asked and Nadya just turned around, gave him the thumbs up, and walked back over to join him.

The night air outside the police station was humid and the sound of crickets and frogs could be heard coming from a retention pond behind the station. Nadya lit a cigarette and stood there with Caspian in silence for a while. The feeling was similar to their moment outside the Waffle House; it felt peaceful but also transitional.

"Twenty questions," Caspian said to break the silence.

"Okay." Nadya laughed. "You first."

"I'm sorry," Caspian said earnestly.

"For what?" Nadya wasn't going to let him off that easy.

"I should have had sympathy, but I think I found a bit of empathy in the back of that cop car," Caspian said, shuffling his feet. "I didn't mean to be the bad guy, the enemy. I see that I was and I am sorry for that."

The doors to the police station opened and Jenks appeared. He stumbled his way over to the two of them. Nadya and Caspian were a bit surprised to see him as they had assumed he would have been taken straight to the hospital. Then again, the police rarely do the right thing when they want something.

"Oh my God!" Nadya said, running toward Jenks. "Are you okay?"

He waved his hand in protest of all the gushing, "I'm fine. I promise."

A black car pulled up to take them away. It looked similar to the vehicle waiting for Caspian and Nadya that evening on the tarmac. For a moment, Caspian wondered if this meant that they would take a similar journey of intrigue back toward the cabin in the woods. It all seemed like a dream at this point; nothing seemed real. For a moment, he imagined the three of them in the woods at the cabin. Him standing there at the edge of the pond, wearing a red plaid shirt and jeans. There is no church, no responsibility. Nadya walks up behind him and brings him a cup of coffee. He follows her inside to prepare some bacon on the cast iron skillet. It would be the perfect escape. Just let it all go, run away, and never look back.

"Do you want to come with us?" Nadya asked sincerely.

"No." Caspian shook his head. "I mean I would love to, but I need to stay here to face whatever it is. I have to face the bishop and figure out what the rest of my life is going to look like."

"It's an open invitation." Nadya smiled.

Jenks began making his way toward the black car. "It was good to see you again, Father. I can't thank you enough. If there is anything I can ever do, I owe you."

"There is one thing," Caspian said.

"Just name it." Jenks smiled.

"What did you find out there that scared you so much that all of this was worth it?" Caspian asked.

"Anything but that." Jenks shook his head.

Caspian gave Jenks a stern look, the kind that only fathers can, and it caused Jenks to look back at Caspian like he was drawing something out of him that he didn't want to give.

"What I am about to tell you I need you to consider it like a confession. You must take this to your grave." Caspian nodded in the affirmative towards Jenks before he continued, "All right, the Russians are developing a weapon. Something so powerful and dangerous it would fundamentally change everything we know about warfare. This whole time we've been worried about nukes. How funny that we've been so terrified of a nearly hundred-year-old technology that we haven't been looking toward the future, just always looking up to the sky waiting for the mushroom dome. Then we started to fear the thought of cyber warfare; what if they shut down our grids? What if they closed the banks? We've feared everything except for this."

"What is it, Jenks?" Nadya pleaded.

"For lack of a better explanation?" Jenks said. "Mind control."

"Shut up." Nadya laughed.

"I wish I was joking." The seriousness of Jenks' response caused the laughter to fall from Naya rather quickly. "You know every single time you hear a story about some guy who ran down the rabbit hole into some conspiracy and the paper always says, 'He was such a nice guy. A family man. Then, one day, he killed them all.' The Russians have been embedding this stuff into their misinformation videos, subtle bits of violence, and then, one day, they just pop. But they seem to have figured out how to streamline the process to the point that just one telephone call and they have control; they can make you do anything: kill a government official, your own family, yourself."

"Jesus," Caspian gasped. "Nadya...."

"The Doctor," she responded. "Jenks, I think we've already seen this in action."

"Then we are further along than I had feared." Jenks turned back toward the car. "I'll leave you two to say your goodbyes."

They watched as Jenks made his way to the car and disappeared inside. They stood there in the beauty of the silence for a moment. Nadya just stood there smoking her cigarette and blowing smoke in unison with the crickets' song before Caspian broke the silence.

"It's weird knowing what's coming and everyone else is just walking around, blissfully unaware"—Caspian reached for Nadya's cigarette and took a drag—"that, at some point, this is all going to activate and turn into something. And everyone is just out there watching their TikTok videos and tweeting and doom scrolling Facebook, and then one day, without warning, the whole world will turn upside down."

"It's always been upside down, Caspian." Nadya took her cigarette back. "Wars and rumors of wars."

"Matthew 24:6." Caspian looked impressed.

"Yeah." Nadya shrugged. "The world has been lighting up forever. There is always a war, a conflict; we've just always found comfort in that the conflict, the war, is way over there. It's happening to kids you will never see, people you will ever know. It's scary all over the world and now it's our turn to face the music."

"I'm going to miss you," Caspian said.

"I mean I was a pretty great presbytera if I say so myself." Nadya laughed.

She began to walk toward the car. "I guess this is my ride."

"Nadya," Caspian said as she reached for the door, "what do we do next?"

"Tell the truth," she said to him. "As Maximos said, that's the only thing that can dispel the lies."

"Whom do we tell the truth to?" Caspian was feeling rather lost with Nadya making her way into the car.

"Whoever will listen," she said. "Bye, Caspian."

"Bye, Nadya." Caspian waved.

He reached into his pants to call an Uber and was suddenly aware that he still didn't have a phone. He wasn't so sure he wanted one ever again. He was beginning to enjoy a feeling he hadn't felt since the '90s: being unable to be found. Just then, a man walked out of the police station and started walking toward him; it was Agent Turner's partner. He was a tall fellow with a trench coat, which was pretty odd considering the heat and humidity of the place.

"You need a ride, friend?" the man asked.

"Yeah," Caspian said as he followed him. "That would be great."

"Know anywhere we could get a good pie around these parts?" the man asked.

"Not a clue," Caspian said, "I am not from around here."

"Damn," the man in the trench coat said as they drove away.

CHAPTER TWENTY-THREE

"In the early evening hours of April 14th, 1912, the RMS *Titanic* hit an iceberg. This should not have been a newsworthy event. The *Titanic* was supposed to be designed to take any number of brutalities; it was an unsinkable ship. The iceberg pierced the side of the mammoth jungle of manmade innovation and the unthinkable happened. The ship began to fill with water and the boat that was designed never to be destroyed crumbled in a matter of hours. In the years leading up to the ship's maiden voyage, countless people, from engineers to steelworkers, constructed what was believed to be a masterpiece of human ingenuity. People from around the world traveled to see it and folks from every station of life boarded the vessel: some for the prestige and others to begin a new life across the sea. Before the fateful events, warnings had been sent out to the captain and crew to alert them to the calamity that lived in the water, but those attempts were ignored.

"Some have theorized that had the *Titanic* decided to take the iceberg head-on, it would have avoided the catastrophic events that followed. Instead, the captain decided to avoid the iceberg instead of confronting it. This decision resulted in a small nick in the steelwork that quickly flooded the entire ship.

"As the ship sank, much like society, the poor and marginalized suffered first. There weren't enough safety nets in place to save everyone on the ship, so the first-class passengers were able to secure safe passage away from the destruction. Those who were poor, slower, or deemed too old were left behind to suffer the consequences of the bad decisions of the leaders and investors who promised that something like this could never happen. They truly believed that they were safe, but that safety was shattered in an instant.

"When the ship began to go under, people responded in many different ways: some jumped ship so they could take control of their own destiny rather than wait for fate to deal them the final blow. Some attempted in vain to pump water out of the ship. Some prayed—others played music. Mothers lay in bed with their children to shield them from all of the fear so that their last little moments would be of peace before the rushing waters of the apocalypse finally found them. There were people who said, "I will see you soon," as their loved ones were lowered on rafts, but they broke those promises. Then, from the safety of their lifeboats, the affluent watched from afar as the lights flickered, the boat sank, and the cries of the third-class passengers screamed for help. Finally, there was darkness and silence at sea as the final chilling moments of the impossible became a reality.

"The iceberg does not, in and of itself, seem intimidating. The small noses that stick up from the sea appear lovely, but the danger is not in the nose but in the body that lies under the depths. The strength of the iceberg is found under the water, in the parts we cannot see. As our climate changes, both in reality and as a society, icebergs are breaking away at an alarming rate. Our seas are no longer safe, much less safe than they were in the spring of 1912, yet we keep treading these waters thinking we will be safe.

"I have seen things that assure me that we are not safe. Much like those who sent out telegraphs on that fateful evening that the *Titanic* met its watery grave, I am here to warn you that we must learn two things from the *Titanic*: first, we must face these icebergs head-on. We cannot avoid disaster by pretending it doesn't exist by attempting to veer and change course at the last minute. By then it is too late. We must crash head-on into the danger of the iceberg in hopes to save us all. That is the answer. We can no longer sit idly by hoping that we can reason with the iceberg or that it will stop being an iceberg if we debate it. We must confront the iceberg. We must use the ship we have been given as it was designed to be used, not to improvise. This ship of democracy and the sturdiness of our Republic is predicated upon the idea that we will use the mechanism of it to be bold, not to call timidity peace. The second thing we must do is decide where we are on the ship. Are you the captain who could have done more? Are you the musicians playing music to calm the fear? Are you the privileged one who will always have a lifeboat no matter which way the storm goes? Or will you be the mother locked away in the ship with no exit, reading stories to her babies while the ship sinks?

"My dear friends, we have already hit the iceberg. The crack is already in the hull of the ship and we are taking on water. We are now at 11:40 PM on April 14th, 1912. We have less than three hours left until the ship hits the bottom of the ocean to become a cautionary tale. A blip in history. That is how fragile this American experiment is.

"On the last day of the Constitutional Convention of 1787, a woman asked Benjamin Franklin, 'Well, Doctor, what have we got, a republic or a monarchy?' To which Franklin replied, 'A republic, if you can keep it.'

"We now stand at the very edge of exchanging our republic for a theocracy, replacing our president of the people with a new king: a tsar. Do we have a republic? A monarchy? A theocracy? Have we appointed a new tsar and replaced our Congress with a Duma? No, we have a republic if we can keep it."

Caspian took a deep breath as he finished reading these words. He could see Nadya wiping her eyes as Jenks sat there solemnly. Caspian was surprised by how alive the cabin looked and he longed to be there with him. Instead, they were only together by way of technology.

"I think it's beautiful," Nadya said.

"Do you think it will make a difference?" Caspian asked.

"Not a chance." Nadya laughed.

"I didn't think so." Caspian smiled back.

"I still think you should do it though," she said reassuringly.

"I agree," Jenks interjected. "We have to do the right thing, even if we aren't heard, even if the ship still sinks, even if it means we lose it all in the process."

"All right, wish me luck," Caspian said.

"Luck!" Nadya and Jenks said together before the screen went blank.

Nadya walked around the room for a moment, picked up her copy of *Chicken Little* off the coffee table and went outside. She had installed a hammock out back by the pond. It had a perfect shady spot under the little tree that rested at the water's edge. She curled up with a cup of coffee, opened her phone, and pushed call. Two bright little faces popped up on the screen.

"Hey, Auntie Naddy!"

"Hey babies." Nadya wiped away another tear. "Can I read you one of my favorite stories?"

Inside, Jenks was sitting down at his computer to finally record that album he had always promised himself he would one day do. There seemed like no more important time than this moment to tell stories and bring moments of peace to the world. After all he had seen and experienced this music felt therapeutic to him. *Maybe if it can heal me, it can heal others,* he thought to himself.

He opened the Zoom call from his producer in Auckland.

"Hey, Karl!" Jenks said.

"All right, buddy, you ready to change the world?"

"Someone has to try," Jenks said with a smile as he picked up his guitar.

Then there was Caspian sitting again in the reception area of the bishop's office, waiting for another meeting with the hierarch. It was time to issue the warning, to sound the battle cry, to attempt to right the wrongs and hope that there was a future. Because that was all that one could hope for, a future. Not just one for himself but one for those who would come after him. He thought of Father Maximos and his children, Nadya's nieces, and the children in his parish; what would the world look like that he was building for them? The bishop opened the door.

"Come on in, Father," the bishop said with a smile. "Have a seat, old sport."

"Your Excellency," Caspian said as he took his seat.

The bishop walked around behind his desk and took a seat. As he placed his hands on the desk, Caspian could see that there was a printout of the *Titanic* parable he had written. He wondered if the bishop had read it and, if he had, did he read it as the pious bishop or had he read it as Nick? Those two people may have shared the same body but were two different characters altogether. One was capable of compassion and understanding; the other was only capable of self-interest. Caspian hoped that it was Nick who read what he wrote.

"You've had quite a few weeks," Nick said. "I can't even imagine all that you've seen. I am glad to see you are all right."

"I am fine." Caspian extended his arms as if to show he was in one piece.

"I see that." Nick chuckled. "And it seems you are a lucky man."

"How is that?" Caspian inquired.

"You should be in a great deal of trouble. But it seems that the FBI has decided not to pursue anything against you and your friends and the local police have also complied with this. I have even spoken with the Metropolitan of the Russian Orthodox Church of the Diaspora; he too wishes this all to be dealt with"—the bishop seemed to be choosing his words wisely—"to become a thing of the past. In a word, my dear friend, you have been absolved."

"I see," Caspian said suspiciously.

"If," the bishop said.

"If?" Caspian questioned.

"If you are willing to let this all go. No papers, no writing. Just look at this as having all been a bizarre dream and move on." The bishop stood up and began to look at his windowed wall. "Don't you think you were doing good at The Mission, Father? I would very much like to see you continue your work there. You could make a difference. From what I just read, that seems to be what you want to do, yes? To leave your mark and make a difference in the world. That is where the difference can be made for you. Not everyone has to grandstand and make definite proclamations; sometimes, the best action is taking no action at all."

"And if I want to take action?" Caspian asked cautiously.

"I certainly can't stop you," the bishop said. "It is a free country, after all. You can print what you wish and post what you want. But if that is the path you choose, then it is a path you must journey alone. I cannot allow you to do this in the name of this sacred institution."

"Sacred institution?" Caspian parroted back.

"Yes," the bishop continued as he paced. "The Church is a sacred institution, as is our government. Both are appointed by God. As the scripture says, 'Let every soul be subject to the governing authorities, for there is no authority except from God, and those who exist are ordained by God. Therefore he who resists the authority withstands the ordinance of God, and those who withstand will receive to themselves judgment. For rulers are not a terror to the good work but to the evil. Do you desire to have no fear of the authority? Do that which is good, and you will have praise from the authority, for he is a servant of God to you for good. But if you do that which is evil, be afraid, for he doesn't bear the sword in vain; for he is a servant of God, an avenger for wrath to him who does evil. Therefore you need to be in subjection, not only because of the wrath, but also for conscience' sake.'

"We are all subject to the governance of God, which flows equally from the Church and the state, you see. Both receive their power and authority from God. But when we rebel, we open ourselves up to judgment and fear. But the righteous man fears nothing. You must have faith in the system."

Caspian knew exactly what the bishop was telling him. That was the longest-winded shut the fuck up that had even been spoken. Yes, the bishop would likely never say it so directly, but that was the point of his little diatribe.

"Faith?" Caspian scoffed.

"Did you lose yours out there?" he asked as he turned back to Caspian.

"No." Caspian contemplated his following words carefully. "No, I reorganized it."

"How do you mean?" The bishop seemed genuinely fascinated.

"What do you know about Grigori Rasputin?" Caspian asked.

"That he was a fake priest who roamed through Moscow, wreaking havoc and helping destroy the dynasty. He fancied himself a healer but was, in fact, just a con man and a fraud. He had an affair with the empress, I believe, if my memory serves me right."

"That is what I thought too." Caspian gave an assuring nod to the bishop. "Then I learned a few things while on the journey. You see, Tsarevich Alexi was diagnosed with hemophilia. It's incurable and deadly. The tsar and his wife kept this secret from the entire Russian World, except for their doctors and Grigori Rasputin. The doctors tried everything but to no avail, and some say his symptoms only worsened. That is when Father Rasputin did something rash; he stepped out in faith and told the royals to stop listening to the doctors. The tsar thought this was insanity; he and the tsarina argued about it, but ultimately her faith aligned with that of Rasputin's and they won out. They stopped listening to the doctors and the boy improved."

"Faith healed him," the bishop observed. "A good lesson."

"No, accidental dumb luck healed him," Caspian shot back.

"Excuse me?"

"See, the doctors attempted to treat his pain and they used the most modern medicine: aspirin. But as we now know, aspirin is a blood thinner. There could not have been a worse drug on the planet for someone like Alexei to consume. So when Grigori told the tsarina not to trust the doctors, he turned out to be right. His blind faith bought the boy more time." Caspian sighed deeply, knowing that what he said next would be going too far. "But Alexei was going to die. Whether it was at the hands of the doctors, the blind faith of Rasputin, or the firing squad of the Bolsheviks, he was running toward inevitability."

"What is your point, Caspian?" Nick asked.

"My point is that the systems were flawed and God didn't stop it." He couldn't believe these words were coming out of his mouth. "The Church and the state, they have been appointed by flawed men who have made grave errors in judgment. Sometimes, they get it right by accident, as Rasputin did about the aspirin. But far more often than not we get it very, very wrong."

The bishop walked over to place his hands on Caspian's shoulders tenderly. "You've lost your way, old sport. I have got to take care of something downstairs. I will return soon and I want you to think honestly about something for me. You've got two choices: to put all of this behind you and remain a priest, fulfill your vocation. Or you can go back to being a peasant. Choose wisely, friend. As long as you are under the umbrella of my protection I can continue to keep you safe. Otherwise, you go your way and may God be with you."

The bishop exited to attend to some duties downstairs and left Caspian to wrestle with his thoughts. He had meant every word he had said to the bishop, but he also loved his job. The ability to help others, he had missed The Mission and his clients. Was it only arrogance to think he could make a difference by exposing something? Maybe this was the definition of vanity. He couldn't possibly believe that his speaking up would somehow make such a difference that he could end a war that was already set into motion. His thoughts were racing, so he moved about the office so that his body could keep up with his rapid thoughts. As he paced about the office he looked at the bishop's filing cabinets. They were the standard kind one would find at any office store, a sort of muted sand-grey color with little locks on them. As Caspian's eyes scanned them, he saw something unusual toward the bottom of the left cabinet. This one cabinet in particular, the bottom of it was hidden underneath the desk, but now that Caspian was freely moving about he could make it out clearly: there was a man with a top hat—it was the symbol of the Statesmen.

Caspian made a panicked rush to the bishop's desk and fumbled around until he found a paperclip. He quickly fashioned it into a device that looked similar to the ones Nadya had given him. He placed it inside the lock and made little maneuvers as she had taught him. Nothing happened. He could feel his heart pumping and sweat building around his brow. At any moment the bishop could reappear. And then he heard a noise. At first, he thought it was the clicking of the doorknob as the bishop entered, but it was not. He had done it. He had finally done it. The cabinet door slowly slid out and there were files inside. He did not have time to peruse them all so he quickly grabbed as many as possible. He stood up and reached around to shove them into his pants above the small of his back and then covered it all with his coat.

Then another clicking noise.

This time it was the doorknob and the bishop entered. Caspian was now standing safely on the other side of the room. But his body was in full-on fevered sweats at this point. The bishop made his way toward him and Caspian felt certain his heart would explode at any moment from the pulsating anxiety.

"Have you made your decision? Peasant or priest?"

"Outlaw." Caspian laughed.

"Outlaw?" the Bishop asked.

"An outlaw for an in-law!" Caspian was laughing uncontrollably.

"What are you talking about?" the bishop asked.

"Oo-De-Lally!" Caspian yelled. "Fortunes, forecast, lucky charms."

Caspian was in full-blown hysterics at this point. The bishop pushed a button on his phone and within a few moments security had arrived to escort Caspian off the property. Caspian could hardly contain himself as he made his way outside. Standing at the edge of the street he saw a cab driving down the ride. Not an Uber or Lyft but a good old-fashioned taxi. He lifted his arm into the air and the minivan pulled up to the curb. The driver pushed a button and the door slowly opened. Caspian lowered himself inside and sat down with relief.

"Where to, Father?" the driver asked.

"All Saints," Caspian said.

"The parish?"

"No, the bar."

EPILOGUE

APOCALYPSE

Kyle was facing up and his eyes were still open. His mouth was slightly ajar as if he was about to scream before his soul finally left his body. The blood that splashed across his face when he was shot had mostly been removed from the deathbed baptism he received from Caspian.

"There is something weird about that kid's face," Detective Lane said to his partner as he leaned in to have a closer look.

As soon as the face of Detective Lane was within a few inches of Kyle's corpse a loud and spooky noise rose up behind him. He jumped so fast that he ended up hitting his head on the desk in the room. When he finally found his bearings, he saw Detective McDowell laughing.

"Real dick move," Lane said as he rubbed his head. "You see these markings on his face? It's like someone cleansed him or something. If I was a superstitious guy, I'd think they were up to something. Something weird."

Detective McDowell pointed his phone toward Lane with the day's Wordle up on his phone. "I can't figure it out."

"Badge," Lane said flatly, still rubbing his head.

"Damn," McDowell said. "You're right."

"Why do you think his face is like that?" Lane asked.

"Who fucking knows?" McDowell was still looking at his phone, bitter that he hadn't gotten the word. "Maybe someone tried to clean up the scene and decided it wasn't worth it."

Two other figures walked into the busy house as the detectives were busying themselves with nothing. The room was mostly hushed as other officers moved out of the way giving Detectives Lane and McDowell a perfect view of the two FBI special agents who had now made their presence known.

"Hey boys," McDowell shouted across the room. "Who the fuck are you?"

"I'm special agent Turner." Then he motioned towards the other agent. "And this is my partner. I'm afraid the fun is over, kids. The grown-ups are here now."

"Wait just a minute," Lane said. "We are in the middle of an investigation here."

"And what have you discovered so far?" Turner asked.

"Well, someone tried to wash this guy's face to clean up the crime scene." Lane pointed at Kyle.

"Baptism," Turner said. "They didn't try to clean up the scene. The son of a bitch baptized him."

Without asking for anyone's permission, Special Agent Turner began to announce to the entire room, "Everyone, it's been a long night for you all, I'm sure. It's time to go home. We will be taking it from here."

It took a few minutes to clear the entire room and there was no end to the grumbling. When the local police got outside they saw that the FBI agents had set up a table with coffee and donuts. They all thought it was hysterical, but none were willing to say it out loud.

Back inside the main house of the compound, the two agents began to explore the place. Agent Turner's partner looked over at him and asked, "What exactly are we looking for?"

"I don't know," Agent Turner said, "but what I do know is this; if we don't find it, there are going to be a lot more long nights like this one, cleaning up bodies of dead kids fighting who think they are playing war."

No charges were ever filed in the death of Kyle. Of course, the FBI knew who killed him, but they let it go as a matter of national security. They also allowed the Brotherhood to eventually continue their activities at the compound. The Krest helped transform the property and, eventually, it was reopened as a summer camp for youth. Kids would travel all over the country so they could begin to learn about traditional family values and prepare for the coming apocalypse.

***

The night of Kyle's death, most of the Krest and Brotherhood members were in town meeting at the local Statesmen Lounge. After a long night of enjoying themselves rather thoroughly they returned to the chaotic silence of a crime scene. It was Orlov who discovered Kyle's body. At first, he felt compelled to reach down and hold him. Just as he was about to act on the impulse, Boris walked into the room.

"Do not touch anything," he demanded. "The prisoner is gone. It will only be a matter of moments before this place is swarming with cops. Follow me."

Orlov silently wiped away a tear and followed behind Boris. A few other members of the society followed as well. They made their way out of the main house and began to walk down the trail that led to the water. About halfway down the path, Boris took a sharp left into the thick woods and the others followed, except for Orlov. He stood there at the edge of the path, looking at a tree. He walked over toward it and placed his hand against the trunk.

"Amin," he whispered.

"Orlov!" Boris shouted. With that, Orlov picked up his pace to catch up with the others.

It was profoundly dark amongst the trees and a humid mist floated around the floor of the woods. Boris seemed to know where he was going, but the others kept thinking about how they had never before ventured to this part of the compound. In the distance, they could make out the outline of a small stone building. It was about 10x10 squared and had a wooden roof. The building appeared to be much older than anything else on the property. A large antique metal lock was hooked through an iron clasp on the door. Boris reached into his pocket and produced a black metal skeleton key. He opened the door and walked inside the dark building.

"Orlov," Boris said again, not shouting this time. Instead, his words sounded solemn, like they had entered a holy place.

The two men left the others behind and stood inside the tiny building. It smelled of mold and dirt and Orlov felt as if something was crawling on his arms. He was sure the place must be entirely infested with spiders. Boris lit a candle and the room illuminated to reveal a small wooden table with a briefcase. He slowly walked over to the briefcase and began to play with the combination pad until all three numbers aligned. He then placed both his hands on top of the briefcase and closed his eyes in prayer:

"Brother will deliver up brother to death and the father his child. Children will rise up against their parents and cause them to be put to death. You will be hated by all men for my name's sake, but he who endures to the end will be saved. Amin."

He then popped the mechanism and opened it slowly. He looked inside for a moment and then went to close the case again.

"Wait," Orlov said, putting out his hand to indicate to Boris not to shut it yet. "What is it?"

"The sword to divide neighbor against neighbor." With this, Boris opened the case and produced an unimpressive microchip.

"That is it?" Orlov was stunned. All this fighting and death was all so Boris could protect a microchip. For what?

"This, my dear Orlov, is everything. It is the weapon to end all wars. With this we can fight without weapons, convincing everyone to hate their neighbor and to dispose of their own children. It is more potent than a virus and more lethal than a thousand atomic bombs. If you want your enemy to kill themselves, we can do it. If we want to swing an election, we can accomplish it. Start wars. End wars. This little thing I hold in my hand is the coronation song of the tsar and will bring about the true destiny of the Third and Final Rome."

"Show me." Orlov was in awe at the power before him.

"Gladly." Boris grinned.

Boris reached back into the briefcase, pulled out a large set of noise-canceling earphones and placed them on his head. He then removed the microchip from its case and placed it on the side of his cell phone. A blue screen with a throbbing circle appeared on the phone. He placed his finger up into the air with anticipation and then slowly placed it on the circle. The tone began to play out from his phone. The blue haze that now filled the stone room seemed to mesmerize them both. Orlov slowly reached toward his side and pulled a large pocket knife from the leather case attached to his belt. He delicately opened it and placed the blade against his own throat. He sliced across his neck in slow motion until the blood rushed down his shirt without him flinching or saying a word. The blood flowed to the ground until he could no longer grip the knife, which fell to his feet. Then his legs gave way and his body joined the knife on the ground.

Slowly, Boris reached down toward the throbbing button, touching it lightly. The sound ceased and he removed the headphones and placed them back in the briefcase. Then he reverently removed the microchip from his phone and put it back inside the case. He closed the briefcase and locked it. Finally, he removed it from the table and began to exit, stepping over the body of Orlov as he walked. Before he reached the door he turned and leaned down to whisper his final words to his former friend.

"I hope you enjoyed the new algorithm, you fucking reprobate." Boris stood to his feet and spit at Orlov's body. "You really think we would let someone like you have a part in the new world we will build?"

Upon exiting the building, Boris commanded the others to burn it with Orlov inside. Everyone watched as the flames engulfed the small building; Boris raised his fist and proclaimed, "For the Fatherland!"

And the others cried out, "For the Fatherland!"

***

Father Caspian could feel the shake of the gravel under the vehicle with tremendous veracity. He dropped some of the papers he'd been holding onto the floor and the driver apologized for their bumpy entrance. Caspian gave the driver a cash tip and then exited the vehicle before making his way down the corridor to a large wooden door that seemed almost out of place. When he entered the building, he couldn't figure out if he was supposed to go left or right but finally chose correctly, entering a large room. Two people were sitting at a table in the corner, waving at him. He was excited to finally see them in person and he walked over with his hand extended.

"Father Caspian?" the man asked.

"In the flesh," Caspian responded.

"Do you mind if we move to this larger table? I have some other friends who will be joining us shortly." The man pointed at a large, round table at the center of the room and the three made their way around it.

"I am Leo; you know that from our Zoom meeting," Leo said, pointing first at himself and then to the woman next to him. "This is Alexandra; she will be keeping notes, if that's okay?"

"Fine," Caspian said, "of course."

Just then, a woman and man walked into the building. She stopped by the bar and was given a drink. The man refused a stiff drink, opting for a tall glass of soda water. They made their way over to the round table to take their seats.

"This is Joy." Leo continued his introductions. "And this is the man I wanted you to meet. He is our resident apocalypse expert. His grandfather not only helped spread apocalyptic theology but he was also one of the founders of the Statesmen, believe it or not. Patrick Thackery meet Father Caspian."

The two exchanged handshakes and pleasantries before the table erupted into everyone catching up with one another, excluding Caspian, who was entirely lost. He was stepping into a world that he didn't quite understand. He had never been a whistleblower before, so he didn't know what that was supposed to look like. But after meeting with the bishop and everything that followed, he knew he was making the right decision.

"To catch y'all up," Leo interjected, finally turning his attention back to Caspian, "Father C here and I have been meeting weekly for a while now over Zoom. He's got quite a story to tell and I think we should help him tell it."

Leo squinted before relenting to put on his reading glasses. He would never admit it, but the red light of the bar made it all that more difficult to read. He read aloud to the group some of the things Caspian had been writing. Everyone listened intently and would stop from time to time to ask questions. Joy reached over, picked up a pack of cigarettes from in front of Leo, and lit one. Caspian missed Nadya at that moment and wished she could be there. But this was the part of the journey he would have to go on alone. He sighed deeply and looked over at Alexandra with a smirk. "Well, it's been a long time since we've had a priest in the friend group. Welcome to the Panhandle Free Press, Padre."

Caspian looked around the table and watched as this group of friends moved intimately amongst one another, laughing and touching. Leo was recounting a story of a friend of theirs who had passed away. He lifted a pretzel in the air and cracked it in half like he was performing the ceremony of the Eucharist. Leo passed each piece to the two on either side of him. *This is Communion,* Caspian thought; *this is community. This is what it is all supposed to be about.*

He reached into his leather-bound briefcase and pulled out all the files he had been able to steal from the bishop's office.

"My brother, it's always my fucking brother," Joy said with a remarkably jovial sound in her voice for such consternation.

Leo began to fondle the pages and files, turning each one delicately. Then one stood out amongst the rest. There was an aged manila envelope at the bottom of the pile. Leo's heart sank. He slowly moved it out of the way to reveal words written in red across the top that said, "EVIDENCE." Alexandra reached for Leo's hand and held him tight. Joy stood up quickly from the table as if the thing was cursed.

"What is it?" Caspian asked.

"A story I haven't finished telling." Leo said, a single tear rolling down his cheek. "I guess the story is never finished."

Caspian sat there awkwardly as everyone discussed things amongst themselves for a while and then the night went on as if nothing unusual had happened. They played a game of darts and enjoyed a few more rounds. Eventually, everyone left except for Caspian and Leo.

"You need a ride?" Leo asked.

"No, I will be fine," Caspian said as they said their goodbyes and made their way outside.

"All right, I'm going to head out." The two clasped hands. "Between your notes, everything we've discussed, and now all this from the bishop, I think we have a clear story moving forward. I can't wait for the world to hear it."

Leo hopped into his car and made his way back to his office. He walked into the building and stretched for a moment, knowing it would be a long night. He walked over to a little desk built of old liquor boxes and looked up at a picture on the wall before setting the envelope atop the little shrine. He walked into his office broom closet, sat down at his laptop and flipped it open. He looked over at his notes and began to type:

The face of Sister Mary Margaret looked almost angelic as her frozen body lay outside the doorstep of The Mission.

Nathan Monk is active on social media…

Follow
@FatherNathan

to get updates

facebook.com/FatherNathan

twitter.com/FatherNathan

instagram.com/FatherNathan

www.CharityInstitute.com

About the Author

Nathan Monk is a social justice advocate, dyslexic author, and former Orthodox priest. He lives in Tennessee with his partner and three children. He is the bestselling author of *The Miracle* and *All Saints Hotel and Cocktail Lounge.*

Having experienced homelessness with his family during his teenage years, Nathan has gone on to help establish programs providing food, clothing, emergency resources, and shelter. When he's not writing, he works with nonprofits and local governments to battle issues associated with homelessness and poverty.

Nathan is also the founder of the Charity Institute, a consulting firm assisting nonprofits, and has served as a board member of the Homelessness and Housing Alliance, the Task Force for Human Services, and the Planning Board of the City of Pensacola. Over his career, he has received notable awards, appointments, and national media for his accomplishments in social justice, neurodivergence awareness, and writing.

Through writing and public speaking, he seeks to educate the public by breaking down stereotypes in our culture about people experiencing poverty and homelessness. His expanded educational programs and consulting work help create nonprofit cultures that are truly client-oriented. With a focus on outcomes over outreach, Nathan believes we can end homelessness and create a more equitable world for all.

Please enjoy this preview of
All Saints Hotel and Cocktail Lounge
Available wherever books are sold

Nathan Monk

ACT I

Two Thousand Nine

Chapter One

Creation

Do any of us start out as saints or sinners or is it just some accident of circumstance, childhood trauma, and maybe access to healthcare? I don't remember ever wanting to give a shit if I was good or bad. I just wanted to survive the next shift so I could pay my landlord's mortgage. Let's be honest; in the sainthood department, most of the best saints are really just naughty little sinners who are better at public relations than the heretics. Who are the sinners anyway? They are just the ones who the saints burned at the stake before they got a chance to tell the truth or at least their side of the story. When our collective trial by fire began upon being thrust into the world, I don't imagine any of us set out to be anything special. We didn't have a fucking plan. We were just a bunch of scared and overly zealous kids grasping for a future we had all been promised, only to find out when we got there it had been reverse mortgaged so our spawners could go on cruises and never retire, just for fun. We did everything we were told to do.

"Go to college so you don't flip burgers!" our parents would say in liturgical unison.

And all the politicians said, "Amen!" with raging boners over the interest we would be paying until the day we died of a preventable ailment.

In the beginning, we never even questioned why we disparaged the culinary artists who prepared our meals, nor did we anticipate that we would all soon be fighting on the same battlefield together begging for table scraps. Comrades in arms of a war we didn't even start. We were casualties of a massive game of Craps our parents were playing with the economy, betting their odds against our planet, our gains, our jobs, our education, our healthcare, our future. We were bitter millennials long before they even told us we had a title. No, we were just the accidental pregnancies, the third babies, a footnote to Gen X, wearing our siblings' hand-me-down shoes, and being told we would never compare.

This was the decade before Bernie would take all our communal rage and turn the hymns of the Occupation into mantras that felt like an authentic version of the hope and change Obama sold us. Even before we had the vocabulary to define our collective anger, we were itching to march somewhere, anywhere, even if we didn't know what the destination was. We needed a map, but we were too busy taking payday loans to finance abortions while telling ourselves that someday, maybe, it wouldn't feel like we would be bringing their grandkids into what felt like a third-world America. We wanted to die but were too afraid we would survive it and be stuck with the medical bills. Plus, someone needed to live long enough to pay off the good time our predecessors were having. So instead of immediate death, we substituted it with drinking our tips each night and chain smoking as a slow motion suicide.

We would spend our nights holding Council Meetings of the Dredges around the billiards table, hoping for a tomorrow that might turn our small coastal town into one of the metro cities to which we always said we would escape. Could Chicago or Nashville or New York City be hiding our potential in a little box, if only we could get there to find it? Anything other than this tourist trap we called home. Our community was nothing more than a piss-stop on the way from Texas to Disney World. We sucked on the teat of the providence of Interstate placement and just hoped to God that someone would become addicted enough to Grits-A-YaYa to maybe stay an extra night and tip us so we could pay the electric bill.

So we would convene at the only altar we knew, the sanctuary for the sinners, heretics, and concubines of the South; the ragtag band of dishwashers, hotel staffers, and spring break attorneys that lined the bar to drink to another successful day of surviving.

"The best damn thing we can hope for is a hurricane," Billy would grunt once a night as he would pour another round. "That's where the money is. No matter what anyone tells you, our industry is not the beach but Jim Cantore."

Everyone knew everyone. Everyone had fucked everyone. Everyone hated everyone. There was no new money in this town. No escape plan. No ladder reaching up or even down. We just floated en masse at sea level hoping not to drown in sin or bills. The same dollars circulated from the Walmart to the military base to the beach hotels and then back to thongs of the strippers at the Angels Gentlemen's Club, money just passing from hand to hand, neighbor to neighbor. There was no accumulation of wealth or prosperity. Even the rich folks were just poor illusions of having made it when, in reality, they were just little fish who were smart enough to escape the big ponds so they could play sharks in one of poorest puddles in the Union.

We all dreamed, but we knew there was nothing on the other side of any of this for most of us. We had all watched as our friends or enemies would escape, knowing full well that something would draw them back like the tide. Off they would run, only to be dragged by the neck back to the town they thought they were finally free from. We would watch them walk back into the bar like a revolving door with grand stories of lives lived outside of the confines of the grips of their conservative roots. New tales of adventures with new drugs, and new bars, and new bodies that kept them warm for a winter or two before the unceremonious return, just in time for the tent revival and altar call to be washed clean again, before becoming clerks at their dad's best friend's law office.

By nature of my Southern upbringing, I'm inclined to believe in something divine, damning, or at least superstitious. But as I look over the landscape of the destruction that followed us all as a generation, I'm less likely to believe there is any grand design or predestination—unless we truly are all children in the hands of an angry God. Nothing that followed over the last decade makes any sense if there is some creator orchestrating our steps. Why would anyone, divine or otherwise, wish this on anyone? But then I take a step back and realize the plan may not be divine, but it certainly was a plan. We are all just puppets in a masterful show for the entertainment of powerbrokers that will never know our names. We are nothing but broken creatures, ants under the magnifying glass of monsters hiding behind suits—Wall Street and Big Pharma and the Prison Industrial Complex. They somehow figured out a way to make our parents cheer on our destruction instead of our success.

We became the suspects, the terrorists living under their new roof, a marauding gang of anti-fascists ready to sell our souls for a couple of social media likes.

Yes, Mom, we did it all for the lolz.

What a laugh riot it has been to live under the highest inflation and lowest economy so we could pay into safety nets that would be consumed before we ever had a chance. We were all giving our lives in some way, over griddles with burger patties, in hallways of our schools to preserve the Second Amendment, or in deserts for you to fill up your SUV. Hell, there wasn't a single one of us that didn't know someone who had fought in Iraq and Afghanistan. They would return through that same revolving door. I sometimes wondered when they would replace the Vietnam vets on the street corners, panhandling on the Panhandle. "Never forget!" Oh, how we would forget their faces soon enough. They would be hidden under scruffy beards and ignored by the VA. Living in a military town, we knew all too well the song and dance. Just another cog in the machine of how our generation was being forgotten before it ever got a chance to begin.

When we weren't being slaughtered in our schools or oil fields, we were the unwilling guinea pigs of technology and possibility. The iPhone was still an infant as we came of age to social media just beginning to move cozily into our beds and bathrooms and relationships. We entered society as we were just moments away from occupying Wall Street and yet a decade away from burning Ferguson to the ground. Stuck somewhere between revolution and a nightcap. Everything filled with a calm rage just before the storm. Each morning waking up and wondering, “Is this the too far? Is this the moment everything changes?” and then ordering another crunch wrap supreme.

This was back when Donald Trump was still just a silly D-list celebrity firing people on television and seemed quite safely far away from being able to fire nuclear missiles.

Here we all sat at our circular table, the vagabond friend group. A collection of leftover misfits from high school with predestined failures to launch because there wasn’t any room left for us in the board rooms because our elders where too stubborn to vacate and make way for us. We could bring them coffee, though, at $7.25 an hour before going back to our apartment with six other roommates. That was super cool of them. But here they have no power over us, not in this dimly lit room filled with smoke circulating through the red lights.

Everything felt perfect in these moments of communal solitude. The five of us were more than friends and less than lovers. Tonight, we didn’t feel as powerless as the elders told us we were. We felt as if we could take over the entire world or maybe just City Hall. It didn’t matter, we had hope. This was the day we would crown our new leader who would carry us into a new horizon. This was Obama's inauguration. Barry came in and took us all by storm with hope. So much hope. Why did everything feel so goddamn hopeless then? Nothing felt like hope when we were still scraping by. At 25 shouldn't I be somewhere else by now? My father owned a home and was well into his second marriage to my mother by this age. Not me, I was scraping by just to not have to move back in with my folks. Only grit kept me living in an 8x10 room downtown with three other people. I felt like I should be worried about having kids or wasn't I still a kid?

It all seemed so disjointed and confusing. In spite of it all, we were swept away in this alluring and seductive idea: hope. Like sailors lured by a siren's song, we came running to the edge of our respective ships and jumped headlong into those waters and swam until our capillaries burst. This tempting serenade of hope and change rang like a promise, a simple promise, and we would sign our fate on a bar napkin, thinking we could make a difference.

So here we were, encircling that table and waiting to savor every moment of this victory. Five friends. One city. And a decision that would change everything.

If I am honest with myself, it all started that night. This was the moment when decisions would be made that would forever change the landscape of everything that would happen. A priest, a hooker, a journalist, a burger flipper, and our resident philosopher all walk into a bar. This was about to be the worst joke ever told and we didn't even know it. Nothing that followed would be funny at all. We just couldn't see it. Only three of us would survive, but we all died that night. There would be no resurrection. No absolution. It all started with the best of intentions. How soon we would find out what happens when mortals charge up Olympus.

Who will absolve our sins? Who will forgive our transgressions? I don't know if there are angels or God. But what I do know is we all found heaven and hell at the All Saints Hotel and Cocktail Lounge.

***

Shane was always the first or last to arrive. He never showed up in the middle. Sometimes he would get there before everyone because he wanted to set the scene. Other times, he would appear last because he had already made a scene somewhere else and needed to re-center himself with a sympathetic audience. He was a candle in the wind and there was no way to hold him down. There would be times when we didn't hear from Shane for a month or two. He would just disappear into the wilderness for a while to commune with the gods and nature and the idea of a woman who would replace for him the need for any other form of sustenance. Then, in an instant, he would reappear again out of nowhere. Our lives would be moving in and out and then he would just be there like Christ in the upper room.

He wrote for the local paper and was constantly certain that today would be the day when they would finally drop the axe on him. There wasn't a single day when he wasn't in some sort of trouble with his editors. See, Shane lived in the future, constantly making plans and sometimes following through with them. His plans' intentions could be gloriously shattered in an instant if something more interesting or beautiful appeared within his line of vision. That's why he missed my birthday last year. Her name was Emma. It was also why he missed New Year's Eve. He was in Egypt. He just disappeared and was gone and then here he was, swearing that he had voted before he left. Talking about how fascinating the world we lived in was. Excited to drink. Excited to party. Excited to be excited.

His hair was long and formed into accidental dreadlocks and he wore a hat that it was rumored he stole from Johnny Depp while visiting a comic convention in LA. He was skinny as a rail and looked always as if he was both coming and going. His style was like a newsboy had been attacked by your grandfather's closet.

When he walked into the bar, our eyes locked. I wasn't exactly sure when the last time I saw him was. He had been gone during NYE and BARE Ball and so it had been at least a month. He sauntered over to where I sat at the table, took me by the hand and lifted me up into a massive hug that defied his frame. He kissed me on the cheek and said, “Let me look at you!” like he was an old man. He cupped my cheeks in his cold hands and smiled even wider.

“Let me buy you a drink!” he shouted, laughing as he took me by the hand to the bar.

We leaned against the bar well waiting for our turn. Billy, the only evening bartender at our little watering hole, looked directly past the line of folks ahead of us and shouted his bartender’s greeting.

“Your usual, boys?” He was holding two tall glasses, one in each hand.

“Two!” Shane yelled back.

“What the hell?” Some guy who I had never seen before was at the head of the line and looking for a fight. “Wait your goddamn turn.”

Billy grabbed the guy’s hand. “You got cash?”

The stranger looked half paralyzed. “No. I … uh … I have a card.”

“Yeah, we are cash only.” There was a clear get the hell outta here hidden in the fine print of Billy’s statement. The guy pulled his jacket down like he was a badass from some teen movie and looked at Shane and me like he was sizing us up.

“Yeah, well, you just don’t even matter. You matter at some useless dive bar, that’s the only place you will ever matter. My dad—”

"Your dad is the milkman, you spoiled brat!" Billy shouted over the jukebox, and with that our new friend exited the building with a huff and a minor puff.

Billy turned back to us pushing our drinks toward us. "Good to see you, boys!"

"I was here yesterday." I smirked at Billy.

"Yeah, but it's not ever good to see you. It's only good to see the two of you. Where is the rest of the crew?"

"They are on their way." And with that, the conversation had reached its conclusion, so he turned around to write a line under our names on our tab. Shane and I made our way back to our usual table and took a seat.

Shane started to tell me all about Egypt, but it was less about the country or the Pyramids or museums and much more about this woman from Australia he had met name Mia. They found each other on the third night after he arrived. She was far more adventurous than he, which was almost alarming in the magnitude of a statement. The thought of Shane meeting his match enraptured me in the stories he weaved of late nights drinking warm wine along bustling market streets. Then, like all of his other romances, it ended with a plane ticket and a return to home base but never an exchange of email addresses or telephone numbers. Just flashes of continental experiences and memories that would morph into legends. It was always an honor to hear the first iteration of a tale so you could watch it grow from infancy into a full-blown Indiana Jones/erotica novel.

It would be unfair to paint Shane as a Don Juan. He wasn't just out there to seduce people. That wasn't even his intention. He was an explorer of life and all of the parts that make life savory and sweet. He didn't fly to Egypt for sex, he went to live, and it just happens that life often evolves to the bedroom. To him, sex was just an extension of a conversation. Admittedly, he had adopted this philosophy from Joy. She was the one who won the debate back in high school that changed everything for how Shane saw, well, everything. Now he lived life as a spirit experiencing the planet. Not free but free to live. He was trapped by the same things as the rest of us—a job, requirements, clothing, and food. He just chose to experience those trappings in a very different way from the rest of us. He didn't let these things encapsulate him; he made those things work for him. If he had to wear pants they might as well be plaid and if he must go to work then it might as well be the type of place that gave him access to more interesting people. As a journalist, he was allowed to ask and provoke and probe to his heart's delight.

I would be lying if I said that he hadn't slept with a lot of people. That was a very true statement. Some of them were famous and some of them served him drinks in Burma. He would start those conversations and ask the right questions and unwrap people so completely that often the natural conclusion would be that, once they were already this naked, they might as well consummate the experience. To him, the package a person was wrapped in didn't matter. He wouldn't fall for their gender or appearance but their mind. The fluidity of his romantic encounters was the benchmark of his ideology that the human experience is not defined by our limited understanding of social constructs.

It was so good to hear his voice again. I could stay there listening to his stories for hours. He didn't talk like other people. It wasn't just him regurgitating experiences. He wove the tales together by asking you a series of questions. You became part of the experience.

"Did you know that Egypt fell under Roman occupation?"

"Since we are on the subject of sex, are you seeing anyone?"

"Have you ever truly felt so completely satisfied by a meal that you could be content never to eat again, everything else would be consuming ash in comparison?"

And then, somehow, organically, he would tie that all back around to his story, his adventure, without it ever feeling narcissistic. You were fully engaged in the experience with him and him with you.

He suddenly stopped just to say, "I love you. You know that?"

"I know, man. I love you too." And he would take my hand again. He touched everyone. He was complete with everyone. And the worst part about it all was he really, really meant it. There was not a single bit of pretense or bullshit in any action that he took, except that promise that he would pay for the drinks. He would absolutely leave me with the tab tonight.

"Hello, boys."

We both turned toward the familiar raspy voice. There she was, our Joy. I hadn't seen her since BARE Ball. She was lovely as ever, but it also felt different to think that today. See, the ball was an annual NYE celebration for those of us who worked in the service industry. It was a massive event. One of the nightclubs in town hosted it. It was the only night of the year that they were ever closed to the public. On that night, everyone would file in like we were the talk of the town. We would rent tuxedos or buy dresses. It was an open bar and they always had an amazing spread with hummus and shrimp as big as your hand and a massive roast. We would eat and drink until midnight, some seven days after the actual turn of the New Year, and it would now be our turn to count down and make promises we wouldn't keep. It was our turn to be served. They would replay the ball dropping at Times Square and we would all pretend like we hadn't seen it yet. And then we would continue to drink all the way up until 2:00 AM and then order a cab and make our way back to All Saints to drink until last call.

It didn't matter that this routine never changed. It always felt new and full of possibility.

But as we raged into 2009, it seemed different. The Bush error was over and change was coming. We were a bunch of blue dots in a massive sea of red. Joy and I had volunteered for Obama's campaign all summer long. We made calls and took signs to people's houses. It was lovely and you couldn't help but feel electrified by the possibility that everything would now be different. Our country would soon be so different. The tide had finally turned and this young Black senator from Chicago had finally shattered the glass ceiling. We would finally see a Black man hold the highest office in the land. It seemed like we would be putting a period at the end of the sentence of racism that had held our country hostage for so long.

We couldn't have imaged then that, right here in our home state, just a few hours away, a young Black kid would be walking home with Skittles and a soda and would be gunned down; that this wound we thought was being healed would be exposed as not just a scar but as a gaping hole that had never even been sutured. We had all been living a big lie. We were fooling ourselves.

It certainly didn't feel that way as we arrived with our signs under our arms, placing them in neighbors' rights of way.

I also don't think I was expecting to see Joy the way I did that night. She wore a gold glittering dress that fit around her as if it had always been part of her form. It was built around her and she was made for it. We stood there watching the ball drop fully unaware of all the chaos that waited ahead of us and believing that hope and change were just two weeks away from transforming all the injustices into a river of justice that would flow down even into these swampy waters of the bayous around this little Southern town.

Five.

Four.

Three.

Two.

She looked at me and smiled. I don't think we had ever been this close to each other on fake NYE. She was always with someone. I didn't think she was there with me, but there we were together. Were we there together? I don't think I knew that. I mean I had picked her up and we had been hanging out the entire night. I hadn't asked her to come with me and she hadn't asked me. There we were, shoulder to shoulder, watching and counting and now looking at each other. And before I could say, "ONE!" the ball had dropped and her lips were pressed against mine and mine hers. We stayed there like that for maybe an eternity or possibly only a second. She pulled away leaving most of her red lipstick on me and she smiled.

"Happy New Year, Leo."

There she was standing in front of me now and I realized that we hadn't said a word to each other since the ball. I had failed to mention any of this to Shane as we discussed all his adventures and mine. I guess I was still processing it all.

"Hi! Hi!" I said. Shane shot me a curious glance. That is the problem with having a friend who is a professional linguist. He notices every nuance. The other problem with your friend being a reporter is, well, he doesn't mind asking the hard questions. As a matter of fact, he is very, very good at asking all the questions. I could see out of the corner of my eye as those questions were being tabulated in a list inside Shane's brain. With each numeration his smirk grew just a fraction of skin until it was a full-blown presumptive grin.

"Holy shit!" Shane exclaimed. He looked back and forth between the two of us. "Did you two fuck? You did. Well, I'll be damned. Just one little trip across the sea and you miss all the good shit."

"No," Joy quickly interrupted.

I also had a no I was trying to get out but it had a question mark at the end of it. Because of two reasons, I was pretty sure she was lying but I was also not completely sure she was lying. See, I couldn't really remember a whole lot of that night. I remembered waking up at her house and I remember that I wasn't wearing anything. But she was gone. We hadn't spoken since. I wasn't sure if I had been the world's biggest dick and had just totally blown off one of my closet friends like I was a cool kid one-night stand. Maybe she was avoiding me. There was no real way to know for certain without communication and we weren't doing that either. I suppose it was also possible that she took me back to her place; that I had thrown up on nearly everything and she washed my clothes. I mean, yes, my clothing was washed in the morning and folded waiting at the end of her bed. So yeah, I didn't know. I was more eagerly awaiting the answers than Shane was.

"No?" Shane said with the appropriate question mark I was hoping to muster.

"No," Joy said with absolute certainty. Then she mussed my hair. "We made love. Leo is way too sweet to fuck anyone. He was just so tender and loving I was afraid he would make a proper Southern woman out of me, so I ran for the hills and hid until I heard that the expat had reemerged stateside."

I looked up at her with curiosity and she looked back at me with complete deadpan. I couldn't tell if she was telling the truth or just telling Shane, in her way, that it was none of his business. I was pretty sure that it was my business though. I just didn't know how to, exactly, ask the question.

Before I could find my feet again to say anything, Joy yelled out across the room, "Nicholas!" A large figure dressed entirely in black moved across the floor toward us. He was a massively tall man. He towered above all of us at 6'4" and this combined with his jet-black hair, just like Joy's, made him an impressive specimen. He would have been the Panhandle's most eligible bachelor if he weren't married to Jesus. Whatever hope we had of completing this conversation was dead on arrival now that Nick was here, not just because Nicholas was a priest but also because he was Joy's older brother. Both of those identity markers made him the outcast of the group because he was completely uninterested in conversations about sex, decadence, or shenanigans. He was a few years our senior, but we were also some of the only people that Father Nick could be his real self around. He just didn't want us to be our real selves around him. We were his reprieve, but it was not reciprocal, we had to be on our best Sunday morning behavior … most of the time. Sometimes we could get him to drop the pretense, not just because Joy was family but because we had all grown up with him. We had watched him go off to prom the saintly son of the DeLuna family and return no longer a blessed virgin.

We also had all seen him that entire next day wallowing in guilt before he disappeared inside of himself and eventually into the Church in order to repent for his sins. He was a very conflicted man. He wanted to be both pious and a peer. He just didn't fit in anywhere. I think we all knew he was going to have to make a choice at some point. I just didn't know which way he was going to choose. Shane used to say that Nick ran into the Church in order to get away from the shame of being human. "The problem, Nicky, is that your brain, brawn, and balls are attached. You can't run from them."

"Shane," Nicholas said without much emotion as he approached our table.

"Nicky," Shane said back in response.

Shane was a long fallen away Catholic. All of us supported Nick when he decided to go to seminary. We even got in line with calling him Father in public, even Joy. All of us except for Shane. No, he hated the idea. Shane used to buy weed for Nick and they were way closer than the rest of us, even Joy. All the way up until that night of Nick's senior prom and that was it. Their friendship was over and Shane never quite recovered from it. That next day, as Nicholas set there in those pews of the church down the street, he swore to God that if He could make this guilt go away he would give everything he had left to God.

He made good on that promise.

I don't know a whole lot about the Bible, but my mom's favorite verse was, "Your sins will find you out." She used to shout that at Republicans when she was watching her nightly news shows. Your sins will find you out.

For Nicholas, that sin was Clementine.

The girl from the prom wasn't just some random crush. Nick didn't really have those. He was scared to death of women and himself. He knew he had a responsibility to either get married, have lots of babies and a good job or become a priest. In an attempt to appease his parents, he found a date for prom and that was Clementine, Joy's best friend in the whole world. She was thrilled to go with him. Clementine despised almost every man in the world except for Nicholas. I think she was in love with the both of them, but Nick was just perfect in her eyes. In his eyes, she was an easy way to get his parents off his back. An annoying friend of his little sister's but she would do. It was an easy fix. His parents' approval meant everything to him. He was built out of baseball and science camp. He was all American but also brilliant. That's a rare and dangerous combination. He probably could have easily been a senator or president. Instead, he chose to put a collar around his neck. I don't think I knew at the time what a political move that was.

Clementine always felt like she didn't fit in and wasn't as pretty as the other girls. She was taller than most and the shape of her body was proportionate to her size but just larger than the other girls at school. Nick was so tall that the two of them made sense next to each other. That didn't stop people from being cruel. The night at prom, as they danced at the school, some guy leaned over and asked Nick how he felt dancing with a whale. Clementine ran out of the room and Nick followed. It was just like a movie. Sixpence played in the background or some such shit, I'm sure.

He found her crying on the concrete stairs that led out of the gym. He told her how beautiful she was and how perfect her dress looked on her. He brushed the tears from her eyes and then her hair behind her ears. They kissed. Then the someday priest and the future plus-size nude model would lose their imaginary construct of innocence to each other in the backseat of his mother's sedan in the school parking lot. Something that he would always be reminded of. Something that would always haunt her because now she felt she couldn't ever admit to the person she truly loved more than anyone else in the world that she did, in fact, love her. Not now that she had lost her virginity to her brother.

That was all then and this was, of course, now. They grew up to be the polar opposites of each other. Our Father Nick found a way to be full of piety and wash away his self-imposed sins. Clementine learned to express herself in a way that allowed her to feel as beautiful as she was. Every time she arrived, she completed our little circle. Tonight was no different. And yet, tonight was completely different.

Tonight, we gathered around our usual table. A circle of friends, all of us intertwined and full of love for one another.

If there is a God and if He would be willing to grant me a wish like a genie, I would go back to that night and tackle us all. I would engulf us all in bubble wrap and never let a single one of them out of my sight again. But it didn't feel like I was bludgeoning any of them to death in that moment. It didn't feel like I was shoving pills down their throat until they would softly slip away. I didn't know I was killing them. Killing us. I just thought we were high on possibility and hopeful that soon this recession would be over and we would finally be able to be adults. The television clicked on as Billy nodded to us to look up at the screen.

He walked out on the stage and placed his hand on the Bible and said, "I, Barrack Hussain Obama, do solemnly swear that I will faithfully execute the office of president of the United States, and will to the best of my ability preserve, protect and defend the Constitution of the United States. So help me God."